Cover design by Nic Wainwright
Library of Congress Cataloging-in-Publication Data
Harem Twins Book Two
Dolores Maria Davis
ISBN 978-0-9976240-3-8
Printed in the United States of America
10 9 8 7 6 5 4 3 2 1

Harem Twins
Book Two

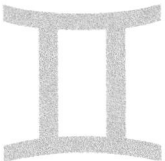

Dolores Maria Davis

Chapter 1

♊

Princess Becataten paused at the bottom of the gangway before boarding Viceroy Merymose's large papyrus ship, The Golden Falcon measured 150 steps long and was constructed of long tightly bound bundles of papyrus reeds about a foot in diameter. Her bow and stern arched up toward the middle of the craft cutting a long sleek and dark shadow in the warm morning sun. The heavy linen square sail brandished her name. At midships stood a platform where anchored wicker chairs offered comfortable seats. Rowers pulled oars painted with lotus flowers. A private structure aft was constructed using poles and fabric for sleeping that could be dismantled. They were heading south where Merymose oversaw the gold mines of Kush for Pharaoh, his half-brother, who had garnered him with the name, the King's son.

In this land of Kush, where Nubians lived, the Egyptians called Upper Egypt whereas the natives called it Land of the Bow.

After Pharaoh denounced his former court astrologer, and also half-brother, he had him disfigured and tortured for plotting against the throne, then immediately gave Becataten to Viceroy Merymose. Princess Becataten never understood why her marriage followed the horrific event so quickly but was thrilled to leave the court, and the sadness behind. Sailing to Kush would allow her to get to know her new husband, and a land he ruled.

Becataten clutched her wrap that early morning and standing very still on the dock sensed someone behind them. Turning to look down the quay, she saw a dock attendant help two passengers board a small craft. A middle-aged man clung to the attendant with nervous uncertainty about where the narrow gangplank lay beneath his feet. A pet baboon tied to the helper's waist whimpered and pulled at his leash. More able on his legs, the animal swayed in time with the rocking of the raft. Both castrated; the beast many seasons ago, thus making him a more docile pet, the middle-aged human, but two moons ago by Pharaoh Amenhotep III's order. The Egyptian man had also been blinded, that too by Pharaoh's decree.

The princess had asked her new and beloved husband Viceroy Merymose a nearly impossible task: find the Astrologer—her true father—who had been cast into the streets of Thebes to become a beggar. She knew not how the Viceroy accomplished this, or how he persuaded Pharaoh to allow her father to journey to Kush with them.

Becataten noted Dwarf Beset, her much-adored lifelong companion, watching the sight of the man and his pet board the small boat behind their vessel with unease. But Becataten was resolute in her decision to save the life of the denounced Royal Astrologer and his pet baboon by arranging that his small boat trail hers. Her father's plight was due to his plotting against his half-brother, Pharaoh, who retaliated with torture then flinging him into the streets.

Long shafts of Ra's light broke the dark sky, turning the Nile to shimmering silver and Egypt's Theban cliffs to painted gold as the time to sail grew near. Becataten rushed up the boarding plank of the Viceroy's long sturdy ship. Her face artfully painted, she chose not to wear a wig for the voyage, though her golden anklets and dangling earrings jingled softly. Rose oil, the favorite scent of the Viceroy, wafted from her bronze-colored skin. Her two long-time companions followed her on board; savvy Dwarf Beset, with her screechy voice, and Nanny Maja, a dark-skinned, bent woman who began her life as a slave. The three women chose light woolen shawls, imported from the Pharaoh's vassal states of the eastern Mediterranean, to fend off the cool morning air.

When Becataten arrived, the Viceroy took her hand and held it tight with the expression of a man who adored his new wife. "Welcome aboard, my Princess. We sail with Ra's first light."

Becataten's green eyes softened as she leaned into him and whispered, "Thank you my husband, for making my wish come true by arranging what I asked." Then with concern, she said, "Yet I must still say goodbye to Lady Nagara."

"I understand," said the Viceroy, "She was at the dock before I arrived. I think she is missing you already."

Not sailing with them, Lady Nagara had been on board before dawn designating with firmness the placement of Becataten's many chests, furniture, and her staff. As the Viceroy's Nubian crew hefted Becataten's coffers onto his ship, Lady Nagara oversaw the workers with scrutiny. The twenty men and women she had chosen to serve Becataten in her new environs

3

were trying to find places on deck to settle themselves and their bundles. Becataten's mentor and second mother, Lady Nagara, had packed every item she could think of to make life in rustic Kush as comfortable as possible for the young princess. She and her husband, Royal Architect Suti, had raised Becataten to adulthood, were childless and would miss her more than they knew.

Looking sad, Lady Nagara again reviewed the cargo on deck. Becataten watched as she fiddled with her cape, and for the first time in Becataten's memory, the self-composed woman looked unsettled. Having stayed well past the time of casting off, the noble-woman appeared upset and on the verge of losing her dignity. Becataten enveloped the woman's rigid body and felt for the first time in her life their roles reversed. "My heart holds much love for you Lady Nagara, and I will never forget you," Becataten whispered.

Quietly, Lady Nagara spoke into Becataten's ear, "You are a beautiful child, Becataten, in both body and *Ka* and we *will* live to see one another again." With a quick turn, the Lady rushed up the plank onto the quay to her waiting chair, not looking back as the litter bearers whisked her conveyance away.

Becataten stood on deck to gaze along the Theban shores where passing temples reminded her how much time she had spent there as a young girl. Now a woman, it was time to say goodbye to the Karnak Temple complex and all the monuments she loved. She offered a silent farewell to her long dead mother, Princess Attah, and to her beloved twin, Prince Jobutaten, who too had died begore he became a man. In the Royal Nursery where she and her bother grew from babes to children, Pharaoh had bestowed their

4

royal names; Becataten and Jobutaten, advised by the royal astrologer. They also had been gifted with golden jewelry and best of all, Dwarf Beset, an adult dwarf that had grown up in Pharaoh's court. Becataten's mother, like many women that bore twins, had not survived childbirth. Yet her mother arrived from Mitani in the Babylonian empire with her slave, Maja, a simple woman who never grasped the Egyptian language well. She was their caring nanny but could not pronounce the children's titles, so she had given them diminutive names of Jobu and Taten. There was much to say farewell to.

Becataten took a deep breath of the last of the cool air and returned to her husband. Questions crowded her mind about sailing south to their new home in rural Kush. Grinning like a child, she said, "How far is it to the first cataract?"

Smiling at her enthusiasm, Merymose said, "We should arrive before dark."

"And, then will we pass over the first cataract?" asked Becataten.

"We probably won't pass over it, but with all the cargo you have brought on board, my ship should hold steady in the water when we near it. I will better decide when we get there and learn how deep the water is."

"And the second cataract?" Becataten asked.

"Rarely do vessels travel over the second cataract, no matter how high the water reaches. Ships and rafts are dragged along the shore around it. That is where the 'belly of stones' begins."

Merymose's lengthy craft now underway moved against the ripples of the Mother Nile, the only river in the known world that flowed south from origins few people understood. And with inundation, her banks swelled depositing a rich and black magical soil.

Becataten felt relieved to sail away from this life. Yet, she had to admit grave events had left her considerably wiser than the fourteen inundations she had lived through. Experiencing the murder of her brother, an intimacy with Pharaoh, a plot to overthrow the crown, and her terrifying abduction had all overwhelmed her young life. Then to learn that her father was not Pharaoh shocked her to her core. All of this *and* being mentored by nobility had given her wisdom beyond her years. Pharaoh knew of her departure, as he had given the Viceroy to her in marriage, but he did not acknowledge her exodus. His reticence about such matters put him into her past, a place Pharaoh rarely visited, Lady Nagara had explained.

Becataten watched Nanny Maja viewing the shore with melancholy, knowing how the unknown frightened her. Dwarf Beset welcomed adventure, but shielding her eyes, she anxiously observed the small raft following them with a frown on her brow. Beset rarely missed anything.

Working in unison, expert oarsmen moved the boat southward toward Kush. The Viceroy and Becataten grasped the arms of their chairs anchored to the elevated platform. Side by side they observed ripples of the river alter into small waves. Speaking over the sound of rushing water, Becataten asked, "Tell me, Viceroy about our lives and duties in Kush?"

"You ask big questions, Becataten," he said, smiling.

She returned his smile. "Actually, I know some things about Kush and the Nubian people. I have been reading scrolls about the great land and how you administer it for Pharaoh."

"Then you tell me what you know, and I will add what you do not," Merymose suggested.

She grew serious, straightened in her chair as she did before her tutors at the Suti Estate, where skilled instructors were engaged by Architect Suti and Lady Nagara for her education. "We will live just past the first cataract in Fortress Buhen, which is garrisoned by five hundred Nubians. You are in charge of Upper and Lower Kush, an area that encompasses about one thousand miles of the Mother Nile, and of course inland where all of Egypt's gold is mined. You have played a very important part in keeping the Nubians Egyptianized. This is crucial, because if you do not, from time to time, a chieftain will emerge and try to revolt."

The Viceroy said, "And did you know that Fortress Buhen is sometimes Pharaoh's residence when he is on campaign?"

With a surprised expression, Becataten's eyes widened, deciding the Fort must be a place of great comfort and beauty.

With a nod the Viceroy reclined in his chair, a smile of satisfaction on his face.

She continued, "Upon Pharaoh's command, you administer Kush as though it were a minor Egypt. The principal materials we import from Kush are: ostrich feathers and eggs, leopard skins, and oils of many varieties. For our jewelry we take copper, amethyst, carnelian and more. Also, Egypt receives some select cattle, dogs, live leopards and their skins, giraffes, and baboons too. Egypt uses much of the furniture made in Kush and boat makers supply us with quality fishing crafts. We take taxes in the form of grain—but of course most of all we want Kush's gold. Shall I continue?"

Relaxing, the Viceroy put his hands behind his head and said, "And I had no idea someone so beautiful, and pleasant to love, could surprise me with such learning."

"I like surprising you."

He settled a long serious look on her. "You suit me, Becataten."

They sat watching the land drift by as they passed into of the Land of the Bow, so named by the Nubians of Kush. The Egyptians preferred the name, Land of Gold.

"Why do the people live so close to the water?" asked Becataten.

The Viceroy stood as his hand swept across the land. "Here we have but a narrow Nile, unlike Thebes where the river is wider and easy to build canals into the interior for farming."

"But why can't the farmers channel in water like they do in Thebes?"

His approval showed at her well-thought-out inquiries. They were not just curious questions; he could see she wanted to learn. "The river here inundates fast and recedes just as quickly. It allows no time to trench water into the land. That means the farmers have but one planting, and that is directly after flooding."

Becataten took the time to observe a parched desert on both sides of this narrowing Nile. Only a few grasses and stunted trees dotted the landscape. Vegetables were planted under date palms, for valued shade. The only obvious livestock were goats that thrived in great numbers.

Becataten stood, feet apart while holding onto the back of her chair. "What is that sound that grows louder, Viceroy?"

Settling his arm around Becataten's shoulders, he spoke into her ear. "Watch what you see as the oarsmen make this turn."

Becataten caught her breath! An enormous tumbling of water cascaded down a pile of huge boulders ending in a fine mist all around them. "It is beautiful!" She said, admiring the waterfall.

Maja's eyes bulged with fear along with the twenty attendants who gasped and huddled together on deck at the sight of the rushing water. Dwarf Beset stood holding tight to a line with her feet apart and in her high-pitched voice said, "By the Gods, look at that beautiful waterfall tumble over the huge rocks. It is so big isn't it, Taten?"

"It may be big and beautiful to you ladies, but *this* is where we moor. We can no longer navigate against the currents. They grow too swift and a north wind will be with us soon. You will feel it on your face." The Viceroy called to give orders to his crew. "When we disembark, we will have a better and safer view of the cataract from your litter as we head overland to Fortress Buhen."

As soon as the vessel moored, in this land between the first and forth cataracts, lank statuesque Nubians showed themselves from the hilltops. They stomped their feet and cheered in unison while beating their hide shields with spears. It sent a reverberating roar up and down the Mother Nile.

"They are paying homage to you, Becataten, to celebrate your arrival," Merymose whispered, holding his wife close to him.

"I am so impressed. Did you arrange this Merymose?"

"I did not."

The powerful voices of hundreds of Nubians resonated over the red stony hill tops. Their bodies swaying and their black skin glistening, they sang a rich and moving welcome to the new princess. The spectacle entranced everyone on board. Passengers gazed, mesmerized by the number of the men from Kush, and their powerful voices.

The ship's crew quickly jumped from the craft to drag the Viceroy's vessel up to a muddy shore, away from the river that was beginning to rage as they grew nearer the first cataract. After firmly securing the vessel, passengers disembarked while waves rushed from the steep rapids to wash the decks, hampering attendants who were unloading Becataten's sizeable cargo.

The land conveyance the Viceroy had arranged nearly matched the length of his boat. It took twenty-four strong Nubians to carry Becataten, Dwarf Beset, Nanny Maja, Isis, the make-up artist and much of the ship's goods. Carefully and in unison the bearers hefted lengthy poles to steady the long sturdy woven litter, with grunts and deep breaths. The Viceroy had arranged a canopy for the conveyance, a center chair and several pillows to make the litter comfortable. As Viceroy Merymose led the group on foot, a few bold pygmies jumped on the giant litter to fan the three women with giant plumes.

"Maja, standing behind Becataten's littler-chair, bent down to whisper in her ear, "Taten, I don't like the tall boy that walks close to the bearers and who stares at us. At you, I mean. He does not look like a friend." Becataten noted the scrawny, tall boy who did indeed stare with dark enticing eyes at her and her companions.

Though unsettled, she managed to say, "He is probably just curious about us, Maja. We must look strange to the Nubians." Maja continued to show concern over the large boy's intense interest in the princess as Becataten tried to ignore him.

Standing on the litter next to Becataten, Dwarf Beset shaded her eyes, and more than once strained for a view of the shore behind them. One of the tallest Nubians plucked her off the litter as though she was an ostrich feather. "Little Dwarf, sit on my shoulders and see what you want to see behind us."

The small boat that had shadowed them from Thebes had moored behind them. The blind man and his baboon were being aided by Nubians as they disembarked. No one spoke of this or appeared to notice, but Dwarf Beset did. Princess Becataten had prayed to all the Gods she knew, and so it had come to pass that her father, Abu, the renounced Royal Astrologer along with his pet baboon, would be with her in Kush.

Chapter 2

♊

Although it had been strenuous to move from Thebes, over rushing water and parched land, Princess Becataten viewed the trip as an adventure. She was determined to make this new home one she and the Viceroy would enjoy. She heard that Kush was a sparse and unfriendly place but kept in mind that Pharaoh stayed at Fortress Buhen when on campaign, so she reasoned it would be a palatial place to live.

The large litter the Viceroy arranged to carry Becataten, Dwarf Beset, Isis and Maja for the long trek to the Fortress move steadily through the arid land. The twelve powerful bearers, six on each side, were renewed daily so as not to tire the men. No one save the Viceroy had understood that this move could take up to ten days through vacant, hot land where comforts were minimal. A good planner, he had arranged that a chariot be sent ahead for he and Becataten to ride in for a change of pace. Beset and Maja would be confined to the litter platform for safety. Beset couldn't manage the long strides set by the Nubians, and Maja was far too timid to walk with foreigners, so he endeavored to make their ride comfortable the best way he saw fit. Merymose ordered small chairs be attached to the large platform and additional down cushions. He ordered the pygmies to remain on board to fan the women. The conveyance carried ample amounts of well water, dried beef, dates and honey cakes. Nights were spent in tents close to fires that kept dangerous animals away. The Nubians nightly prepared a variety of fine roasted meats of gazelle, alligator, native birds and fish, cooked over open fires. Her father and his keeper remained in the shadows of the nightly dinners, but Becataten always saw that they were sent food. And when the fires grew low, she would steal away to visit briefly with her father.

On the sixth day, the litter arrived at the rear gates of Fortress Buhen, a dismal walled compound constructed of mud brick. The castellated fortification presented a serious military presence. Built on the edge of a steep escarpment, the fortress loomed high above the Nile. A narrow footpath wound up the escarpment from the river to its face. Nubians hauled water jugs and freshly caught game to the top where a small portal allowed a one-man entry. A wide bending road around the fortress led up to the rear of the compound where massive gates stood to accommodate wide loads.

They arrived in the early evening up that bend.

Once inside and while there was still light, Becataten directed her attendants to build her father a temporary shelter deep within the compound in the form of a lean-to. She wanted it to be near the entrance to her dwelling where she was told two long corner walls would form the beginning of her apartment. Natives quickly built a bench about six paces long against a wall, set two sturdy poles into the earth and four paces from the wall then fastened a thick linen cover from the top of the poles to the wall for a canopy. Unlike Dwarf Beset and Maja, Becataten set aside the fact that the fortress was a rough and dreary place to live. Making a comfortable area for her father and creating a new life with the Viceroy absorbed her.

Maja and Beset stared at Abu as they watched Becataten settle him into their new abode. Becataten had tied a scarf low about his head so as not to expose his mutilated eye sockets. Maja rung her hands and said quietly to Beset, "Why do you think Pharaoh let Taten bring her father here, Beset?"

"I am not sure. And I'm not sure Pharaoh knows that Abu *is* Taten's father. You and I, Maja, are two of the few people who know that."

Maja nodded. "I know because Taten's mother, Princess Atta, told me in the Harem when we live there, that Abu is her father, not Pharaoh."

Beset stood with her hands on her hips. "Probably the Viceroy knows," was all Beset said.

Maja gave Beset a wondering look as she covered her lips with her scarf. "You once said Abu is half-brother to Pharaoh. Maybe that is why he allows Abu to live."

"Maybe," Beset's stubby hand reached to scratch the back of her head, and speaking softly she said, "But Abu did plot against the crown, and I am still surprised he was allowed to keep his life."

Abu wore a soiled loincloth, no longer carried a rotund middle, his power and dignity gone, his flourishing presence a thing of the past. He and his baboon were a pitiful sight sitting on a wooden bench against a stark mud brick wall as natives finished covering the sides with palms fronds to shelter him from the sun. Abu's body ran with sweat and Huni's mouth poured with drool as he whimpered, leaning into his master with a fearful look.

As Becataten fussed over her father, Abu cleared his throat and said, "Becataten, you need not worry about me. Huni and I just need a bit of shade and water. We will be fine."

"Father, I will always fuss over you. I have appointed a man to care for your needs. He speaks some Egyptian; a Nubian who is retired from one of Pharaoh's campaigns. He arrives tomorrow."

"Thank you Becataten, I will look forward to engaging him in his tongue. I learned to speak with the Nubians years ago on a campaign with Pharaoh. These people don't have a written language."

Becataten took his hand. "I knew you would like to speak with an informed native. And you need an able attendant as well."

Abu grunted. "You know when I accompanied Pharaoh here several inundations ago, Fortress Buhen was the first stronghold along the Nile, and I guess it still is. The walls here are ten or more feet thick and nearly forty feet tall, as I recall. I know this must seem a strange place, but you should be safe here, Princess, while the Viceroy conducts his business."

Becataten said, "I think it will take some time to adapt to the heat and bareness of the land, especially for those of us who grew up in the Palace grounds and are used to gardens." Becataten looked around at the vast barren courtyard that was confined by thick fortress walls, with not a plant in sight. The huge enclosure served a number of dwellings along an east wall for several simple dwellings. The open sky offered only stifling heat. She missed the gardens of home already. She was distracted back to her conversation as her father reached out to pat her hand, saying, "How can I thank you, Princess, for including me in your life?"

Becataten said gently, "You can start by calling me 'daughter.'"

Abu struggled for emotional control and finally spoke in an uneven voice. "I am grateful for the second life you and the Viceroy have given me. Did you know your Viceroy found me in the streets of Thebes begging for food? He even had his men scour the animal markets for Huni." Abu's voice broke." I am told Huni was found on a bidding block about to be sold to a trader and depart by caravan for Babylon."

She laid a hand on his shoulder. "Put all of that behind you Father, you are safe now and with me."

When he reached out to her, the mutilations on his arms stunned her. Becataten's voice nearly faltered, but she was determined to be strong for both of them now. "This small bench and table are temporary, and I will soon see that you have a cot and more amenities before Ra leaves us, Father."

Nearby she could feel a young man watching her, the one that had caused Maja to warn her of his persistent presence. Her nervous movements signaled Abu to say, "Princess, are you upset about something?"

Becataten said, "I think it is just the move."

Huni's screeches grew loud as he rose from the bench baring his teeth, jumping up and down. Abu sat erect. "Princess, I can feel someone nearby is distressing you, and so does Huni."

"Well, yes there is a young man who seems to spy on me. It started when we traveled inland. I thought he was just curious at first, but he continues to watch me, and it does give me an uneasy feeling."

Abu motioned her nearer to whisper in her ear. "Child, listen carefully to me. See that you tell the Viceroy of this immediately, and have him get you a pair of dogs, preferably a male and female. Keep them near you always. I have Huni, but you need dogs. And don't let anyone give you a monkey. They are a poor choice as a protector."

Becataten smiled, touched him gently on the cheek, and said, "I will do as you say, Father."

Turning away, she thought maybe it was a good idea to have some animals around her for protection. She knew of an old proverb that advised keeping beasts not just as guards or pets, but also to take injury and blunt any harm that may be directed at their masters.

In the clamor of sounds, she walked toward the development of her new quarters, looking about for her stalker and thankfully not seeing him. She watched a living space being quickly developed in this most distant corner of the fortress. The Viceroy had Nubians working to enlarge his old headquarters into a home while they lived at Buhen. How unlike this structure was when she compared it to the buildings that she had seen the architects Suti, and Hor work on. Only briefly did she think of how long their stay here might be. She could see a private bedchamber being created for her and knew she'd have a place to sleep for the night. Nearby cot rooms for Beset, Maja, as well as for other attendants were coming into view as the bricklayers rushed to form walls. Not sure where the balance of her staff would find quarters, she decided to ask the Viceroy that later, as he seemed very busy delegating workmen. Mud bricks were quickly being laid to create rooms using a corner wall to build out from. Keenly woven mats were were set for flood coverings that awaited her carved wooden furniture. Trying not to react, Becataten made a face and shivered every time she saw a native pick up a stone to smash a scorpion. This was a much larger domicile than the modest apartment in Pharaoh's palatial compound where she grew up. Yet she had to admit that down deep the fortress almost felt hostile. She knew she would make the best of it, and later that evening when she saw the final wall enclose their quarters, as well as a pair of heavy doors waiting to secure the entrance, she stated, "Oh, how quickly the men worked!"

Only the open sky delivered a minimum of light from the stars. The air was fowl with animal fat from the many lamps it now took to see in the beginning darkness.

Becataten, Maya, and Beset were led by a worker to a makeshift sleeping area in the dark corner of a new room, where they quickly prepared for sleep. Though work continued well into the night, occasionally waking her slumber, Becataten was able to rest until the early rays of Ra announced a new day. She awoke, anxious to learn all about her new home. When the huge back gates opened for daily commerce, the feeling of air and light was welcomed

Standing, she wrapped herself in a linen covering and looked around, noting the heavy ornate doors of her area that had been added just the night before. Next to the doors, Nubians had delivered and stacked goods off their large conveyance that brought them to Buhen. It was unclear how all the items would fit into their quarters. Lady Nagara had sent so much for Becataten's new home, and the Viceroy had tolerated the Lady's indulgence.

As the compound grew brighter, and Ra reached the open skies of the fortress, Becataten walked about the huge courtyard, thinking her father was right as she judged the walls to be approximately forty feet high. She moved to the small opening where workers hauled water, and animal catches of the day up the slender foot path that zigzagged up from the Nile. She looked down the precipitous path and felt light-headed. Now she understood how secure the fortress was. At the bottom of the formidable escarpment flowed the Nile where a narrow harbor with a substantial quay received river crafts. A fleet of sturdy boats tied there were filled with regular tribute from Kush and hauled back to Pharaoh's warehouses. A smaller line of boats ferried necessities for the compound such as water, freshly caught fish and game, as well as vegetables.

Becataten estimated the narrow and winding path leading up to the fortification from the Nile were hundreds of steps high. The natives nimbly navigated the restricted path up from to the river carrying most items on their heads. And on this day, adding to their loads they carried heavy bricks on their backs. It made her dizzy looking down on the activity, and his was not a place to explore, she was in their way and had to step back. But the prospect of going out the two main gates at the back end of the fortress and driving a chariot around the exterior walls excited her. This was nothing like the Karnak Temple where she had grown up. This was a garrisoned stronghold, one of ten, built through the 'belly of stones' with additional fortresses all the way to the fifth cataract. She promised herself to one day see them all. Buildings were constructed differently here, and she wanted to know more.

That morning when the two back gates were open, tall black Nubians entered with ease, shouldering sacks of grain, balancing cages of monkeys on their heads plus hauling Becataten's items from her large litter. She observed that Nubians of a lighter color seemed to have jobs managing or negotiating, not laboring. Later as the dark fell, small cooking fires were beginning to ignite on the grounds within the compound on this second night. People were settling into family groups. Caged animals were crying less, and workmen were gathering up their tools.

Becataten jumped when she heard the boom of the fortress gates close. She gathered this signaled the securing of the compound and Ra's departure. Soon came the smells of cooking, pungent odors of crowded humans and animals—things to which she must grow accustom.

On this second night, the dark time was better illuminated and helped her see her way. She studied her new residence, a large and well secured living space taking up a sizable corner of the compound.

On the third morning, Becataten was examing the inside layout of her living space, when she was startled by a diminutive person who stepped before her and with a deep, almost manlike voice said, "Welcome Princess to Fortress Buhen, I am here to be your servant." This short, brown-skinned figure wore a skirt of grass and had enormous dark eyes. Her feet were long, and her exposed breasts, pendulous. Her teeth were filed to sharp points. She looked like no one else in the compound or anyone Becataten had ever seen. Becataten stepped back with a start by her voice and appearance. "I do not know you. Have you been sent by someone to aide me?"

"Yes, it is my guiding spirit that sent me. I am here because you will need me to show you Kush. And when you bear your first child, you will need me."

Becataten composed herself and analyzed the woman. "We will speak when Ra is low in the sky. I am still tired from our long journey and need to rest." The pygmy nodded, left, and casually walked toward the exit. Dwarf Beset, who had been listening, tracked her with a suspicious stare until the strange woman disappeared.

Beset turned to Maja, "*That* was a rash pygmy, as most of them are."

Maja fanned herself with a palm frond. "I don't like this place, Beset. It is hot and ugly with strange people."

"It is true. This may not be a good choice for a home, but remember it is temporary. The Viceroy has promised to build a big house for Taten near the first cataract, so we must make do until then."

Late in the evening, permanent cots were set in designated cubicles for house servants and many furnishings were in place. However, there would be soft goods to unpack in the morning. When Ra left, it was difficult to adjust to the intense blackness and Becataten was grateful when attendants went about lighting many oil lamps. With the petitioned rooms complete, the fortress secure, the Viceroy still stationed two guards outside their newly installed doors, as quiet finally settled on the compound.

Becataten sunk into her large bed of fluffy down next to the Viceroy. She heaved a great sigh and said, "Mosie, how long will we be in this place?"

"Not long, Princess, and I promise you when Ra returns, you will not experience the turmoil of the last two days. And what is this new name you have given me?"

"I want a private name for you. I will of course call you Viceroy in public."

"You can call me anything you like in bed, Princess, just as long as you always share it with me. He turned toward her. "Now, I sense you wish to talk."

She snuggled up to him. "Yes, I do. I would like you to find me two dogs, preferably a brother and sister from the same litter. I want to have them near because I know you will be away from time to time while we live here. And I would like you to find me a guard, who will accompany me on chariot rides, so I may drive about."

The Viceroy said, "So it will be: Two dogs, a guardian and a chariot. Tonight, I ask for less." He turned and reached for a potshard to extinguish the flame of the oil lamp.

Becataten didn't know why she withheld the information about the boy who had been stalking her.

The follow morning, Becataten entered their dining space where the Viceroy was being served freshly baked flat bread, goat cheese and herb tea. He looked at her with tenderness in his eyes. "You are very beautiful this morning, my Princess." She wore a sheer pleated gown, strapped with a gold cord at her waist, knowing how he liked the transparency of fine linen.

He cleared his throat. "I meant to tell you that you will have a guard of six of my finest Nubians when you choose to leave the fortress, in a chariot or a litter, not but one guard. And I do *not* want you to make a habit of going too distant from the fortress or staying away too long. Do I have your word on that?"

"You do, Mosie, and thank you for that."

"I hear you had a visit from the Pygmy Lady."

"I did. Who *is* she?"

"She is one who reads fortunes and wants to be your attendant. She is well-known in Kush and can be trusted. But it is up to you whether you wish to include her into your household staff. Now I must go. I will return to you before Ra leaves us."

Becataten wished to run her household as efficiently as Lady Nagara did at the Suti Estate. With a large staff, she planned to make a fine home for the Viceroy, and as soon as possible explore Kush in her chariot. She swept through her new home, dressed in a light but not transparent honey-colored shift, gold earrings and cuffs at her wrists, "Nanny Maja, Dwarf Beset," Becataten called in a new, authoritative voice. "Maja, I want you to find our cook, and have that person learn where vegetables and meats are found. Beset, you locate where beer is made and bread is baked. Both of you take attendants. I will order our chests unpacked and furniture put in place. I want a fine dinner waiting for the Viceroy when her returns."

The pygmy appeared out of nowhere. "It is all taken care of. I have directed your cook to the marketplace. Beer and bread have already been delivered, and I have a man who will play a flute while we all dine tonight," Pygmy Lady said.

When Beset saw the pygmy, in an unhurried fashion she took up a place behind a piece of thick hanging flax and stood to listen to the women with her fists clenched.

Becataten directed Pygmy Lady to her main sitting room that was partitioned with thick wicker screens. She was uncomfortable with this bold fortuneteller, and realized she needed to understand why this peculiar woman wanted to serve her. She motioned the pygmy to sit on a stool.

Lady Nagara came to Becataten's mind, and how she would handle such a self-confident stranger. Becataten sat in a high-back chair of woven palm fronds, folded her hands in her lap, sat up straight and said, "Tell me about yourself pygmy, and your name."

"You could not pronounce my name. Just call me Pygmy Lady."

Going right to the heart of the matter, Becataten spoke her mind. "Why do you choose to attend me? I have many attendants."

"I do not choose to serve you, I must! My spirit has willed it so. I'm sure Viceroy Merymose told you that I read fortunes. I once read his and told him that he would marry an Egyptian princess and bring her here to Kush. And here you are!"

"No, he did not mention that. Is there another reason you should be serving me?"

"Yes, the biggest reason of all. You will go through much suffering in childbirth, maybe even deliver a lifeless child, unless I am with you."

Becataten sat motionless, feeling uneasy in her chair. She shuddered at Pygmy Lady's words, shocked, but she wondered if this may be true. They stared at one another in silence. It crossed Becataten's mind to send a scroll to the Heka Priest and ask him if this pygmy's magic was real. But she remembered that the old Priest told her she too carried the magic and decided to use her Heka to make her own choices.

"You may be a fortuneteller to many, but not to me. It is a distressing thing to tell me that I will have a child born dead if you do not attend me. And you were insolent by taking over the duties of my staff early this

Ra without my permission. Can you not see that you have begun badly?"

Pygmy Lady appeared unruffled by Becataten words. "I did not want to shock or offend. I am here to warn and help."

"You have a poor way with words, and you are far too rude to my staff."

Pygmy Lady, with arms folded, said, "If you want apologies, I can give them. But do not dismiss me and be deceived that I cannot help you."

Becataten's Heka said, *try her.* Adjusting her golden cuffs and sitting tall in her honey colored day gown, she said, "You may work as an attendant for me for one moon. You will do only as I say, and you will ask permission to accomplish anything I have not granted."

Calmly Pygmy Lady slid off her bench, nodded her head, and on her way out, slapped at the flax weaving that concealed Beset.

Becataten watched her walk out of her quarters, cross the large enclosed courtyard to converse with a man Becataten could hardly make out. Both were in in animated speech, when Becataten realized Pygmy Lady was talking to with none other than the boy who had been stalking her.

Chapter 3

♊

It took more time for Becataten's staff to organize her new home than she had planned, but once things were in order, she went directly to her father to invite him to live within her new domicile. He firmly refused.

"But Father, we have space for you, and I want you to be with us, not in this outdoor lean-to that just offers shade and a bench.

"I cannot do that, Princess." Abu said.

"Why not?"

"I do not deserve to live with you. Let us leave it at that."

"Please, Father."

He raised his hand and said, "No more talk. Now, did you tell the Viceroy about the young man who has been following you?"

"I plan to tell him tonight, I promise. And I did ask him about getting me some dogs and a chariot."

"A chariot," he answered with enthusiasm. "You can handle one, Princess?"

"A little, and I love it. Do you suppose you could come out with me sometime, Father?"

"No, child, my driving days are over. But I was thinking about passing on to you some of my knowledge about the heavens. If you could get me a board and some pebbles of varying sizes, I believe together we can reproduce the night sky."

She knew that as the royal astrologer of the court of Amenhotep III, one of his myriad responsibilities was to establish a commencement date for all royal events, which he did by reading the heavens with great acumen. Casting birth charts, recommending favorable times to wage war or begin a major royal undertaking like temple building, was once all within his purview.

She grew excited and lapsed into fast-talking, a style of speech Lady Nagara had worked hard to eradicate in her. "I would like that, and languages too. Tutor me in all the tongues you know, Father."

"First things first, Princess."

Huni began tugging at his leash and jumping as a crowd assembled near a young man who was being dragged to a post. It was too far off to know all that was happening, but it looked like he was being tied there to receive a lashing, someone nearby said. It brought to mind her long-ago punishment when Lady Nagara learned she had fraternized with the outdoor staff and ordered her to kneel on pebbles until her knees bled.

Abu asked, "What is going on, Princess?"

"Someone said there will be a beating. Several guards are restraining some sort of prisoner."

Abu said, "What type of guards brought the man into the compound?"

"I'm not sure what you mean, Father."

"Describe for me the clothing of his captors."

Becataten squinted and said, "Red loin cloths, I believe."

Abu sat a little straighter, and said, "You said you *didn't* tell the Viceroy about the young man who was stalking you?"

"No, I did not. Do you think he is the captured one?" Becataten asked.

"I think that is a possibility. I'm quite sure that the Viceroy's men dress in red garments."

Patting him on the cheek, she added nothing to the conversation, but left him with cool well water, and a basket of dried salted goat strips and fresh dates, which she lay on his bench. She ordered an attendant to bring him some hide pillows. Then she looked toward the gathering crowd where the young man had been taken but was unable to see anything and decided to go back to her quarters.

Merymose assigned the six Nubian guards to Becataten that he had promised. They were available all day should she wish to drive or be littered about. He also chose one other protector to watch over her within the walls of the Fortress.

The following morning outside her door, that man was waiting. "Greetings, Princess Becataten," he said in a friendly manner.

Becataten smiled warmly. "You must be Nehesy. The Viceroy told me about you. I am happy to consider you a part of my staff." She hoped his kind face reflected a gentle *ka* in his aging body; a man shorter than his countrymen with his bowl-shaped greying hair and deep-set knowing eyes. She noticed that he garnered respect from passing Nubians.

Nehesy bowed before her and said, "I am honored to be of service, Princess Becataten of Thebes."

The early morning brought smells from cooking fires, the odor of dung from animal cages, and the loud clatter of people moving about. "Would you please come into my quarters, Nehesy, so we may talk?" She scanned the huge courtyard for her stalker before stepping through her doorway, grateful she did not see him this morning, and thinking he maybe the captured man they were going to punish.

Dwarf Beset had been lurking near the doorway, trying to learn who this newly appointed man was that was talking to Becataten. As the two entered, Dwarf Beset carried a small stool to sit behind one of the wicker screens in Becataten's sitting room.

Becataten offered Nehesy a stool but he preferred to stand. She chose the woven highbacked chair and said, "Tell me of your life?"

Uneasy, he shuffled his feet, adjusted his red cape over a shoulder and said, "Not much to tell. I serve the Viceroy."

"Yes, but in what capacity?"

Standing at attention he said, "For many years I have tended Viceroy Merymose on campaign and on his travels to the mines where smelting takes place."

"So, you were like a butler or a personal aide to him?"

Nehesy nodded, with pride showing in his eyes.

Obviously feeling out of place in the home of a Princess but wanting to please, he abruptly said, "My family raises dogs, and tonight a male and a female will arrive for you."

With a broad smile, Becataten said, "That will be wonderful." She felt relief to know she would be better guarded in this strange new home.

Nehesy looked surprised by her delight, and added, "At the back of the Fortress is a chariot waiting for you with six guardsmen, all strong men."

Becataten beamed again and thanked Nehesy for the news.

He stood still while his eyes darted about as though trying to find something else to please her. So charming was her response that he blushed.

When his interview was over and he left, Dwarf Beset went to Maja and with some distaste reported, "We have yet another staff member. We are getting dogs, and the Viceroy gave Taten a chariot."

Maja shook her head at Beset's words. Then they both turned to hear someone talking in a loud voice, delivering commands to the household staff. With tight lips Maja pointed in the direction of the noisy dialogue.

Beset wiggled off her stool, grabbed her staff, and with short determined steps went toward the commotion. "What is going on here? Oh, I should have known, it is *you* causing the trouble, pygmy. Our Princess did not give you the right to direct our staff!" Beset screeched.

Pygmy Lady looked down at Dwarf Beset and in her low voice said, "My name is Pygmy Lady, short one."

Leaning on her staff, one hand on her hip Beset looked up at her. "And my name is Dwarf Beset, of Pharaoh Amenhotep III's court in Thebes." She looked at Pygmy Lady with disdain. With little left for either to say, they turned from one another and walked away.

That night in bed, the Viceroy said, "I am sorry you had to see the capture and restraining of the young boy today. It is my fault that I did not direct the punishment to take place outside the walls."

"I am assuming you are going to punish him because he followed me, but how did you know it was him? I did not tell you."

"You must know that I have eyes and ears everywhere, Princess."

"Yes, but did you think he was going to cause me harm?"

The Viceroy paused for a moment. "Probably not, but stalking my wife garners a severe punishment."

"Who is he, Mosie."

The Viceroy said nothing.

"Please, Mosie, tell me who he is. It bothers me terribly not to know."

He put his arms behind his head, looked up and said, "He's my son."

Chapter 4

♊

The Viceroy rose well before Ra graced the eastern sky. He quickly dressed in a plain leather kilt, tied on sturdy woven sandals, applied circles of kohl around his eyes, didn't speak to Becataten and left their bedroom in haste. An attendant rushed to set a small table with ginger tea and flatbread for him. He shook his head swiftly passing the attendant on his way out the door. His mood strange and new to Becataten, he was gone before she got out of bed to say goodbye. It was her first encounter seeing him so remote. After slipping on a long white linen gown, she waved off Isis, the makeup artist to sit and drink the tea and flatbread left by her husband. Dwarf Beset paddled in to share breakfast with Becataten and explained that the Viceroy had headed to a village where a dispute required his handling. How Beset learned such things always mystified Becataten.

Later in the morning Beset rushed to keep up with Becataten as she followed her about. Walking through her new living quarters, Becataten checked the linens that had been unpacked but not yet put into their proper chests, she fused over the placement of stools and two large carved mahogany chairs for she and the Viceroy, all the time being preoccupied.

"Taten, Taten, can we talk. I wanted to speak to you about something."

Not looking at Beset, and examining her wardrobe with a heavy hand, Becataten said, "In just a bit, but first I must dress! I'm trying to find the thinnest of linen, where are my light shawls and my jewelry chest." She glared at Isis. Before Isis could speak, Becataten, clearly upset with the Viceroy's stark exit, made a mess of unfolding and tossing garments from a neatly packed trunk. Weary of answering questions from attendants earlier who wanted to know where to put kitchen supplies, where was the household water supply, and where should household goods for food service be placed and where should they sleep if no place in the house was available – all these questions from her domestic staff was becoming overwhelming. It was enough to worry where to store her wigs and their stands, her heavy shawls, which hardly had a use in this climate, she thought. Should she keep her woven sandals handy rather than her fancy ones. And, her glass perfume bottles, they needed a special place, maybe in her makeup chest they would be safe from breakage. Currently, Becataten had no appropriate attendant for organizing her personal items or her household goods. She stopped to collect herself and remember that Lady Nagara had a proficient butler who did all of this and more. The size of her attendants was beyond her scope. And no one among her staff that arrived with her stood out as someone who could lead them. Perhaps she could make Nehesy the one to run her house.

Anxious to get outside the walls and drive, she cast away thoughts about her household, and slipped on a pleated blue knee length shift and belted it with a rope of golden threads. Impatiently she sat before her painter, Isis, near her large cosmetic box Lady Nagara had so generously gifted her.

As the makeup artist reached into the chest for a pot of kohl, she said, "I will paint your eyes heavily today, Princess. Thick black lines of galena paste will protect you from the tsetse flies and bring shade from the strong rays of Ra so you will not return to us the color of a Nubian. Now, would you like me put on your leather sandals?"

Absently, she nodded.

Due to the heat, Becataten rarely wore a wig anymore and had Isis keep her head neatly shaved. She dressed more simply than she had at the Palace at Thebes. Daily, she chose her sheerest linens. The only adornments she hadn't given up were her long golden earrings and gem-studded cuffs.

The Viceroy had asked that in this environment she keep her breasts covered when she left their residence, and she complied. He explained that in Kush it was the lower-class Nubian women who moved about bare-breasted.

At the dinner table, however, Becataten often appeared bare-breasted, her face properly painted with a light dusting of gold dust on her checks. She also would sometimes wear the costume Viceroy preferred, the one she had to sit very straight in with narrow straps that barely covered her nipples.

Dwarf Beset waited patiently for Becataten to go through her frustrations of taking on her new household then poked her head into Becataten's private chamber, holding her tea in one hand, staff in the other. "Taten, Taten, now can we talk?"

Becataten took a deep breath, settled herself on a low stool and said, "Yes, Beset, come and sit near me while the artist finishes my face."

Beset set her tea on a table and took a footstool. "Taten, I do not wish to upset you, but did you know the boy they dragged into the courtyard yesterday for punishment was the one who had been stalking you?

Becataten frowned and said, "That is what my father suspected."

Dwarf Beset's face grimaced. "Did you know that he is the son of the Viceroy?"

Sitting erect Becataten looked shocked and said, "I did, but how did you know?"

"You know I have my ways of learning things, Taten. I came to tell you the boy escaped from the guards in the night and went back to his village."

Becataten turned away from the painter to look at Beset. "Do you think that is where the Viceroy is headed?"

Beset nodded.

"And I can see in your expression, Beset, you think danger is lurking."

Dwarf Beset nodded again.

"Do you want to tell me something else, Beset?"

"Just that there are many tribes in Kush, and some are war-like, while others are not."

"Is the village that the Viceroy traveled to war-like?" Becataten slowly asked.

Beset said, "Of that I am not sure, Taten."

Isis spoke, "Here in Kush, Princess, I will apply no facial colors of ocher when you go outside the walls. It is better that you sweat to help you stay cool, but I will rub your skin with castor bean ointment to protect your skin. We don't want you to return looking like a native."

When Isis was finished, Becataten shook her head and walked outside. Preoccupied, she nearly fell over a small child asleep next to a basket that held two small dogs. The girl awoke.

Becataten said, "Oh these are my puppies, aren't they?"

The scrawny child stood, put a finger in her mouth, and nodded. She picked up one of the animals and held it up while talking in a tongue Becataten couldn't understand. She took the youngster's hand and led her to her father's lean-to. "Good morning, Father, are you well?"

"I am, Princess. You are up early?"

"Yes, I was on way to my new chariot when I found this waif with my new pets. She speaks a language that maybe you can understand. She wants to tell me something. And, Father she has brought me two puppies for guarding just as you suggested."

Abu spoke to the girl and put out his hand. The girl showed no fear but seemed leery of Huni. Abu and the child chatted briefly, then she put her finger back in her mouth and looked at Becataten with a grin.

"What did she say, Father?"

"It seems she comes with the dogs."

"Oh no, not another attendant! I'm stepping over them like cats at Pharaoh's abode."

Abu said, "I would keep her for a while. She will probably sleep outside with the animals and wander off one day. She may be of some use."

Becataten nodded. "I'll rely on your words because right now, I just want to get to my chariot."

"Go to your new conveyance, child, and enjoy yourself."

Becataten watched the young girl sit next to her father and chat with him as though they were friends.

When she turned around, Nehesy had a chair waiting to take her outside the walls. She smiled at him and anxiously settled into the seat. Four bearers carried her across the courtyard expanse while the natives gawked.

Both Maja and Beset waved her off. Maja looked frightened. "Is Taten safe to go with these people outside the walls, Beset?"

"I hope so, Maja, but I have a bad feeling about today," Dwarf Beset said as she turned to walk away.

Becataten's chair moved swiftly across the indoor settlement, but she got a glimpse of Viceroy Merymose's headquarters and barracks. The two-story headquarters took up a great part of the corner of the interior wall at the opposite end of the fortress and built into the garrison walls like her domicile. Hammocks, looked to be numerous, stockpiles of weapons crowed corners and men dressed in red kilts were busy organizing equipment getting ready to leave the garrison. Were they to follow the Viceroy? She also noticed a tangle of workshops next to a small open temple with statues of Egyptian Gods and Gods that she assumed were of the natives. This looked worth visiting on another day.

Once outside the Fortress walls, Becataten finally felt free. She stepped from her chair to the chariot. She smiled at the Nubians with such delight that they nearly lost their composure. The driver bowed. In perfect Egyptian, he asked where she wanted to go. "Now that we're outside the compound, drive around the walls of the Fortress," she said. Becataten decided to let him take the reins so she could watch him drive, but knew ultimately, she would ask to handle her new conveyance alone.

The chariot wheels had been stained red, the body handsomely woven of sturdy wicker and the floor made of laced leather. An ostrich feather that adorned the mare's head bobbed as they trotted off. A small canopy had been rigged to afford shade for she and the driver. The other five Nubians jogged behind. She smiled as a warm wind touched her face, and the fast trot of her high-stepping horse gave her a feeling of joy. "I want to look at the construction of the walls of the Fortress so don't drive too fast." Becataten said.

Her Nubian guards were of a lighter color, and once again she noticed these were natives that garnered the higher positions. No doubt some intermarriage had taken place with fairer Egyptians like herself. The Viceroy's son from a Nubian mother must be lighter, she thought. Not having gotten a good look at the boy, she remained curious about him. Why had the viceroy not mentioned his son before? She would not judge him even if the boy's mother was a Nubian. The viceroy had spent much time in Kush and met the woman long before they knew one another. He did tell her about his son born of an Egyptian mother. She would like to get to know this young boy and hoped he would not be punished on her account.

Once outside the compound, Becataten was drawn to the enormous ditch that surrounded the Fortress. She guessed it kept the enemy from scaling the walls. Scrolls had told her that these fortifications had begun fifteen hundred inundations before her birth. With reverence she stared, realizing this structure was as old as the pyramids. Amazed at the protruding towers studded with loopholes from which archers could direct their arrows, she stood in the slow-moving chariot, shading her eyes with her hand, unable to take her eyes off the high walls.

The immensity of this embattlement amazed her when she heard a sharp call from a rear guard. Her able driver abruptly drew the chariot to a stop. He looked east to a glowing horizon that covered a high mound and was about to deliver Ra's rays. Standing in silhouette, with the sun at their backs, were thousands of Nubians. Spears and shields in hand, looking down on Becataten and her six guards.

Chapter 5

♊

With strong arms and firm hands, Becataten's chariot driver raced back to the Fortress, charged through the opened gates and across the settlement enclosure, ignoring the regulation never to race a horse-drawn vehicle through the confines of the walls, and shouting a phrase she did not know. The huge cedar doors, that the Viceroy had imported from the eastern shores of The Great Sea, boomed shut behind them. That sound triggered panic among the people within. Shutting the Fortress gates during daylight hours meant great danger was near. Becataten held hard to the rails of her transport. They flew by the barracks where commanders marshaled their troops, who poured from their quarters. Hundreds of bowmen took to the wall-stairs. With full quivers slung over their backs, they raced up the steps for a position of height to defend the stronghold.

Crying women gathered up their children, and family men were arming themselves. The charioteer drove the mare toward Becataten's entrance holding the horse hard when he arrived. After the abrupt stop, the foamy-mouthed animal pawed the earth.

"Thank the Gods you are safe, Taten," said Maja as she ran to her.

Beset followed. "Taten, we must leave Buhen immediately. A rebellion is taking place, and Nehesy has arranged our escape," Beset said, hobbling to the chariot.

"And how is it to happen that we leave without my husband?" Becataten asked.

Nehesy stepped forward, "Princess, the Viceroy's boat is on the Nile waiting for your departure to Thebes. It will accommodate you and your attendants, but we must move with great speed. Many warring tribes are assembling across the river as we speak."

She saw her frightened household staff packing only what they could carry, then disappearing through a small door that led to the steep narrow footpath to reach the landing on the Nile. Becataten turned to Nehesy with her head held high. "Please see that Dwarf Beset, Nanny Maja, my father and my staff are all aboard the Viceroy's craft, and make sure that they leave at once."

Nehesy stood at attention looking alarmed. "Princess Becataten, you must come as well. It is very dangerous to be within these walls. The Fortress will be under full attack soon."

"But I have heard nothing from the Viceroy, and I do not plan to leave until I do," she bolted back.

Nehesy implored. "We have no word as to the exact whereabouts of the Viceroy, but we do know with certainty that the fifty guards he left with have already been taken prisoner, Princess."

Becataten's eyes widened. "But surely we will hear soon were he is."

As Nehesy and Becataten continued to debate, Dwarf Beset shook her head and slipped away. In haste she struggled toward Abu's lean-to.

Huni was screeching and baring his teeth at the gathering pandemonium while Abu tried to quiet him.

Dwarf Beset put her hand on Abu to gain his attention. Over the noise of panic, she explained that they were in the midst of a rebellion, and Becataten was unwilling to leave using Nehesy's escape plan until she heard from the Viceroy.

As Pharaoh's half-brother and paramount aide, Abu had been a brilliant royal astrologer who made major decisions throughout his career. After listening to Beset, he sat in a brief silence. Then he said, "Have a healer make a poultice of the poppy and send Nehesy to me."

Beset promptly did as he said.

Nehesy arrived to confer with Abu, and then summoned Becataten's six Nubians and marched into the quarters of the princess. She looked up from her scroll, "Nehesy, I was just going to summon you. I want this scroll sent to the Viceroy. I'm sure someone can find him. I have written that I will wait for him here, and that I have sent my staff on to Thebes."

Nehesy looked at her the way a person looks at someone who doesn't understand imminent danger. "Princess, it is quite possible that the Viceroy has been taken hostage along *with* his men. We must leave now!"

"How can you be sure? Have you received word of this, Nehesy?"

With a resigned look, Nehesy moved aside, and nodded to one of the Nubians, who swiftly covered Becataten's mouth with the poultice of the poppy. Her resistance to the drug was brief. She slumped on her stool while a guardsman caught her up and carried her outside to a waiting litter chair. Maja and Isis watched, holding one another in disbelief.

It was a short trip for the barers of the chair to carry an unconscious Becataten to the top of the steep path that led to the harbor below. The Nubian guard who held the poultice to Becataten's mouth, jogged next to the chair. When they stopped, and lowered the litter in front of the egress to the steep foot path, the guard picked up Becataten, carefully settled her over his shoulder then took long, slow steady strides down the precipice where below the Viceroy's vessel was moored on the Mother Nile.

Nehesy sent word ahead to the captain of the Golden Falcon to be prepared to receive a full load of passengers for an immediate sail. Then Neshey sent a guardsman to Abu and to lead him from his lean-to across the courtyard and down the narrow exit. The man encouraged Abu to hold on to his shoulders as they traversed the long and winding precarious path. Huni followed Abu holding on to his loincloth whimpering all the way.

The boat had been quickly boarded by scores of Becataten's staff who anxiously awaited the Princess. The decks were crowded, and the crew eager to sail. Sounds of Nubian natives rustled through the wind as they mounted mountain tops. Off to the side Pygmy Lady scanned the hills with the eye of a falcon. Abu's baboon screeched as Nehesy's men moved unconscious Becataten to the boat, settling her on a wicker chair at midships then helping Abu into the chair next to her. Pygmy Lady stepped forward, yanked the baboon's tether, and growled at him. Huni calmed. Neshey snapped his fingers at a half dozen of his men to board too, which surprised Pygmy Lady. Abu was settled in the chair next to the Princess. Pygmy Lady, the last to board, took Huni leash in hand.

Abu settled his arm around his daughter. "This is the second time I have been responsible for you being carried off with a poppy poultice. But this time, my daughter, I do so for your safety, and in memory of your mother, Princess Attah." Abu held her tight, softly speaking his words into her ear. Once the boat got underway, Abu called out, "Where is my baboon?"

"He is here with me and needs to be more obedient!" Pygmy Lady called. The square sail was set, and rowers maneuvered the tumultuous waters, while terrified attendants looked up from seated positions on deck at the towering cliffs noting more Nubian tribes assembling. As the Nile rushed at them from the second cataract, the ship traveled rapidly away from the Fortress. High waves slapped at the craft's hull. But the sounds of war cries competed with the sounds of tumbling water.

After a swift sail to the first cataract, the captain shaded his eyes from the sun, squinting ahead at the grumbling river. "If all the gods are with us, we will be able to sail across the first cataract, but everyone hold hard to the vessel." As they advanced, the women screamed, the men held their jaws tight. Polemen, with their long shafts, stood to help the rowers maneuver through the belly of stones.

Abu held Becataten tight. When she awoke, at first frightened, then angry, she refused to speak. The strength of the poppy potion she had been given was strong and sent her back into a sound sleep. Abu's face showed concern that she may have been given too much of the poppy.

The morning had been fraught with panic when sailing away from the impending rebellion at Fortress Buhen. Even though he Viceroy's sturdy boat was well over one hundred steps long, it was never designed to accommodate the numbers she now carried. The only good thing about the excess weight, the captain mumbled to his mate, was it might stabilize the craft and help get them through the tumultuous waters ahead. Gratefully, three days later, the passengers were as calm as the Mother Nile had become. Becataten had not yet spoken and was intermittently vomiting.

At the front of the boat, Dwarf Beset stood holding on to a line enjoying the vast display of growing fields and the aroma of blooming flowers coming into view. "Look at the rows of beautiful iris. Can you smell them, she called?"

Abu could smell them and hear cattle too. "We must be passing the southern end of the Suti Estate." Abu called from midships.

Beset's interest perked. She could hear Abu say something, she thought about the Estate, and her active mind quickly developed a plan. She made her way across the long deck to Abu, hanging onto one line and then another along the way, where he and Becataten sat. He held is daughter upright with a strong arm while Maja sat at her feet. The dwarf bent to his ear and whispered. "Abu, I was thinking, little awaits any of us at the Palace in Thebes. The Suti Estate would be an ideal place to stop, especially when Lady Nagara hears Becataten is without a home."

Maja eyes widened at Beset's words as she stood to take in the vast number of crops and animal herds as they passed.

Abu turned away, looking to be in deep thought then heaving a great sigh, he said, "This is a fine location for the Princess, Dwarf Beset."

The captain and Nehesy were told of the plan and motioned the rowers toward the Estate dock. Waves of relief came from the Becataten's attendants when it was announced they were headed home to the Estate.

In the distance came three hard-driven chariots with Stable Master Senzar in the lead. After a dramatic halt, and a tight hold on his reins, he called, "Are you here at the invitation of my master, Royal Architect Suti?" The lowered sail did not identify the Golden Falcon.

Dwarf Beset stood and formally introduced herself, explaining that they had just escaped a beginning uprising in Kush. When Becataten came into Senzar's view, he bowed his head and said, "How may I serve you, Princess."

"The Princess is not well. We need a litter for her," Dwarf Beset said.

Neshey's Nubians hastened to set the boarding plank for disembarking. Another, at Nehesy's command, rushed to Becataten's side, deftly lifting her into his arms, and rushed to Senzar's chariot. Stepping on board the chariot, the Nubian turned to the Stable Master. "Nehesy says we go now, no need for a litter," as he held Becataten firmly in his arms. Senzar nodded and turned his vehicle wide toward the great house. A crack of his whip triggered his steed into a gallop.

Lady Nagara had been alerted to the commotion and stood shading her eyes at the top of the stairs to see the Stable Master's chariot rush toward the villa. When Senzar's transport slowed, the Nubian was quick to mount the stairs three steps at a time to the large entry where he was directed to a grand chamber.

When the Nubian passed Lady Nagara, she looked horrified, and directed him to the downstairs sitting chamber. "Carefully place her on this lounge," said Lady Nagara as she knelt at Becataten's side. The receiving chamber held four lounges, all covered in the worm-silk imported from far eastern lands. The walls were painted with verdant Nile scenes.

"She has been drugged with the poppy, that is all," the Nubian guardsman said before he turned and left.

"My Healer, send my Healer at once!" called an alarmed Lady Nagara.

As the Healer rushed to Becataten's side, he and Lady Nagara looked at one another, perplexed.

"It does appear that the Princess was drugged with the poppy, My Lady. I can smell a residue of the poultice. I will prepare a strong herbal tea that will revive her." He strode out of the room.

Almost as if Lady Nagara didn't believe that Becataten was alive, she began speaking to her and rubbing her hands. "Becataten, wake up. You are safe at the Estate. Wake my child. Your attendants are here, I am here. All is well." Becataten made a small breathy noise but did not awaken. Worried, Lady Nagara looked for her Healer, but he had not returned yet with the promised tea.

Dwarf Beset arrived at the Estate house in a chariot, but on the shoulders of a standing Nubian. They had raced toward the villa as she tussled at the top of his back, hanging on to his bowl-shaped hair with all her will. When the vehicle stopped, and she was set down, she staggered to a seat at the bottom of the stairs to collect herself. Her age betrayed her patience, and her dignity. In a controlled calm, she sat quietly. Walking toward her were Becataten's attendants, headed to their familiar places of work. Maja had chosen to walk with them.

"You don't look well, Beset. What happened?" Maja said as she took a seat on a step next to Beset.

"One of those giant Nubians sat me on his shoulders as we raced here in a chariot. I had to hang on to his hair so as to not fall!" Reaching for her staff with a shaking arm, Beset said, "Just because we are small, people always think we are toys."

"I am glad I walked," Maja said.

Beset's head shook and she started up the stairs. "We should go into the house and see to Taten and get something to eat."

"I have something to tell, Beset," Maja said.

Beset turned to Maja, whose dark eyes shone with fear. "What is it Maja?"

"When I walked here from the boat, I heard some bad talk."

"Tell me what you heard, Maja."

"Some of Taten's attendants understand Nehesy's language, and said he was a bad man, and we should not trust him."

At that moment, Nubian guardsmen jogged passed them, spears, and shields in tow, led by Nehesy. They were a small but disciplined force, Beset observed, contemplating how to learn more about them when she didn't speak their tongue. Abu was someone to confer with in this matter.

Back at the boat, it appeared that the only passengers who were still on board were Abu, Huni, and Pygmy Lady. And no one noticed the small child and basket of two young dogs that were sound asleep at the rear. The driver of the third chariot was offering Abu a ride and swift delivery to the Estate.

"I will not be going to the big house," Abu said.

"The Princess would want you at her side. Go!" Pygmy Lady said.

Abu needed help getting off the vessel, and as an attendant aided him, Abu disregarded Pygmy Lady's words. "You have a large stable, do you not?" Abu asked the charioteer.

The driver nodded, noting that Abu was blind, and of a high station. "We do indeed have a grand stable, My Lord, and I can take you there."

Abu noted he had been addressed with respect, and a title. That hadn't happened since he had been tortured and expelled from Pharaoh's court, nearly an inundation ago.

After he and Huni were loaded into a chariot and were driven to the stables, Abu said, "My baboon and I shall take our quarters there."

"And me too," said Pygmy Lady, as she took Huni in tow.

The Stable Manager settled Abu into an ample stall, where a groom was ushered out. "Are you sure that you wish to stay in this accommodation, My Lord?" asked the Stable Manager.

"I am," replied Abu.

Pygmy Lady's deep voice commanded, "This will do us fine. Now leave us."

In the far corner of the large stall was a pile of barley hay Huni spied where he collapsed to rest, curled up and faced the wall. Abu sat beside him.

Pygmy Lady stood over Abu and said, "I am going to guess you were a man who suffered disgrace." She stood over them both, hands on her hips.

"You offend me. Leave now!" Abu said, not liking the voice he heard.

"Ha, you *must* have been important, the way you order people around. Let me see," she said, rubbing her chin. "You... were maybe someone from Pharaoh's court, I think. And you wear that cloth around your eyes, probably because they were burned out of your head. You must have been very bad, very smart too, I wager. But in the end, the Gods pissed on you."

Abu waited for a time then spoke. "Why are you here?"

"I met the Viceroy some time ago and educated him about 'The Land of the Bow.' Now, I am here to assist the Princess when she bears her son, and maybe help with something else too."

With tight lips, Abu's head shook in disgust. He stood to feel about for a cot. His hands ran across a meager straw mattress that he shook well before settling it back on its frame and lying back down. Nearby he heard Pygmy Lady settling herself into a makeshift bed.

Before they fell into sleep, Pygmy Lady said, "Can you understand the tongue that Nehesy speaks?"

Abu grunted.

Pygmy Lady said, "If that grunt was a yes, you had better start listening to him and his guardsmen when they talk. They are not friends," she said in a warning voice.

Abu thought of her words as he fell asleep.

Chapter 6

♊

Sitting up on her lounge in a dirty shift, kohl running down her tear stained checks, Becataten choked out, "Where is the Viceroy?"

Lady Nagara settled herself on a stool at her side and said, "We do not know, Becataten, but I am glad you are here, and most happy to see you alive."

Becataten looked around the familiar room, as if just now noticing where she was. She reached out for Lady Nagara's face and touched it. "How did I come to be here? I was drugged, wasn't I?"

"Yes, you were." She motioned a slave girl to attend to Becataten with damp linen cloths scented with peppermint oil.

"Whoever did this to me? I hate them, and I will punish them!" Becataten cursed.

"Will you, Becataten?" Lady Nagara said as she took her hand.

"Who drugged me, Lady Nagara? Do you know?"

Lady Nagara sat rigid, looking hard into Becataten's eyes, "I'm not sure. But you should be grateful to them. That act saved your life. The Nubian, Nehesy, tells me you were unwilling to leave the settlement and by the time you did, it was surrounded by rebel tribes."

Becataten had a far-off look in her eyes at the memory of what had happened. "Lady Nagara. What of the Viceroy?"

"I think you must brace yourself for the possibility that he has been captured by hostile tribes, Becataten."

"That is what I did not want to hear," Becataten said as she covered her face with her hands and wept.

Lady Nagara's heart hadn't ached for a man since she was a young girl in Pharaoh's court when he had turned away from her to marry Lady Tiye and make her his queen. As she began to relate to Becataten's stress, she tried changing the subject. "There are a few things you must know, my child. The military establishment at the Fortress got word to Pharaoh of the uprising, and he has responded by sending his royal navy and ground forces to secure the Fortress. I will see that a scroll is sent to him explaining you are unharmed. I must also tell you that Pharaoh's child did not recover from his illness. Your dream of the demise of the heir-apparent was evidently prophetic. Because of this, Our Living God is in deep mourning, and will not lead his troops to Kush but instead has given command to his generals."

Becataten collected herself, and said, "Oh, I *am* grieved to hear Pharaoh has lost his oldest son."

In the distance, loud cheering could be heard. Lady Nagara's Butler appeared, bowed before her, then stood tall and said, "My Lady, Pharaoh's troops are sailing past us on the Nile to defend Fortress Buhen and put down the rebellion. The Estate attendants have rushed to the Mother's shore to cheer them on."

"As they should," replied Lady Nagara with her head held high.

Becataten struggled to rise from the lounge and said, "I would like to see them from the stairs."

But after standing, she wavered and covered her mouth to avoid vomiting, which brought the slave girl rushing toward her with a bowl.

That night, Dwarf Beset and Nanny Maja were each assigned an upstairs chamber in the grand house of the Suti Estate. Because the residence was so formidable and the rooms vast, they decided to occupy a large chamber together. This decision, and the life-threatening event they had been through, marked the ending of any animus the two had previously held for one another. The large space had an attached sitting room. The mattresses on their cots were plump with goose down. Urns of flowers and bowls of fruit arrived as they settled in. Attendants followed, lighting tall floor candles.

After their evening meal, Maja concealed a smile and said, "I never had someone empty *my* piss pot, Beset."

Beset nodded. But she wasn't displaying her usual enthusiasm for life, or even the familiar food that had always enticed her. Resting on a lounge and with a wistful response she said, "It *is* lovely and peaceful here, isn't it?"

Maja nodded. "And the trays of meats and vegetables are like the Pharaoh-food you once brought to our apartment."

Beset agreed with a nod but added no more.

Maja cocked her head. "Are you sick, Beset?"

Beset said, "I have something to tell you, Maja. Please listen and understand my words."

Maja stood and went to sit on Beset's lounge. "What is it, Beset?"

"Maja, I am going to die soon, and there are some important things you must help me with before my death."

Maja looked confused. "Oh no, that cannot be true, you don't look sick."

Beset said, "You must trust me in this matter. A dwarf always knows when their death is near."

With a sad face, Maja said, "I will listen to you and I will try to understand your words." She folded her hands and sat to listen, her left eye drooping more than usual.

Beset said, "We must help Taten in three ways, Maja. First, we must learn more about Nehesy and his guardsman, and how dangerous they might be. Second, we must establish a line of communication with someone at the Palace; a person we can pass information to. And lastly, we must become friends with Pygmy Lady because she is like me; she feels and knows much."

Maja made an ugly face and said, "It will be hard to like Pygmy Lady. But because you ask, I will try."

The next day as Ra washed over the white walls of the Estate, Nanny Maja slipped away from the villa to seek out Pygmy Lady. She did so because Beset had explained that this strange woman must become their ally, and although this troubled Maja, she chose to obey Beset's request. Walking in the morning heat, her bent body plodded toward the Estate dock where she had last seen the pygmy.

"Greetings, Poleman." Maja said as she stepped near the river's edge. She startled the man who was absorbed in the repair of his small raft, and he took his time to answer.

Maja waited.

He stood looking annoyed and scratched his crotch through his filthy loin cloth.

Maja asked, "I am sorry to interrupt you, but have you seen the Pygmy Lady? She came in the boat with all of us from Kush?"

Stable dogs barked from a stall, and Maja jumped.

The Poleman said, "The dogs are shut up in a stall, and won't bother you. You want the one who went in the chariot with the baboon and the blind man?"

Maja nodded. "I think so."

The Poleman pointed toward the stables.

Turning in that direction, the mild smell of horse manure drew her to the large structure that housed the Estates horses, chariots, and carts. It was an orderly, well-tended barn with slaves clearing the stalls of manure while others were assigned to swat the ever-present flies. Certain attendants fed and groomed while others exercised the revered horses that were largely traded from Babylon. Leathers hung on pools where workers sat cleaning bridles and harnesses. The smell rising from metal workers braziers made Maja's nostrils flare. She didn't know that they were fabricating bits and fittings for horses and chariots. Her eyes grew wide at the bustling of another world at work.

She was directed to a large horse stall, cordoned off with thickly woven papyrus walls and as she approached, she called, "Pygmy Lady!"

Abu answered from within and asked, "Who calls?"

Timidly she said, "It is Maja, Princess Becataten's Nanny."

"Enter," said Abu in a strong voice.

With trepidation Maja entered the stall. Huni frightened her, and she planned to avoid him.

"Greetings," she said, staying close to the entrance and looking around to assess the situation.

"Greetings Maja, is your Mistress well?" Abu said in a calm voice.

Stepping further into the stall, she said. "Taten, I mean the Princess, is sleeping, but she is well, I think." Maja was still scanning about for the baboon that seemed strangely absent. She wondered where Huni was, and if Pygmy Lady had him with her.

Abu said, "You have a message for me?"

"No, Beset sent me with words for Pygmy Lady."

The stable dogs continued to bark.

Abu was seated on a narrow cot filled with grain stalks, unlike the soft goose-down mattresses in the grand house Maja now slept on. In one corner of the large stall were Becataten's puppies sound asleep, and in another corner sat a small finely woven wicker chest.

Abu asked, "Why does Dwarf Beset want to see her?"

Maja seemed unable to tell Abu why, and instead stared at her feet.

Abu asked again with more authority, "You can tell me why she wants to see Pygmy Lady, Maja."

Abu's booming voice of so many years ago had commanded Maja and her mistress, Princess Attah, in Pharaoh's harem. Hearing him speak intimidated her into servitude, she jumped, then straightened her posture as best she could and approached Abu.

Nervously and with haste, Maja related everything Beset had told her the night prior. "And there is one more thing," Maja added nervously. "I have heard talk in the big house that the Viceroy may be captured, and attendants are whispering that Becataten may be with child."

The night they all arrived at the Estate, Nehesy and the guardsmen had jogged in the dark well beyond the growing fields to make their camp. They too had watched Pharaoh's royal troops sail the Nile to put down the rebellion at Fort Buhen, but with scorn. While one gathered sticks for a fire, another quietly raided a pen of geese, choosing a plump gosling for roasting. After the fire was sparked and the young goose was set to roast, Nehesy said, "The Viceroy is held prisoner in the village of his Nubian wife. Who among us will rescue him and return him to this place?"

The six men all looked at one another in amazement shaking their heads. Nehesy smiled. "I know now you are all loyal to Our Land of the Bow." Nehesy continued, "We stay here for now. I have a runner who will bring us news of our rebellion. If enough of the tribes come together and take Fortress Buhen, we can keep the gluttonous Egyptians out of our land. And I have a plan to take the life of the Viceroy."

In agreement, the men all brandished their spears, and shouted a war cry.

The Poleman Maja had earlier talked to had returned to complete his raft repairs and was sitting on his haunches waiting for passengers to ferry across the Nile for a small fee. The tallest of Nehesy's Nubians slinked toward the craft and said, "How much to take me to the first cataract?"

The Poleman said, "So you want to return to the rebellion and join your kind?"

"How much?" the Nubian asked.

"I will take you *not* to the first cataract, but close, for a piece of silver debon that weighs heavy in my hand."

The Nubian stepped on board and reached into his pouch.

Chapter 7

♊

Abu, Huni, Pygmy Lady and Ne Ne, the small girl who came with the dogs, were all sharing the barn space. It was surprising that Ne Ne had found her way onto the boat through the turmoil of leaving Kush. She even brought the two pups along in a sack. The ten-year-old, with eleven brothers and sisters managed well on her own and had attached herself to Abu. She was learning quickly the language of the Egyptians, and she liked being Abu's eyes—even occasionally referring to him as father. The stall was kept quite orderly with slaves emptying their pots of waste and refilling their jars of well water and beer. But it *was* crowded, and Abu needed more privacy to think and plan a strategy that would ensure Becataten's safety after hearing all that Maja had to tell him. He had surmised that cunning Nehesy, and his small force of Nubians, were traitors and need an inroad into the Estate as spies. He needed to learn more of the whereabouts of the Viceroy, and he needed a scribe.

"Attendant," he loudly called. "Quiet those dogs!"

"Yes, My Lord," answered a passing slave.

"And summon me the Stable Master," Abu growled.

The slave fumbled his words. "The, the... Stable Master is away but will be back, back before Ra leaves us."

"See that he comes to me when her returns," Abu said with authority.

The slave nodded and ran from the stall, frightened by Abu's booming voice.

Ne Ne rushed into the stall returning with Pygmy Lady and Huni from an early morning walk. She and Pygmy Lady had eaten at the outdoor Estate kitchen where they were fed and treated well. Pygmy Lady walked to Abu, grunted, and placed a basket with warm bread and two boiled goose eggs in his lap. Ne Ne brought him a handful of figs from her pouch. The pups sidled up to Ne Ne as she greeted them in the far corner where they were kept.

Ne Ne sat at Abu's side while he ate and jabbered excitedly about all the wonderful things she had seen during their outing. Huni sat on Abu's other side, sweating and eating a pomegranate. He too was in bright spirits having been outside, and off his leash, which hadn't happened in some time.

"Old Man," Pygmy Lady said, "I saw Nehesy's tallest Nubian, Kombo, take a raft back to Kush this morning. Why do you think he did that?"

Ne Ne took the floor at Abu's feet with the small dogs. In her tongue, Ne Ne said, "I know why."

Abu patted her and said, "Tell me, Ne Ne, what you know."

She looked very serious and speaking words in her tribal dialect, mixed with the Egyptian language, she said, "Kombo said it was a secret and I should tell only you."

Abu pointed to his ear.

She leaned close and whispered, "Kombo said that he has gone to rescue the Viceroy."

Becataten lay in bed in the morning feeling as ill as she had the night before. The slave girl attending her had told her she was pregnant. She chose not to entertain the thought too much, as it didn't make her feel any better knowing that the Viceroy was captured. But she wouldn't think the worst. She loved her Mosie and together they had just begun their future. This happiness and love for him couldn't be taken from her, and she refused to admit to what she knew many believed; that the Viceroy was being brutally tortured or was already dead. A baby, now, was a complication she could not think about. She had tried to believe her recovery from the poppy poisoning was causing her pregnancy-like symptoms, but so many had said she was pregnant, the possibility was becoming real to her.

Maja entered Becataten's chamber and as if on cue bluntly said, "Good morning, Taten, are you really going to have a baby?"

Becataten smiled weakly. "I think I might, Maja. I haven't seen the healer yet but everyone around me tells me I am. And when I think about it, I have missed a moon visit, maybe two. Everything is so complicated right now though. Where is Beset?"

Maja moved to sit on Becataten's cot. She ran her dark, rough-skinned hand over the smooth material. Her round black eyes grew large and filled with tears. She hadn't touched Becataten since childhood but reached out for her. With a grave face, her hand on Becataten's, she told her what Beset had said about dying. Maja left out what Beset had told her about Nehesy. Before Maja could get her words out her checks spilled with tears and she began to sob.

Becataten took Maja in her arms and the two sat hugging one another until Becataten said, "Oh Maja, we must do something." Becataten sat up in bed, clapped her hands for a servant and asked for the Estate healer to tend to Dwarf Beset. Then she quickly rose, dressed and together she and Maja went to Beset where the healer was already examining her. Rushing to her bedside, Becataten said, "Beset, tell us this is not true. It must be a mistake."

The healer shook his head and said, "I am sorry to say that Dwarf Beset is very weak."

Beset reclined on the same lounge where Maja had left her. In a frail voice Beset said, "Taten, you look better than you did last night, and a rumor says you are going to bear a child. I would like to say that I will live to see your baby, but I don't believe I will."

Becataten sat next to Beset, her green eyes sparkling from tears flooding them.

Dwarf Beset said, "Don't weep, Taten. We have had a fine time together, you, Maja, and me. We lived the life of great luxury in the Royal Nursery, we were happy in our small apartment together, and although we lost Jobu, he lives with Osiris and in our hearts. And you, Taten, survived a clergy-plot showing us all that you possess the Heka. And Pharaoh blessed you with the Viceroy, who you have come to love. He returned your love and saved the Royal Astrologer. And you now have your father in your life. But, Taten, what I want to talk about is your future. You have difficulties yet to face. You have heard me say that great tests are given to great people. To face those challenges, I believe you must have protection, and that will come from special people."

Becataten took Beset's hands in hers. "Beset, please, do we have to talk about this now? Can't we just be together and stay happy for a while?"

Beset said, "Yes, we can, but not until you have heard me out."

Maja saw that Beset was failing while Becataten could not. Putting her hand on Beset's shoulder, she said, "Taten, we must listen to Dwarf Besets words."

Becataten swallowed hard and nodded.

Beset continued, "I want you to keep the Pygmy Lady close. She has the Heka, which she calls magic. She will aid you in the birth of your child, and I believe she has an eye that sees into the future. Also, I want you to talk to the Royal Astrologer about everything. He has a fine mind, and I think he can reestablish his influence at the Palace when you need it most. Find your father a scribe. Lastly, Taten, do not be so trusting of people. There are those around you that would do you harm."

When the Stable Master Senzar returned, he sent a slave to inform Abu that he was available to meet with him. Senzar had been told by his assistant that Abu was blind, an unknown person but of some importance, and that Abu remained adamant that he didn't wish to be a guest at the villa.

Little Ne Ne, with the pups following her, had walked Abu down a long barn corridor ending at an open-air office, canopied by a thick linen canvas, supported on pools where the stable master conducted his business. He was an experienced and professional horseman who liked being near his horses and their needs. Running the barn at the Estate meant acquiring horses, breading them, and keeping the animals fit, along with overseeing the fabrication of tack, vehicles, and carts. Senzar's very name was that of a city where great horse masters came from in Babylon. He had carried the title Chariot Master on several of Pharaoh's campaigns, and when he retired, came highly recommended to run the Suti Estate barns.

"Greetings, Abu. Should I be referring to you by a title?" Senzar said, directing an attendant to bring a folding chair of horse hide for his guest.

Ne Ne helped settle Abu in the folding chair and stood next to him. Abu said, "Just Abu will do, Stable Master."

The Stable Master said, "How can I assist you, Abu?"

Abu said, "I should like quarters more fitting my needs."

The Stable Master said, "I understand you do not wish to live in the Estate house. But I can assure you there are fine rooms and many servants there."

Abu said, "No, I do not, or rather, I would not be welcome."

The Stable Master looked both uncomfortable and confused by Abu's comments and said, "I do not wish to be rude, but may I ask why you are here?"

Ne Ne interrupted and said, "He is Princess Becataten's father."

The stable master stood and said, "My Lord, I, I apologize for not knowing. Please forgive me. You are the father of Princess Becataten and Prince Jobutaten. May I offer my condolences on your loss of the young Prince."

Abu put his hand on Ne Ne as if to quiet her and fell silent for some time. Then he said, "Just find me quarters that seclude me from the Estate house."

At that moment, rushing toward the Stable Master's office came Princess Becataten and Maja. "Father, I have found you! I am *so* happy you are here." She took his hand then looked at the Stable Master. He remained standing, bowed, and snapped his fingers for another horse hid chair to be unfolded.

"Father, I am pleased that you have met Stable Master Senzar. Do you know that he may well have saved me from a foreign assassin that tried to take my life when Lady Nagara and I were caravanning to the Palace?'

Abu looked away, appearing to hide the shame he felt at his involvement in the crown-takeover that initiated that event. In a rough voice, he said, "My gratitude to you, Senzar, my gratitude."

"But of course, My Lord. Now, we were talking about a residence for you. There *is* a dwelling far behind the barns that once housed the manager of the Estate. He was released of his duties many moons ago when Lady Nagara took control. Since that time, we all report to her directly, and there has been no need to use the home."

Abu said, "Let us walk through this place."

"Of course, My Lord."

Becataten took Abu's arm and they soon found the residence. With pleasure, she pointed out its appointments to her blind father, and together for the first time she felt they must look like father and daughter. Abu soon became serious and said, "You must not reveal to Lady Nagara that I am staying here. Maybe one day, but not quite yet, Princess."

She embraced him and said, "Whatever you say, Father. I will ask the Stable Master to also hold his tongue for now about your new arrangements."

The dwelling sat in a shady grove of date palms, constructed of sizable whitewashed bricks, adding thickness and further coolness to the home. Both privacy and distance from the villa was assured. Three large chambers; one for working, another for dining and one for lounging, plus several sleeping cubicles for servants, appealed to Abu as his daughter described the dwelling while he felt his way around.

"Oh, this is a good location for you, isn't it, Father? Look, it has a stairway to the roof so you can escape inundation. I will arrange for a cook, a butler and a slave or two," Becataten said.

Pygmy Lady came sauntering in with Huni and said, "This *is* an improvement," and flopped on a dusty wicker lounge.

Chapter 8

When Kombo stepped off the raft, once again on Nubian soil, he moved about with stealth. He could be recognized as a part of the Viceroy's guard while wearing a red kilt and carrying his Egyptian-crested shield. Finding a small child, he paid the boy a few pieces of copper debon to find him a kilt made of common hide and a round Nubian styled shield. With care, he avoided villages that were empty of men who had left to join the insurgency.

Having changed his appearance, he headed toward the settlement where the Nubian woman lived who bore the Viceroy's son, Ahmose. Rumor suggested Viceroy Merymose was being held there. Along his path, Kombu encountered spirited rhetoric by tribesmen on their way to join the revolt calling out, *Kill the Egyptian dogs. We are greater warriors. Take back our Land of the Bow.*

When Kombo arrived at the village where it was believed the Viceroy was held, it too was nearly abandoned. A few old men and children with their mothers were the only people moving about. He strode into the center of the circle of thatched huts showing confidence, loudly requested water, and said that he was on his way to join the rebellion. In quick response, from one of the huts, the Viceroy's weak speech called for a drink. Kombo's voice had been recognized.

An old woman approached with a jug to well water to quench Kombo's thirst. He thanked her and said, "Who is calling from that hut?"

"It is the dog, Merymose," said the old woman.

"You mean the Viceroy, himself?"

The woman nodded.

"I am surprised he has not been killed," Kombo said.

"Just tortured. When the men return, they will take their time to kill him."

"May I see him?"

"She gave him a curious look and asked why.

"When I join my brothers to fight for our 'Land of the Bow,' I can tell them I saw the great Viceroy Merymose, captive."

She muttered something and motioned him to follow her.

Kombo entered the round dwelling built of flimsy, acacia sticks. Adjusting to the darkness took time. Once inside his nostrils flared at the stench from human waste and rotting injuries. Unable to stifle a cough, he moved forward to a bound body lying in the dirt. The viceroy's neck was red with old blood. A circular wound caused by the rope that collared him was spotted with flies. His kilt soiled with waste. In a corner, what first appeared as a shadow, became the image of a young boy, Ahmose, the Viceroy's son.

Kombo put on a brief performance of spitting and cursing at the Viceroy, then marched out of the hut. It would have been unwise to stay, as the boy knew him to be a part of the Viceroy's loyal guard. If Ahmose exposed him, Kombo would suffer a long and painful death as a traitor. The guardsman picked up his pace and sprinted away from the village. Along the way he collected any spears he could find.

After running a safe distance, Kombo gathered small twigs and some dry grass to build a fire. He found a rag and some animal fat in a herder's shed. Then he circled the settlement and returned to squat behind the hut where the Viceroy was held captive. On his haunches, he arranged the sticks and kindling he had gathered into a small mound and wrapped his spears with strips he tore from the cloth smeared with tallow, then waited in silence. When the half-moon moved low in the heavens and the sky would darken no more, he struck his flint to start a fire. Setting the tips of his spears with tallow, he set the rags aflame then one by one sent them flying toward the most distant huts. This set the roofs of dry palm fronds ablaze, drawing the villagers of women and children to the spectacle.

With the swiftness of a hyena, Kombo raced back to the captive's hut, reached the Viceroy, and sliced his rope constraints. His long arms lifted the Viceroy over his left shoulder, turning his face away from the reek of his urine-stained kilt. The villagers arrived at the fire hooping and gesticulating with alarm, thinking the fighting had reached them. In haste, Kombo saw that Ahmose quickly understood what was happening and began to gather spears and clubs. Kombo exited the shelter as quickly as he had entered. With each of his long strides, the Viceroy groaned, and his head bobbed like that of a dead man. Kombo's gait gained momentum, knowing that the barren land offered no cover, and a grey sky would soon follow with light.

Following behind was Ahmose, mute. As a shy restrained young boy, his silence served him well. The

Nubians who held the Viceroy captive had never grasped that he was loyal to his father. During the Viceroy's capture and punishment, Ahmose had remained in the background. Not quite old enough to join the rebellion, he had been saved from fighting against Egypt.

As soon as Kombo reached the Nile, he lowered the Viceroy into the water to conceal him. It also ridded him of the tenacious flies that clung to the circular wound deeply set into his neck. Revived by the water, the Viceroy looked up at Kombo, and in a raspy voice said, "Greetings old friend. You saved my life."

With a wide grin, Kombo held up his long forefinger and said, "I did, and I must do so *one* more time to pay you back for saving mine, *twice.*"

"But not today, Kombo," said the Viceroy.

Kombo nodded and stepped into the water, "Hold on to me here." He pointed to his mid-section. "We will let the strong currents of the cataract float us down river before we reach the beds of crocodiles. We will travel fast. And Viceroy, I believe Ahmose has followed us by land."

The two men entered the Nile, the Viceroy hanging on to Kombo's waist. On his belly, arms outstretched, Kombo began the daring river journey. With no other choices of transportation, the two men were about to use the rapids to distance themselves from the warring tribes that had captured Fortress Buhen. The waterfall of the first cataract shot them forward as currents now projected them around the belly of stones that Kombo adroitly navigated. The swift movement of rushing water cast them through narrow passages, carrying them away from the enemy. They twisted and slithered between some sharp broken rocks and large round ones that swirled around islets. The white, foamy water hurled them into whirlpools, around huge black shinning boulders that gleamed in the sun as the Viceroy clung to Kombu for his life. As they entered calmer eddies, their speed slowed. They had distanced themselves from the rebellion and had found safety. Over the river sounds, Kombo called, "You hold me strong, Viceroy, we leave the Belly of Stones now!"

Kombo had taken a great risk using the Nile as their escape route. But in the full light of day they needed to be concealed. The only cover *was* the raging river. Few men ever traversed this part of the Nile, other than some occasionally by small boats. Kombo had omitted mentioning to the Viceroy that a certain breed of crocodile lived in these tumultuous waters.

But luck had been with them. It was a good time to stop, as the Viceroy appeared seriously fatigued. Kombo soon reached the shore; however, the shoreline was not necessarily a safer place. The giant crocodiles, that grew to be fifteen to twenty feet in length, often sunned themselves on the warm rocky shores.

As Kombo helped the Viceroy to his feet, he said, "You stand strong, Viceroy. The water gives back strength."

The Viceroy had planted his feet into the muddy shore for stability, his hand reached to touch his neck wound that would forever brand him as a man the Nubians had once captured. Both men stood still, breathing heavy, leery, and silent. No adversaries appeared. The clatter of fighting was gone. They were beyond the rebellion. The only sound was of the distant rush from the first cataract. The barren land offered almost no form of life. But behind them came a fast-moving boat headed toward the shore. The rowers, royal navy men were maneuvering through the last of the rapids moving as adroitly as they could so as not to capsize.

"Who are they, Viceroy?"

The Viceroy shaded his eyes and said, "A terrified bureaucrat; a high-ranking scribe is my guess. He's probably headed for Thebes with meticulous accounting records." With eyes squinted, he added, "There looks to be some wounded on board as well."

"That's better than Nubians, Viceroy."

"*Yes*, it is, Kombo, and the Gods have given us a craft so we may return to Thebes."

The official waived vigorously when he recognized Viceroy Merymose. The man was indeed escaping the onslaught, clenching his wicker chair. The Viceroy hailed the vessel to commandeer her. All Egyptian royal solders knew Viceroy Merymose, and immediately rowed toward shore and surrendered to his command.

At the same time, Ahmose appeared from the western desert. He was smiling and brandishing spears held high in his hands. The Viceroy's face showed pride. His son had chosen to leave the village of his birth to join him and bring weapons. Viceroy Merymose's stance showed renewed energy. He would live to report to his Pharaoh, and return to his beautiful wife, Princess Becataten.

"No!" Kombo's voice roared across the stark desert. He put up one hand toward Ahmos and pointed with the other at a large crocodile that was slithering out of the Nile, but a few yards away.

Once on land, the predator focused its green eyes on Ahmose. Raising its head and trunk above the ground revealed his purple colored underbelly. Then it began a high walk toward the boy, who was not yet a man.

"No, oh no." called the Viceroy in a ragged voice.

A rower in the boat assessed the imminent attack, stood to release an arrow at the beast, but the vessel bumped into the shoreline and the shot went astray.

Ahmose dropped his weapons at the approach of the giant lizard-like animal and froze.

Kombo ran toward the boy, gathered up a few of the crude spears and threw one at the dark coarse hide of the giant water demon. Like a palm frond, it bounced off the creature's tough and scaly backside. The agitated beast snapped its tail and threw Kombo an angry glare.

Ahmose began to run, but his adolescent legs tangled under him and he fell. Kombo began running alongside the killer reptile, trying to fight it off with mettle few men possess. He was near enough to poke his spear at the softer but thickly scaled underbelly.

Trying to save Ahmose, Kombo continued to harass the predator. With another projectile, he taunted the beast and it worked to draw the predator away from Amos. Now, too close, Kombo began to run away from the crocodile. It was clear to all watching that these creatures could outrun any man. Kombo stumbled and tried to regain his footing, which attracted the beast. The crocodile turned to pursue Kombo, who was scrambling in the sand to stand.

"Get up, Kombo, get up," screamed the Viceroy as he advanced toward the horrifying scene. A bowman jumped from the boat and ran to Merymose to restrain him.

"Rowers, release your arrows on the beast," the viceroy roared, trying to escape from being held back.

Half a dozen men jumped to the shore and took aim at the crocodile. Two of the Egyptian bowman hit their mark, penetrating the beast's underbelly, which had little effect on the animal's speed.

The Viceroy screamed, "No God Sobek, let him go, let him go..." His pleas echoed through the hot, dry land.

The giant reached his prey, made and abrupt stop and opened its powerful jaws wide, then snapped them around one of Kombo's long arms. With a powerful jerk of its head the beast tore off Kombo's arm, above the elbow. Kombo's screams resounded across the desert landscape as he lost consciousness.

The animal's hold was firm on his body-part and his trot quick back to the river. With the two arrows bobbing from his giant frame, he entered the Nile where he had exited. Once in the river, the water thrashed as a float of crocodiles arrived to ravish Kombo's arm, as his lifeless body lay bleeding.

Chapter 9

♊

A full moon had come and gone since the rebellion was put down. In the late morning sun, Becataten sat on her purple linen lounge. Her jewelry chest of carved cedar in her lap, filled with mementos and jewelry the Viceroy had given her. Sadness clouded her eyes and her heart was heavy with pain as she held a ring of turquoise set in a delicate papyrus blossom of hammered gold. Dark blue glass bottles of perfume that only Palace artisans new how to make filled with oil of the rose, scented the chest. As she unrolled a small scroll from the chest, her eyes welled with tears when she read poetry Mosie had given her:

To hear your voice is Pomegranate wine to me
I draw life from it
Could I see you with every glance
It would be better for me
Than to eat or to drink

Then without announcement, a loud disturbance occurred, and Pygmy Lady charged through Becataten's chamber door. She usually stayed away from the big house, preferring the residence Abu had taken in the palm grove. The Estate butler followed her brusque entry and climbed of the stairs, trying to preeced her. Out of breath, he said, "I regret, Princess Becataten, this... this woman has come unannounced."

"Do not apologize, Butler, she is a friend and in the future she *is* welcome. Thank you for your concern."

Butler backed out of the room saying no more.

Pygmy Lady flopped into a large cedar chair. She adjusted the goose down pillows that were covered in the hide of the spotted leopard, and relaxed as she swung her large feet back and forth. "You live like a *queen* here."

Becataten dabbed her eyes with a linen cloth, and said, "Yes, it is a grand house. Lady Nagara and Royal Architect Suti were my mentors and have been very generous to me here. They are responsible for my education and have given me many worldly items."

"Worldly items, humph! Explain that to me?" Pygmy Lady said with a flourish of her small arm.

Becataten looked at Pygmy Lady and said, "We should not begin a conversation as though we were drinking sour wine. Let us start anew. Tell me why you are here."

Pygmy Lady stood, rubbed her chin, and paced. "I had a dream about crocodiles attacking someone near the Nile, and the Viceroy was there."

Becataten caught her breath, sat up straight and said, "Are you telling me my Mosie was killed by the God Sobek?" She placed her hand across her chest in anguish.

"No, I am saying the Viceroy was there." Pygmy Lady called back harshly. "And a God, Sobek or any other, had nothing to do with it. You Egyptians make a deity of anything that swims, walks or crawls!"

Becataten tied the rolled scroll with gold twine that she was reading, needing time to respond. It was taking some effort getting used to the harsh ways of this woman, but she was going to do so because Dwarf

Beset had said to, and because the Viceroy believed in her too. She would begin anew with a bit of praise, as Beset had always recommended.

With composure she began, "Pygmy Lady, it is Beset's wish that you stay near me when she departs to the underworld from us. She believes you have the Heka. I think you call it magic. Beset says you can guide me through difficult times that lie ahead. I must tell you that Dwarf Beset, who I have lived with my entire life, says she will not be with us much longer and that I must prepare myself for life without her here."

At this news, Pygmy Lady no longer paced but strutted, and straightened her posture, though it did little to lift her pendulous breasts.

"That is very interesting, Princess. I must speak with the Dwarf. I may be able to lengthen her life, some. I need to have many talks with her." She turned abruptly and walked out of Becataten's chamber.

Becataten swung her legs off her lounge, stood, and decided she had felt sorry for herself long enough. She clapped her hands, which brought her slave girl running.

Just then, Pygmy Lady stuck her head back into Becataten's chamber and said, "Do not trust Nehesy and his men, they are traitors." And just as suddenly, she was fast gone again.

Becataten shook her head. *By the Gods, could that be true?* She hoped that Pygmy Lady would not quarrel with Beset but have talks that would be polite and useful. Her mind was full now with traitors, her dear Mosie perhaps encountering Sobeks, Beset's near death, Pygmy Lady's predictions, and the child growing within her. She felt faint.

Becataten turned to the waif at her side and said, "Send me Isis, and tell Butler before Ra grows higher that I want a chariot waiting for me." She needed to be out of the grand house, in Ra's light and fresh air.

She sat with her makeup artist to comply with Lady Nagara's firm request not to leave the Estate without a properly painted face. Today she would begin asking Isis about the gossip of the day. The painter arrived, and Becataten settled herself on a stool next to her large cosmetic chest. "How did my chest get on the boat when we sailed so quickly away from Fortress Buhen?" Becataten asked.

"Oh, that would be Kombo's doing, the tallest of Nehesy's Nubians."

"Really? And what possessed him to do that?"

"He asked me what you valued most," Isis responded, "and I said your chest of paints, because by then I had put all your jewelry in the coffer too."

Becataten thought of Kombo and found it sad to believe he was a traitor, let alone Nehesy.

"That was kind and thoughtful of you. Thank you, Isis," said Becataten.

"May I say something rather personal, Princess?" Isis asked as she drew dark kohl around one eye.

"Of course you may."

"This morning workers tending crops near the Nile's edge said they thought they saw the Viceroy sailing toward Thebes." Isis pulled the kohl stick away at Becataten's quick jerking reaction.

"And why wasn't I told this!" Becataten demanded to know.

"It is just worker-talk, and I cannot be sure that it is true," the painter said, trying to remain calm, although she looked upset.

Becataten patted Isis's hand and said kindly, "Finish quickly, I must go."

After her face was complete, she had Isis put her favorite earrings on, the ones that jingled with gold and silver beads, and requested her finely woven leather sandals. She rushed to the stairs refusing a wig having gotten used to not wearing one during her short stay in Nubia. Nearly stumbling along the way, she bumped into Maja.

"Be careful, Taten, remember you are with child."

Taten nodded, patting her newly swelling belly.

Once outdoors, it pleased Becataten to see the two spirited stallions harnessed to her chariot. She knew Senzar's horses could run like the wind. Today she would not drive, but instead command the charioteer. Stepping on board, she took a corner seat with a pillow. It must be common knowledge that she was pregnant because the stable manager had the chariot rigged with a canopy over her chair. The oversized chariot would be a smooth ride for a long trip. This larger chariot Senzar sent was designed with a full square basket bordered in a woven blue turquoise papyrus.

"To the river, and then north until I ask you to return, and I won't be driving today," she said, settling into the seat for the ride.

Becataten reasoned that the Viceroy would pass the Estate on his way up from Nubia and head to the Palace in Thebes, not knowing she had stopped at the Suti Estate to reside.

It was a day's ride north to the Palace from the Estate, and Becataten hoped she could catch him before he was too far passed the Estate.

As the chariot raced forth, the hot wind jangled her earring until she used her light linen shawl to cover her head as Ra rays grew director. They searched until late in the day for the boat that she prayed held the Viceroy, with no results. Realizing how Ra would soon leave and she could go no farther, she ordered her driver to return to the Estate. "You may return at a slower pace," she said as she began to tire.

Once returned to the Estate, Isis took one look at Becataten's shift soiled with perspiration, her eyes running kohl and whisked her into a copper tub that slaves filled with cool water. "You must rest after you cool down."

Becataten nodded, but not admitting she was exhausted from the long ride that ended up being halfway to the Palace with not a sign of the Viceroy.

The next night Lady Nagara and Becataten dined together in the formal dining chamber of the grand Estate. Becataten remembered that Lady Nagara dined only in this manner. They sat at their separate benches and tables. She ran her finger over the edge of the cedar tabletop. With much care, a slave boy set their stands with alabaster plates, finger bowls of marble, calcite goblets and small crystal vases containing blue flowers from the herb, rosemary. Becataten admired the beauty before her but remembered what a happy time it was when she, Dwarf Beset and Nanny Maja ate sitting on the floor off wooden plates. The small apartment accommodated two small cubicles, one for Beset and one for Maja. One sleeping cubicle just slightly bigger she shared with her twin. The food was humble faire, but it mattered not because Jobu was there. That seemed a long time ago.

Lady Nagara peered at Becataten over their decorated tables. "So, I take it that you did not find any more answers after your chariot ride to find the Viceroy yesterday?"

"No," replied Becataten in a solemn voice. The ride had been dirty and exhausting, and she had slept much since her disappointing journey. She was glad this was her second night back.

"I was not pleased to hear that you were in a chariot, Becataten. I hope your ride was not a long one."

To change the subject, Becataten sipped her blended wine then turned to Lady Nagara, "Did you find an opportunity to send a scroll to Pharaoh explaining that I am well and safe here at the Estate, and of course extend my deepest sympathies for the loss of his son?" Becataten asked as both women began to eat their meal.

"I did, Becataten, but I understand that Pharaoh is receiving little of his correspondence and even fewer audiences. I am told that grieving for the loss of his son has consumed his days and he is in deep mourning."

Becataten nodded as she bit into a piece of her skewered lamb that she rolled into lettuce leaves after drizzling them with chickpea sauce. "We do know that the rebellion goes well, do we not?" she asked.

"Yes, that we do know. The tribes of Kush tried to unify and rebel as a group but could not get all the villages to cooperate. You know how those primitives are. So, of course within one moon cycle, royal troops put them down. I do not want to give you false hope, Becataten, but there is gossip that the Viceroy has escaped his captors."

Becataten held her tongue but wondered how long Lady Nagara had this information and had not told her.

She set her skewer of meat aside, took a deep breath. "Where did you learn of that?" she asked.

Lady Nagara too pushed her food away and clapped her hands for the plates to be removed. "It comes to me from my secretary, but it *is* gossip, and that is precisely why I don't want you to take it too seriously. It is common knowledge, Becataten, that envoys who arrive from the Palace also arrive with gossip. These couriers are bearers of news that one does not find in a scroll. I have made it a firm rule that this information be delivered to me by my secretary." Lady Nagara sat rigid with a twist to her mouth.

"But this gossip could mean that the Viceroy has been released?" Becataten exclaimed.

Lady Nagara clapped her hands for their tables to be removed. Standing, she said to a servant boy, "Bring date wine to the sitting chamber."

After they were settled in cedar chairs ample with down pillows covered in hide, and their sweet wine before them, Becataten asked, "Please explain why it is believed that the Viceroy escaped?"

Lady Nagara took time to adjust herself in her chair and after a sip of wine said, "Brutal as it may sound, Becataten, if the Nubians would have killed the Viceroy they would have paraded his body for all of Egypt to see, and that hasn't happened. So, it is believed he is still alive ... somewhere."

"That's a strange way to arrive at what I hope is the truth," said Becataten.

They sat for a time then Lady Nagara said, "I understand that you may be with child, my dear. Is that true?"

"Yes, the healer and I spoke, and together we calculated that I am. He says I have been carrying my baby the same amount of time I have been here at the Estate, two moon cycles."

Lady Nagara who rarely smiled, produced a broad grin and said, "Becataten, that is wonderful. Suti is due here in a few Ras and he will be delighted with this happy news. We must thank the Gods that you escaped Fortress Buhen. That would have been a ghastly place to bear a child," she said, shaking her head and wrinkling her nose.

Butler quietly entered the chamber and said, "There is a small girl at the steps calling for the Princess. She says her name is Ne Ne."

"There must be some mistake." said Lady Nagara.

"No, no I know the child. She accompanied us from the Fortress. She is in charge of my dogs," Becataten said.

"Dogs," said Lady Nagara, "There will be no dogs in my house!"

"No of course not, Lady Nagara, they live elsewhere... just let me see what she wants."

Becataten found Ne Ne standing at the main entrance to the house always with her finger in her mouth, a habit she hadn't abandoned since early childhood, her brows furrowed. The puppies at her feet wiggling with curiosity. "Papa Abu says come, quick."

Chapter 10

♊

Becataten wondered why Abu sent Ne Ne for her when slaves were available. It was quite a long walk from his house to the Estate residence. But she was happy to see the child, and that her father took an interest in teaching her the Egyptian language. She guessed Abu would be a loving grandparent, and teacher.

After speaking with Ne Ne, Becataten returned to extend a proper good night to Lady Nagara and thanked her for dinner. She asked a slave girl to bring her a shawl, then requested a chair littler from the Butler making him promise not to reveal that she was going out for the evening. Becataten explained she would not leave the Estate grounds. The chair soon arrived with a torchbearer to light their way. Becataten took Ne Ne's hand and together they settled in the wicker seat of the litter.

As they jostled along Becataten looked about, feeling that someone was following them. She adjusted Ne Ne on her lap and said. "Did you walk all the way in the dark from my father's house?"

Becataten saw shyness and intelligence in the child's large dark eyes, as Ne Ne nodded.

"Did you come alone?" Becataten asked, gently removing the child's finger from her mouth.

"No." Ne Ne said.

"Who did you come with?"

"The dogs."

"Where are they now? And how long did it take you to walk from my father's house?"

The child seemed to struggle with the answer. "As long as it takes to eat a big pomegranate," she said.

Becataten smiled noting the red stains on the child's face.

"How *are* my dogs, Ne Ne?"

"Getting big." she said. Pointing to one of them running ahead of their chair.

"How old are they now?"

Ne Ne's shoulders rose and lowered.

"Well, let's try and figure it out. How old were they when you brought them to me at the Fortress?

Ne Ne sat still with a blank stare on her face.

"Were they about two moon cycles when you took them from their mother?" Becataten asked.

Ne Ne offered a nod.

"And we all lived together at the Fortress another moon cycle. So how old were the puppies when we left?"

Ne Ne quickly held up three fingers.

"Now, add two because we have been at the Suti Estate for two moon cycles." Becataten said.

Becataten saw Ne Ne hold up five fingers as her eyes shown like glass from the torch held by a bearer running beside them. "You are learning your counting skills, along with the Egyptian language, aren't you?" Becataten thought, here I sit for the first time with a child on my lap, and soon I will have my own.

Ne Ne's head bobbed.

Becataten could feel Ne Ne fingers touching her golden bracelets.

"Ne Ne, hold my earrings so they don't jingle, I want to listen." She quickly removed and handed the girl her earrings. After dark, animal sounds of marsh birds, jackals, hyena, baboons, and more were everywhere. On this moonless night, silence prevailed. She turned to the slave running alongside them, lighting the way. "Are you armed with a bow?" She saw surprise on the bearer's face as he shook his head. The night was as dark as a pot of kohl and she could see nothing. Something was amiss. What was it?

About to dismiss her thoughts, she was reminded that she was gifted with the Heka and should listen to her inner feelings. Had her father become ill or was there some problem with him staying in his new house? Ne Ne would have told her if her father was ill, and she felt sure that Lady Nagara didn't know of Abu's dwelling, at least not yet.

Once they arrived, Ne Ne jumped to the ground and took Becataten's hand then ran to Abu's door. Becataten banged on it but failed to wait for an answer and barged into the entry. "What is it, Father?" she called as she hurried to his sitting chamber.

"Come, Daughter, I am pleased you are here and safe. The Stable Master tells me that he has ordered security for the stable area and my house. He says the horses and the Senzar's stable guard dogs are acting up. I'm hoping the pups that Ne Ne has brought us will soon be your guard dogs."

She rushed to her father's side and embraced him. Then from the shadows, moving toward her stepped a familiar figure. She squinted, not believing her own eyes. A man stepped forth, her heart pounded in her chest, and her knees buckled. She sat on the chaise next to her, unable to hold herself up. The Viceroy stood before her, bent huddled and worn looking. Yet to her, he was beautiful, and proud, and a love she had never experienced before welled up inside her at his presence. Before she could say anything, he reached for her and enveloped her in his arms. Never had she felt such relief before as she held him back in a tearful hug.

"Oh, Mosie, I thought I may never see you again, and here you are! The Gods have given you back to me."

"Yes, they have, Princess, with some help from Kombo." The Viceroy said in an unsteady voice.

They stood in a long embrace, and Becataten got a glimpse of the deep scar around the Viceroy's neck.

"You were all I thought about when I was held captive." He whispered in her ear.

Becataten looked up into the Viceroy's face and said, "So you *were* taken prisoner? And what happened at the Nile when you encountered God Sobek?"

"What did you say, Becataten?" the Viceroy asked with a confused look on his face.

Becataten watched Kombo rise from his chair using the arm the sobeks didn't take, the other heavily bandaged above the elbow. "It was I who met the crocodile, Princess, but how did you know?" Kombo asked.

"Through a little used side-entrance, Pygmy Lady appeared "Greetings Viceroy, she whispered, "I see you escaped the ruthless Nubians." With a finger to her lips, her eyes grew large with alarm.

Ne Ne was looking about for the pups, but they were nowhere to be found. "Did anyone see the pups?" Ne Ne said, after looking through the house.

"Ne Ne did you leave them outside?" Becataten asked.

"They must have gotten loose and run back to the stables for their meal. That is where I take them to eat each day." But Ne Ne looked worried and ran to the door to go and find them. Pygmy Lady reached for her and held her back just as a squeak came from the bronze hinges of the entry door.

The sounds of men grunting were followed by a small opening of the door, then a thud of something thrown inside the entry, and the door shutting again. An air of stilled fear filled the room. The Viceroy moved Becataten to an alcove and motioned to Kombo to take a dark corner. Kombo nodded and drew his knife. The silence was broken as Pygmy Lady ripped through Abu's cache of weapons stored in a conical shaped basket at the front door. A clatter of sounds came when she turned the basket upside down grabbing two spears, a handful of arrows and two knives. She handed one to the Viceroy, another she laid on Abu's lap. Abu took it in hand and held Ne Ne tight. Then the door closed. The Viceroy and Pygmy Lady looked at one another, suspicious and troubled as they rushed to the entrance. On the floor lay a sack of coarse brown linen. The Viceroy cut it open with his blade. It contained Becataten's young dogs. Their throats were slit from ear to ear.

Chapter 11

♊

Stable Master Senzar rushed to Abu's dwelling to see the slaughtered remains of Princess Becataten's young dogs and dropped to his knees. "I am responsible for this killing. I am at your mercy, My Lord," he said to Abu, and then he bowed to Becataten, who stayed on her chaise as the Viceroy stood. She felt distraught but knew now was not a time for weak tears.

"Yes, you are in part responsible, but it is also clear you have no men here to defend any of us. Did you lose any slaves or attendants during this attack?" Abu said.

"Two slaves, My Lord," said Senzar.

Ne Ne cried soft tears for the loss of the pups she had cared for and was the only one who remembered to get them on the boat when they sailed from Nubia. Abu spoke quietly to her and wiped her tears, then slid her off his lap. As Abu slid Ne Ne off his lap, Huni moved in close to him. "I can help some with this Nubian problem. My daughter the Princess Becataten has provided me with an able scribe, and I have already requested soldiers arrive from Thebes to guard this Estate. After a rebellion has been put down, like the one at Fortress Buhen, it is not uncommon to expect incidences like the one we witnessed tonight." He announced in his strong voice, one Becataten remembered from the past.

The Viceroy stepped forward and bowed to Abu from habit, not thinking about his blindness. "I have much appreciation for your insight, as you know after my capture Kombo and I traveled to the Palace where I filed my report to the Vizier. Pharaoh is still in deep mourning, and I did not have an audience with him. But I lacked your awareness in requesting protection for us, Royal Astrologer."

"So, you were Pharaoh's astrologer!" Pygmy Lady said.

Ignoring her interruption, Abu said, "You are a good man Viceroy, but you errored when you believed that certain Nubians were your friends. For fifteen hundred generations passed, we have subjugated the Nubians and taken from their land. This is not the first time they have revolted, and I don't expect it to be the last. And Viceroy, please, no longer refer to me by that title. That is no longer my station."

Becataten took Ne Ne to her side. "I think we should all be happy that we are alive, and I would like to thank Stable Master Senzar for doing what he could. And Father, thank you for sending for the royal militia."

Ne Ne pointed to what looked like a figure in the dark corner. Becataten peered into the darkness, picking up a candle and moving toward it cautiously. She smiled, then settled her hand on the shoulder of an adolescent boy seated quietly on a stool. "You have been here the whole time, haven't you?" she asked.

The Viceroy cleared his throat. "This is my son, Ahmose. He escaped from the Nubian village with me and Kombo. I asked him to remain quietly in the room."

Ahmose stood awkwardly, already taller than his father and stared at his feet. His light brown skin and tall scrawny body portrayed a Nubian youth in body but not facially. There was a semblance of the viceroy's features in his expression. The Viceroy approached him. "This is my wife and your second mother, Princess Becataten, Ahmose."

Ahmose stared at Becataten, as if stunned by her beauty up close, and bowed.

"Ahmose, you remind me of my twin brother who left us last year for paradise. I am happy to know you, and I must tell you that soon, you will have a brother or sister," Becataten said coyly, patting her belly gently.

The Viceroy stood perplexed for a moment, then with surprise he said, "Becataten, I didn't know. You are with child! Are you well? This is a joyous day!"

Becataten looked at her father, who sat with his head turned with an ear to her voice and saw him reveal a rare smile.

Pygmy Lady walked about the apartment, her large feet slapping the stone floor. "Now that we all know the Princess is going to have a prince or princess, can we plan further to stay alive? The enemy is outside our door!"

Stable Master Senzar, shuffled his feet and stood at attention. "I have called in all the field workers and armed them with spears, and as you suggested, Viceroy, your crew from the Golden Falcon is standing by also. These men now surround this house. I have alerted Butler to arm the security at the Estate residence and to be on alert."

"My Palace contact says we will see troops when Ra appears next," Abu said.

The viceroy turned to his wife. "Becataten, you must stay the night here in your father's home. I will not allow you to risk a litter ride back to the Estate house.

Ahmose, I expect you and Kombo to be on guard here in this room, I will bed with Becataten in a chamber," he added. But on the viceroy's mind was the liaison at the Palace that Abu knew, and if they would come to their rescue.

"Yes, that is best," said Abu.

"Well, you can all stay in this house, but I will be outside on the roof." Pygmy Lady said.

"What does she think she'll do on the roof?" Becataten said quietly to the group as they stood to prepare to settle in.

"Have you ever seen her throw a spear, or fire a bow, Princess?" Kombo asked. "We can all sleep well if Pygmy Lady is on guard above us!"

Before dawn, Pygmy Lady rushed down the ladder from the roof of Abu's house and entered the cool home embedded in the shade of the date grove. She stood in an obstinate pose, hands on hips, wearing her hide kilt, her pendulous breasts exposed as usual. She faced Abu. "Are you sure these famous royal troops you ordered to defend us are going to arrive, Old Man? I have seen no traffic of royal ships on the Nile or Pharaoh's chariots."

Annoyed, Abu ignored her.

The men looked at one another, rousing from a troubled night. Fear had returned. The men took up arms as they heard a knock.

Pygmy Lady listened. "It *must* be a friend. Senzar has this house surrounded by armed attendants. I saw them from the roof, but I did not see Nehesy's Nubians," she said.

The knock came again.

Abu knew that a knock on the door would likely not come from the enemy. "Enter!" said Abu, adjusting his cape. He had remained the night in his chair with Huni crouched at his feet.

Kombo rose unsteadily his black eyes growing. He leaned against a wall, spear in his free hand, a dagger in his belt, the bloodied bandage on his other arm looking ragged. The Viceroy stood like a statue, held his hand back to Becataten, his dagger firmly held in his other hand. He motioned to Ahmos nodding to the spears on the floor. Pygmy Lady, the most cautious of all, backed into a shadow with her bow pulled taught but first kicked a spear toward Ahmos with a stern look that said use it if you must. Ne Ne crouched at Abu's feet with Huni, both she and the baboon whimpering.

The door squeaked on its hinges and Nanny Maja poked her head in the opening. "Taten, are you here?"

Becataten rushed to her. "Maja, why are *you* here? Is something wrong?"

"Oh, Taten, come quick to the big house, the healer says Beset has little time left."

"You cannot leave this house, Princess," commanded the Viceroy.

"I agree," said Abu in a loud voice.

The men watched Pygmy Lady suddenly run outside. It sounded as though she was arguing with someone near the door. Huni began to screech and jump up and down. Abu tried to settle him, with no results.

Pygmy Lady sprang back into the house. "Maja, go outside and get into the chariot that the stable master is harnessing and wait there. You, Kombo, get some spears and come with me!" He did as she asked, wincing as he moved to the weapon-cache, able to grasp but three spears with his one hand.

Becataten put her arm around Maja and pulled her aside. Please comfort Beset with all my love and explain that only because I am with child, I cannot go to her.

Pygmy held a hand up to Becataten. "Princess, we must go. It is only I who can help the dwarf, now, and I fear she is in danger from not death alone." she said.

Becataten pulled Maja aside. "My heart is with Sweet Bes, and tell her that. Tell her that I love her as a mother, as a confidant and as my guiding spirit."

The Viceroy interrupted. "Kombo can't go with you, he is too badly injured. Can't you see that, Pygmy Lady?"

"I can see that he can throw a spear with his good arm as well as I can, and so, he's coming." She rushed to the door, impatiently waiting for Kombo to exit with her.

With help, Kombo was positioned into the crowded chariot. Leaning against the wicker frame, his face twisted in pain. "Maja, hold my spears upright," he said. Maja did as she was told, then squatted on the floor of the conveyance in silence.

Pygmy Lady stepped on board and turned to Senzar. "Tell your driver to race like the wind to the Estate house."

Ra was nearing his rise as they galloped toward the grand house. The skies began to brighten as they could see steam rise from the sweat of the galloping horse. In the ponds, lotus blossoms were opening toward the emerging brightness, and finally the Suti residence came into view, washed in golden light. The drive had been swift and their arrival safe. No weapons had been hurled at them, as was feared.

Pygmy Lady climbed the steps to the residence calling over her shoulder to Kombo. "You hide yourself,

I don't want to come back and find you dead." Hauling Maja by the arm, she said, "Take me to the dwarf."

The women startled the butler as they rushed past. "Call for the herbalist," Pygmy Lady yelled at him. As they ascended the second story, she could feel Maja's body shaking. "Why are you so afraid, Maja? We are safe now."

Maja's eyebrows shot up and her black eyes showed fear. "Pygmy Lady, is Nehesy really a bad man?"

"Yes. Why?" answered Pygmy Lady.

"I, I heard him and one of his Nubians asking the butler where the Princess was when I was leaving for Abu's."

"Doesn't this household know by now that Nehesy is the enemy?" Pygmy Lady hissed.

Maja shook her head and continued up the steps. Once upstairs, Maja pointed to Beset's chamber. The door had been left partially open. Both women peered in for a view, and Maja nearly stumbled into a stinking chamber pot. Pygmy Lady scowled at her.

In the large suite Maja and Beset had recently come to share, they were tended by slaves and fed like Pharaoh, and the chamber pot should have long been emptied. Dwarf Beset lay on a lounge bedded with fine linen, as nearby braziers wafted the aroma of frankincense to comfort her in her last days. She looked gravely ill. Her skin was grey in color and her hair matted; a linen cloth covered her eyes. Nehesy in his red kilt showing false allegiance to the Viceroy, was looking down at her, and had not come alone. A tall, armed Nubian hid in a corner. Shorter than most, and lighter skinned Nehesy looked out of place among other Nubians as he carried some Egyptian blood. His graying bowl of hair gave him a wise look. His respect from most tribes during the uprising had grown in The Land of the Bow, especially since he had secretly switched allegiance away from the Viceroy. When Becataten hired him as a personal aide, she noted many full-bloodied Egyptians even thought him superior.

Beset removed the cloth from her eyes and rose on shaking elbows, drained and weary.

Nehesy moved closer. "Greetings, Dwarf, I see you are not well."

"Yes, I have seen better times. Why are you here, Nehesy?" Beset said in a weak voice.

"The Viceroy has sent me. He has just arrived safely from Kush. He wants the Princess to come to him." Nehesy said in a voice as though he were speaking to a child.

Beset lay back down. "I am not sure where the Princess is, Nehesy. Tell me again why are you looking for her?" she asked quietly.

"The Viceroy has returned from being held prisoner. He is anxious to see her and sent me to find her," Nehesy said in a smooth tone.

"I think not, Nehesy," Beset responded.

"What do you mean, Dwarf?"

"I mean, I believe you are looking for Princess Becataten to do her harm," Beset said.

Nehesy took a cushion off Beset's lounge. "One more time, I ask you, where *is* the Princess?" he said, holding the pillow just above her head.

Beset smiled weakly. "It is not you who will have the privilege of ending my life, Nehesy."

Nehesy covered Beset's head with the goose down pillow. Her feet kicked and her small arms flailed.

Pygmy Lady drew her dagger, pushed open the door and rushed to Nehesy. Using all her force, she plunged her blade into his back. With the knife sunk deeply into him, he fell with a thud on the stone floor. When Nehesy's Nubian bodyguard appeared, she stood motionless. He headed toward her, jabbing his spear into the space between them.

"You touch me with that spear, and I will place a curse on you and your tribe for centuries to come," she growled.

He shook his head and kept coming, but less aggressively.

She took a deliberate step toward him. "I will see your first child born dead."

The Nubian's face flashed with conflict and his pace slowed.

On the floor, Nehesy was writhing in a growing pool of blood. Looking up with agonizing pain, he said with hate, "Kill her!"

The Nubian gained some courage and walked more deliberately across the stone floor toward the pygmy.

Maja stood at the open door, fear-ridden, her mouth covered with her hands.

Beset took large breaths and lifted herself onto her elbows, able only to watch.

Pygmy Lady, without a weapon, looked for something that would suffice but found nothing.

One more step and the Nubian would be close enough to thrust his spear into her.

She reached for the tall unlit brazier and pushed it to fall between her and her oncoming slayer. Stepping over it, the bodyguard tripped, and his long legs landed him on the hard floor. His spear went askew, and together they scrambled on the floor for the weapon.

The Nubian pulled his dagger as the spear skittered across the floor out of their reach, in an attempt for a close kill.

Maja looked about for anything to do harm to the Nubian, but all she saw was the unemptied piss pot. She picked it up, ran to the Nubian, and threw the contents into his face. He dropped his dagger to reach for his burning eyes, sputtering and moaning, as Pygmy Lady stood and got up out of the way.

The Butler arrived at the door with attendants to subdue Nehesy's guardsman as Nehesy himself moaned in agony on the cold floor, his very life leaving him.

Chapter 12

♊

Architects Suti and Hor were in the field, standing over plans for temple repairs when an envoy headed toward them carrying what appeared to be a scroll. The breathless runner approached Suti. "I was told that this is an important message from your Estate, Royal Architect," said the bowing dispatcher.

Suti reached for a hefty piece of copper debon from his pouch and handed it to the messenger. He broke the seal, unrolled the document quickly and scanned the scroll. His hands trembled as he read, and the news caused him to collapse in his field chair.

"What is it, Brother?" asked Hor.

"I am told that Royal Troops put down a rebellion in Kush. And they also hunted down a small band of Nubian insurgents that were encamped on my land. The rebels have all been killed, and the bodies were given as offerings to God Sobek. Large floats of the giant lizards met them at the shoreline to devour the corpses. This was to commemorate the crown's *final* victory over the Nubian uprising."

Hor's jaw dropped. "Who sent you this message? he asked.

Suti reviewed the scroll again for credibility. "It is unsigned, but a General Nesu is in charge of the operation and is reporting to... to Abu?" Suti said with raised eyebrows." I can tell that his scroll has been dictated by Abu, who now seems to reside on my Estate."

Hor slumped heavily in his field chair. Suti rolled the scroll tight looking into the distance. "He lives on my land, and I assume without Lady Nagara's knowledge. It sounds like Abu has lost none of his tactical abilities, blind or not, and was the planner behind this defense. I must leave at once."

It usually took from sunrise to sunset to arrive at the Suti Estate, but this trip took half the time. Driving fast and hard in a four-horse chariot, with a change of steeds at the half-way point, Suti got there in half a Ra. Lady Nagara and the Princess Becataten had not been mentioned in Abu's scroll, and that caused him much concern. Reaching the northern border of his landholding, Suti viewed Royal Soldiers swarming his land. He raced for the Estate. Reining his horses to a quick stop at the steps of his grand house, he was greeted by Stable Master Senzar.

"Welcome home, Architect Suti. Much has happened during your absence," Senzar said with a deep bow, then proceeded to give Suti an overview.

"Was it Abu alone who was able to amass this number of Royal Soldiers?" Suti asked.

Standing tall, Senzar said, "Yes, Royal Architect."

As Architect Suti rushed up the steps, he turned and said, "Wait here, Stable Master. I will meet with you in the Royal Astrologer's quarters – I mean, Abu's quarters, after I see Lady Nagara."

"Yes, Royal Architect," Stable Master Senzar said.

Suti paused deep in thought. "You say Abu is living in the old manager's dwelling in the palm grove?"

"He is, My Lord, and a fine man he is, if I may say so."

Rushing now to the top of the stairs Suti muttered to himself, "How could Abu manage to amass Royal Soldiers after being stripped of his court life?" Confused he strode hurriedly down the corridor toward his wife's chambers.

Butler bowed when Suti appeared at her doors and found his wife was not there. "Where is Lady Nagara?" Suti demanded to know. "She has never failed to meet me when I arrive."

"She is with Princess Becataten in the chamber assigned to Dwarf Beset and Nanny Maja. The healer believes that the Dwarf is near death, My Lord," said the Butler, "and there is more to tell..."

"Not now," Suti said, clearly frustrated as he rushed up to the second story and entered the large chamber. Late afternoon rays from Ra shown down on Beset's reclined body from the high clerestory windows at the ceiling. Smoldering braziers of charcoal were burning, frankincense for protection and healing. There was a smell in the room, not of life, but of death.

"Greetings," Suti said softly as he lessened his pace, trying to catch his breath. He stepped curiously around attendants cleaning the floor of what looked to be blood as slaves cleaned remains from the brutal fight Pygmy Lady had waged.

Lady Nagara rose from her chair to greet her husband. "But I only just sent a scroll to you. How did you arrive so quickly?"

"Another source told me of the events taking place here, My Lady. Are you well?"

Lady Nagara nodded. "We have been through much difficulty in such a short period, Husband."

"What is this bloodlet on the floor?" Suti asked as the last of it was cleaned up with linens and the slave rushed out the door.

"It was Nehesy, a traitoress aide to the viceroy. He tried to kill Dwarf Beset, and others," Lady Nagara said, not wanting to overwhelm Suti with all the dire news at once.

How is the Dwarf?" asked Suti, as he reached for Lady Nagara and hugged her.

Lady Nagara shook her head and sat back down with a frown.

A distraught Becataten rushed to Suti's side. "Oh Suti, I am so glad you have come. Beset has been asking for you." Becataten's brave face showed a new maturity. Suti knew the Dwarf had been Becataten's only true mother from birth and could tell she knew she was about to lose her, and that Dwarf Beset was soon to join Osiris.

Moving to Beset's lounge, Suti took her hand. "My friend, Dwarf Beset, it is I, Suti."

Beset released a sigh. "It is well that you are here, Suti, for I must now say a few things." She spoke in a soft voice that didn't screech anymore. The dwarf's grey colored skin wrinkled and drawn was a picture of sadness.

"Don't trouble yourself, Beset, perhaps it is better that you rest and speak later." He glanced at the nearby Healer, who shook his head to the contrary.

"No, it is best I speak now," she said in a peaceful way, her voice nearly inaudible. She turned to Becataten. "When Pharaoh presented me as a gift to you and Jobu, it was the happiest day of my life," she said, turning to look into Becataten's eyes. "Maja and I didn't always agree on how to raise you two, and we were slow to get along, but finally grew to love one another, didn't we, Maja?"

With tears streaming down her dark wrinkled cheeks, Maja nodded. Princess Becataten nodded too, fighting back her own tears.

"You children arrived with a conundrum. You were not recognized at court and had no Royal privileges. Being a dwarf, I felt obliged to learn why."

Becataten stood tall and said in a proud voice, "You learned who my true father was, the Royal Astrologer Abu, not Pharaoh. And as a result, I was able to save him, so he can now live with me. And I am so grateful for that, Beset."

Lady Nagara sat erect in her chair and gasped at the news. She looked hard at Suti and whispered, "Did you know?"

Suti nodded.

Dwarf Beset continued, "Many years ago, Princess, did you know that Abu asked for your mother in marriage, but Pharaoh refused him?"

Pygmy Lady, who was hunched in a dark corner listening, stepped forward with authority. "The Dwarf must be allowed to rest. She is very ill."

The shock on Suti's face caused him to look at Becataten, then Lady Nagara for an explanation of this eccentric creature giving orders in his home. Becataten seemed to accept her. Lady Nagara sat stunned by the news of Becataten's parentage.

Beset raised her small hand. "No, Pygmy Lady—thank you—but my time is short. Soon I will be with God Osiris. I must speak now."

A vigil had begun to gather in the hall as word circulated throughout the Estate that Dwarf Beset was dying. By now, several dozen Estate dwellers stood by to honor Dwarf Beset. She had come to Egypt representing their God Bes, incarnate, the great protector of households and childbirths.

"I have a few words about the future," Beset said, gathering some momentum, and reaching for Becataten's hand. "I believe you will have a son and a daughter, Princess, who will bring joy to you and the Viceroy. And because few lives are lived without trials, I must mention yours to come.

"Your delivery would be a difficult one, without the help of Pygmy Lady. Remember she has the Heka and is loyal, and that is why she has come to you, Princess. Keep her close and forever your ally.

"Also, Pharaoh will change and become possessive of you, even claim that your son is his, not the Viceroy's. This is the result of the deep loss he feels from losing his heir apparent. Seek help from Pygmy Lady when this happens."

Beset's eyes closed, and her small hands went limp. The surrounds grew still as attendants knelt outside her door. The last shafts of light retreated through clerestory openings high up the wall, as Dwarf Beset left Egypt with the Sun God Ra.

Becataten collapsed on the floor, sobbing at Besets bedside. An attendant offered her a square of linen. Becataten covered her face with the cloth and wept. Her guttural sounds were of someone who didn't know how to cry never having had a life that offered the sadness that she now suffered. She soon realized how she sounded and made a failed attempt to compose herself. "I want the Viceroy, the Viceroy!"

Lady Nagara stared at Becataten. "Is he hear?"

Maja nodded.

Lady Nagara called for Butler to fetch the Viceroy and to shoo everyone away. Even Suti rose to leave. Maja stayed with Becataten and when Lady Nagara stood to go, she placed a hand on Becataten's shoulder as she exited. Maja remained on the floor next to Becataten softly crying.

Dashing up the staircase, the viceroy flew past Lady Nagara then paused to find Becataten on the floor, still weeping at Besets bedside. "Come, my love, you must rest. He reached for her to help her stand. Lady Nagara watched as Becataten faltered and he took her in his arms to carry her to her bed chamber.

She whispered, "I'll send a healer with a tonic of the poppy for her."

The next morning Becataten turned to look at the Viceroy and fully notice for the first time the deep scar that circled his neck. She touched it and he awoke immediately. He smiled at her and she felt their missed intimacy immediately return. With no words spoken between them, he reached for her and they made love until Ra was in his mid-heaven. Lying on his back out of breath, he said, "Are you sure all this love making is alright for our unborn?"

"I'm sure, let's continue."

Late that night, Suti and the Viceroy took a chariot to Abu's quarters. In the dark, Senzar trotted his vehicle toward the date grove. Standing in the chariot, Suti turned to the stable manager, "How long has Abu lived on the Estate?"

"He arrived with the Princess and her entourage when the rebellion began in Kush, two moons ago, my Lord," said Senzar.

"And do you know who this pygmy person is?" asked Suti.

The Viceroy replied, "She is one who tells fortunes and is a friend."

The Stable Master drew the chariot to a stop, jumped from his vehicle to announce his master's arrival. Suti hadn't visited this house since his long-departed Estate manager resided here. Inside two men and a baboon awaited Suti and Merymose.

The Viceroy held the highest rank at court, next to Pharaoh, but offered Suti deference; standing and delivering a slight bow allowing Suti to enter first. Abu remained seated, his baboon at his side enjoying a basket of dates.

As Suti took a chair, Abu snapped his fingers for sma to be served.

"I may be blind, but I remember what a long and dusty ride it is from the Palace to your Estate, Architect," Abu said, his strong voice a reminder from the past. At court, the once-Royal Astrologer had also outranked Suti.

"Thank you, Abu, but I arrived yesterday. I spent time in the chamber with the Dwarf, the Princess, and others. Beset left Egypt with Ra and is surely now with God Osiris. Dwarf Beset is the mother Becataten knew from birth. It is a shame that most women who bear twins die in childbirth, as Hor and my mother did."

Abu adjusted himself in his chair and cleared his throat. He opened his mouth to speak. but seemed to change his mind.

A silence intervened. Kombo sat in a corner holding the remainder of his arm with a pained expression, the bandage needing attention. "Well, it seems I am to assume that my Estate was in the hands of two able men during the last of this Nubian insurrection, and that kept Lady Nagara and Princess Becataten safe." Suti showed a lack of his usual composure.

Abu began to speak, but the Viceroy interrupted him. "Royal Architect, rather than we being in charge, events dictated our acts. When the Princess and her household had to escape the insurrection that began on the attack of Fortress Buhen, they were accompanied here with what I thought to be my loyal, Nubian guardsman, who proved to be traitors. I was myself captured in Kush and held there for two moons. It was with Kombo's help that I was able to escape my captors." The Viceroy motioned toward Kombo standing with Ahmose. Kombo saved my life at the expense of most of his arm, and my son from a Nubian wife remained at my side through my captivity and during our escape.

Suti noticed for the first time, the deep wound that surrounded the Viceroy's neck.

The Viceroy cleared his throat and continued. "Upon my return, I learned that Abu, blind as he is, soon understood that these Nubians were insurgents and recruiting their countrymen to encamp here. Abu quickly grasped the danger to the women and the Estate. He immediately petitioned the Palace for Royal Soldiers," the Viceroy said, ending his short speech.

Suti rubbed his head. He was silent for a time, taking in the chamber, again with the strange primitive pygmy in a dark corner. "Abu, I knew Princess Becataten saved you from begging in the streets of Thebes and took you and your baboon to Kush. And for her sake, I am glad she did. I wish to add, for all our sakes, we are in your debt for saving the lives of our women, as well as perhaps the Estate itself. You took charge accordingly, although I don't look forward to explaining this all to my Lady." Suti added, "And further, I don't understand how you have any sway at the Palace, you, old dog."

Abu grunted but chose not to speak. He had a source at the Palace that he did not wish to reveal.

Chapter 13

Evenings, when Ra left Egypt, Becataten had taken to walking around the large fishpond that fronted the Estate, and Lady Nagara had made it her habit to accompany her. With Becataten's protruding belly adding extra weight to her small frame, Lady Nagara rubbed her back as they walked.

Shadows grew long, when a Palace envoy bearing a canister had been allowed to enter the gates and was running alongside the lotus pond toward them. The carrier's kilt was of fine linen and he wore silver cuffs, his scroll-holder decorated with gems. He approached Princess Becataten and bowed with grace. Becataten thought, *how grand all things are, that come from the Palace.*

Lady Nagara appeared anxious when asking Becataten to read the message.

"It is of course from Pharaoh, and he wishes me to have an audience with him, as well as remain at the Palace for the birthing of my child," Becataten said, concern showing on her furrowed brow.

"I think you should find a way around that. I can respond saying you are unable to travel in these last two moons before you give birth. Remember what Beset said about Pharaoh becoming possessive of you and your child," said Lady Nagara.

"I am afraid I cannot refuse him, Lady Nagara. He adds that Dwarf Beset's mummification is complete, and her burial ceremony is to be attended. It says he is sending his royal barge for me. Pharaoh says that I should have my child with the aid of the Royal Healers. An apartment near him is waiting for me where the Viceroy and I may reside. I miss not traveling to the Palace with the Viceroy, but we all know Pharaoh has him busy advising and reviewing Pharaoh's counsellors about the rebellion." Becataten paused, deep in thought, her brow still creased. "I wonder if the Viceroy will return here and sail to the Palace with me?" she asked, as if she were alone talking to herself. "Pharaoh also says that I have stayed away far too long from the court. It almost sounds like a demand rather than an invitation!" Becataten surmised.

Lady Nagara adjusted her cuffs. "Yes, doesn't it? May I see the scroll, my dear?"

Becataten handed her the missive and wandered off to think about Pharaoh's words.

Lady Nagara went to her chamber and summoned Pygmy Lady, who on rare occasions she now spoke with. When Pygmy Lady arrived, Lady Nagara handed her the scroll.

"I don't read your gibberish. You will have to tell me what it says," said Pygmy Lady flatly.

Lady Nagara shook her head. "I am only allowing you to know of Pharaoh's words because Dwarf Beset asked that you be consulted when we needed help with difficult matters." Gaining her composure, she read Pharaoh's words to Pygmy Lady.

Angry and with loathing in her eyes, she said, "So Beset's vision was correct, your gold-hungry king wants Becataten, *and* her child. Well, I will see about that." Pygmy Lady turned and left abruptly. And send one of your healers to Abu's house to clean Kombo's wound," she added on her way out.

With a stunned look, Lady Nagara sat motionless.

From his royal apartment, Viceroy heard the news of Becataten's invitation by Pharaoh to the Palace and raced to his ships mooring to outrun Pharaoh's *Ka-em-Maat.* With his Golden Falcon being the much lighter ship, he arrived first and slipped into the Estate dock. He ran to the Estate house and leaped the steps to Becataten's chamber.

"I am so happy you have come back to be with me. I was just off to father's house and to say goodbye before sailing to the Palace." They held each other for a long time in silence. She knew her father, like everyone else, had misgivings about her leaving.

After a short visit with her father, she returned to the Estate and when she reached the steps, a runner from Pharaoh's royal barge waited at the top. He announced to the butler, "The *Kha-em-Maat* has moored at the Estate's dock and is awaiting Princess Becataten to deliver her to the Palace."

Lady Nagara walked toward Becataten, her demeanor showing signs of concern. "I hope you are able to return to the Estate and have your child here, my dear. But if that should not happen, I am pleased that you are taking both Nanny Maja and Pygmy Lady with you. Take Isis, too. And, of course Pharaoh's healers *are* the finest."

Becataten could feel Lady Nagar's anxiety as she spoke. The two women watched the loading of chests onto Becataten's second litter in silence. The women embraced. Viceroy Merymose stepped forward to assist Becataten, now heavy with child to settle herself into the chair of the grown conveyance. I will follow the *Kha-em-Maat* in my ship back to the Palace, My Love.

Muttering under her breath, Pygmy Lady said, "If I have anything to say about this, Becataten *will* return *here* to bear her boy-child." She stepped on to the second conveyance that followed and settled herself among Becataten's wicker chests, Nanny Maja, and Isis.

The Viceroy held up a hand to the bearers as Ahmose arrived, out of breath and with a message from Becataten's father. "Abu wants a scroll from Becataten describing Pharaoh's mood, and how he is running his court. Those are his exact words, I memorized the message as I came here," said Ahmose. Becataten nodded and thanked Ahmose, though she thought the message curious.

"We must leave now!" called Pygmy Lady in a loud, demanding voice.

On the litter ride to the *Ka-em-Maat*, Becataten remembered the tone in Pharaoh's scroll, almost commanding she return to him. Pharaoh had always treated her with kindness, so she tried to put aside any anxiety she and Lady Nagara may have shared about her forthcoming audience. And after all, she must attend sweet Beset's funerary ceremony. It surprised her that Pharaoh may even attend himself, considering his extended mourning period over his son. As her litter approached the craft, her troubled mood soon changed to a happy one, as she found her beloved Viceroy ship moored behind the *Kha-em-Maat*. Merymose jumped from his ship and caught up with Becataten to walk up the gangplank where they lingered at the top. He said nothing but held and kissed her hands as they made their final goodbye.

Then he made a quick decision by calling to his Skipper to sail without him, and that he would be sailing with the Princess on the *Kha-em-Maat.*

"You look beautiful, Princess. You remind me of a lotus, in full bloom." His eyes animated as he noticed images of the Goddess Bes, recently painted on her breasts.

The male God Bes, depicted in the form of a dwarf, and Goddess Hathor, who protected all women in childbirth, adorned her skin. Their magical spells were invoked during a women's labor to hasten birth. Dwarf Beset, being born female, carried the feminine moniker. "You are but a moon away from the birth of our child, are you not, Princess?" the Viceroy asked.

Becataten turned toward her husband. "Yes! And we have not seen enough of one another, Mosie. Has Pharaoh kept you so very busy?" She asked. As they sat holding hands in their gilt armchairs of cedar, panels of intricately woven papyrus were swiftly placed around them for privacy by the crew.

The Viceroy nodded with a somber expression that concerned Becataten. "Yes, Pharaoh has done just that, my Princess." With a deep breath and a serious face, the Viceroy added, "I am pleased to see that you have brought Pygmy Lady with you, Becataten."

"She would not let me leave without her. Even Lady Nagara approved." Becataten adjusted her silken pillows of gold and red to support her back. She squeezed the Viceroy's hand, noting how solemn he seemed. They floated up the Mother Nile on the royal barge to the quay at the Palace, the grandest craft afloat in the land, Pharaoh's royal *Kha-em-maat* (appearing in truth). Fishermen ignored their lines, farmers stopped working their crops, herdsmen turned away from their animals to bow in reverence to the barge. But the couple were enveloped in one another, oblivious to that around them. They did not hear or see the twenty rowers on each side of the royal papyrus boat, nor did they see the bare footed men in in their loincloths tending the lines of the thirty-foot sail.

Pygmy Lady sat cross-legged behind the couple with a placid expression, but her face was soon clouded by the Viceroy's mood. Many inundations, ago she and the Viceroy had met in Kush when she had read his fortune. All she had foreseen in his life had come to pass, including marrying a royal princess. Over time they had developed a mutual respect for one another. But Pygmy Lady could feel his sorrow and concern even by sitting near to him. Once she told someone a fortune, they somehow became bonded to her and she could always feel the same things as they were feeling, empath that she was.

"You must be prepared for a Pharaoh that has changed, Becataten," said the Viceroy quietly to Becataten.

"How has he changed, Mosie?" Becataten asked as the reflection of the water peered through the golden screens that surrounded them.

"Since the death of his robust son, only his withdrawn and peculiar boy-child remains, whose interest is in religion alone. In his household, Pharaoh and his two daughters are all viewing their lives quite differently than before their father suffered the tragic loss of his heir apparent."

Pygmy Lady rubbed her chin and edged closer across the deck of tightly laced papyrus where Princess Becataten and the Viceroy were seated. The standard bearer, *Siese,* eyed her with a scowl as she drew closer

114

to the couple. She looked at him with an equally serious face, then decided to show a rare smile, exposing her manifold of teeth, all filed to points. *Siese* returned a small grin then looked up to view the mild wind ruffle the large square sale of the *Kha-em-Maat* as the rowers swiftly but silently drew their oars across the dark silken waters of the Nile.

"How so, Mosie?" Becataten asked.

"He is a more demanding Pharaoh, and much less patient with everyone around him. New favorites appear in his court, while old friends are forgotten. He has thrown himself into the building of his mortuary temple at Luxor. The entrance is said to be flanked by two huge seated colossi in his image, facing the Mother Nile. He had the quartzite sandstone brought overland from the north. His workers journeyed some four hundred miles."

"But it is common that Pharaoh's create glorious memorials to their life, Mosie, is it not?" Becataten asked, holding the bulge of her middle as the baby inside of her moved. The Viceroy laid his hand next to hers on her belly and smiled at the princess.

"Perhaps, but these effigies are to rival the Sphinx, Becataten. They will be sixty feet in height and his mortuary site covers more than eighty acres," he explained, pulling his hand away.

"That *is* grand. How old is Pharaoh now, Mosie?"

"He and I are twice your age. We have both lived through nearly thirty inundations."

Pygmy Lady leaned back on a nearby basket with a pensive expression.

The captain called orders to tend the square sail as the currents were with them sailing north, making it easier on the rowers returning to the Palace.

"It appears that this craft is trying to reach the Palace in haste," Becataten noted.

The Viceroy nodded, and Pygmy Lady's lips closed tight.

As they arrived at the Theban royal quay, Ra's long rays were settling on the white-washed Palace. Panels that had offered privacy abord were quickly removed, a plank was set from boat to quay where a large canopied litter awaited them. They were carried with speed and comfort toward Pharaoh's chambers.

"Are we allowed to freshen ourselves before we are received by Pharaoh?" Becataten asked the Viceroy during the ride.

Taking her hands in his, the Viceroy said, "We have been allocated a large apartment, and I look forward to our stay there, my love." He hesitated before continuing. "But you should know, it is Pharaoh's wish to see not the two of us, but you alone, Princess," the Viceroy admitted in a quiet but steady voice. Becataten grew quiet, contemplating what that might mean.

Becataten called for Isis, then pointed to a wig box. "Arrange this on my head, we are going straight to see Pharaoh. "Not the beautiful new one from Lady Nagara? Asked Isis.

"The less jeweled one will do, Isis."

Pygmy Lady's nostrils flared at the Viceroy's words. Sitting behind the couple in their conveyance, as they moved through the Palace grounds, the pygmy was stared at with delight by the locals. Egyptians loved exotic creatures, and she fit that image. She glared darkly back at them, her mind in deep thought.

When she and Pygmy Lady stepped off the litter they found they had arrived at Pharaoh's massive double doors that led to his private chambers. Here

Nubian sentries clad in kilts of leopard skins received Princess Becataten but moved to block Pygmy Lady's entrance, crossing their spears before her. She stood erect, hands on hips, looked up at them, and said, "A curse I will place on you and your family if you do not allow me entry with the Princess!"

With their ancestry in Kush, they carried the knowledge that pygmies held great powers and the giant-sized Nubians acquiesced allowing Becataten to pass through the great portal with Pygmy Lady.

It was the beautiful room she remembered, with the vast wall map painted lavishly to show Egypt's numerous vassal states, studded with gemstones. There he was, but not as sublime as she had remembered him. A young woman was fondling Pharaoh's genitals while another fed him olives. He took his time to turn to her, but when he did, he swept the two women away with a hand gesture.

"Princess Becataten, I have been waiting for you," Pharaoh said.

His smile was crooked, not full, as she remembered. She noted that he was missing a tooth and thought maybe that was why his grin was different. And as she approached him, she saw that his expression was no longer a savory one. Stepping into his presence, she bowed deeply, wobbling some due to her full belly. Pharaoh did not rise but reached for her and settled her on his lap.

Rubbing Becataten's belly he said, "So, we are with child, Becataten, and when is this blessed event to come about?"

Becataten was surprised at his words, but smiled carefully and said, "At the end of the next moon, My Lord."

He reached for her breasts to liberally fondle, and Becataten caught her breath. "There is nothing quite like the breasts of a woman with child, Becataten. Allow me some time to explore."

The sound of gritting teeth came from Pygmy Lady, as she stood motionless nearby.

Pharaoh continued to pursue Becataten's body with his hands and his mouth, until she became too uncomfortable at his advances and rose and said, "My Lord, I am quite tired from the sail, can you allow me a rest in the apartment you have so generously appointed the Viceroy and I?"

She slid off his lap, to rearrange her shift and wig.

"You may, Becataten, but when we next meet, I want you to come to me with names for our son, for I am sure we will have a boy."

Becataten's mouth dropped opened, but she did not speak. She walked to the Butler who held a tray of filled goblets, and reached for a glass of pomegranate wine, drinking it to its finish before she turned to Pharaoh. "My Living God, there may be some confusion, but do you not remember when you gave me as wife to Viceroy Merymose?"

Pharaoh nodded with little interest, as he was served his stronger vintage beverage of *sma*, made from grapes.

"My Lord, that was nearly two inundations ago. This is the child of the Viceroy's."

Not looking up from a scroll that he had reached for, he waved her away with his hand as he said, "Leave me now Becataten. We will speak again in two Ras."

Pygmy Lady rushed Becataten out of Pharaoh's chamber as a royal attendant walked them to their nearby suite. Becataten saw that the Viceroy was waiting for her outside the door. She ran to him with outstretched arms and tears streaming her cheeks, her wig falling to the ground. The Viceroy held her as she sobbed.

"Do you know what Pharaoh said to me, Mosie?" Becataten asked.

"Yes, I believe I do, My Love," he answered in a soft voice.

Pygmy Lady stepped very close to the two of them and whispered, "How do I reach Pharaoh's kitchen from here?"

Chapter 14

♊

After getting general directions from the reluctant Viceroy, Pygmy Lady disappeared into the Palace, while Becataten and the Viceroy settled into their new apartment. All was comfortable and familiar; Becataten remembered the soft light linens, the décor, and even the servants from her previous time of living under Pharaoh's roof. But this time, it all felt like a devious trap. As she sat reclining on the decadent hide chaise longue, she tried to recover from Pharaoh's unexpected advances as tears fell down her face again.

"Why does he want our child, Mosie?" sobbed Becataten.

The Viceroy's embrace was firm as he enveloped her roundness. "Pharaoh has become demented since the loss of his heir apparent, my Princess. Both the Vizier and Chancellor are very careful when in his attendance, as his moods are erratic. I have spoken with them, and they have grave concerns about his new intentions and desires. They say he grows angry easily, and they are hoping this is a phase in his life that will soon pass as his grief ebbs."

Though Mosie's words offered some solace, it took Becataten a long while before she could collect herself from the sting of Pharaoh's suggestions and the crude fondling of her body. After some time passed, she called for and attendant to bring her an inkpot, a roll of papyrus and a stylus. A house slave brought her the items, as well as a scribe.

Becataten glared at the scribe. "I do not need you, I shall write my own scroll."

"Be careful what you write, Becataten, your scroll may well be intercepted by one of Pharaoh's new inquisitors, and you must think about how to send the missive safely," Viceroy added. "By the way, to whom are you sending a scroll?"

"I am writing to my father about Pharaoh's appalling demand for our child. I need his wisdom in this matter. After all, he and Pharaoh are half-brothers, and he was the Royal Astrologer for longer than I have been alive."

Becataten failed to note that the Viceroy too was Pharaoh's half-brother, but Merymose chose not to remind her.

When Becataten tried to draw a bench up to a table, the size of her belly wouldn't let her get close enough to execute a scroll. Averted smiles came from the Viceroy and Nanny Maja.

Harshly she called to Maja for a pillow and a footstool. Together, Maja and the Viceroy helped her to arrange the cushion on her lap, and to get her feet on the stool as she grumbled showing her frustration. With fire in her eyes, she looked briefly at the Viceroy, then reached for her stylus. Rubbing the end that was pounded into a fine brush, she ruminated. She dipped the stylus into the pot of inky liquid made from black soot, and with resolve began to scribe.

As the others stayed out of Becataten's way, the Viceroy whispered to Maja, "My mother used to say, 'Beware of the anger carried by a woman heavy with child.'"

Maja response was to roll her eyes, and nod appreciatively.

"I can understand wanting to inform your father, Princess. He clearly has some remaining influence in the Palace. Otherwise he couldn't have mustered the Royal troops that he did to crush the rebellion at the Suti Estate." Under his breath he added, "I have been here several moons, and not been able to learn where his influence lies."

Becataten looked up from her scroll. "My father once nearly managed a takeover of the crown. Too bad he didn't succeed."

With surprise, the Viceroy and Nanny Maja sat up at her comment. The Viceroy moved over toward his wife, to massage Becataten's back as she wrote out her scroll.

"Not now, Mosie, please," she said.

Silently, Maja remained at Becataten's side as the Princess furiously scribed her message.

All the Viceroy could do was pace. "Becataten, this scroll must be sent with the surety that it will not be opened and read before it reaches your father."

"I heard you the first time, Mosie," Becataten said harshly, but she caught herself, realizing her incident with Pharaoh had left her nerves on edge. "Don't repeat yourself, husband," she added in a gentler tone.

The Viceroy squeezed Becataten's shoulders and moved away as Pygmy Lady burst into the room, surprising the sentries assigned to their entry doors. They jumped to attention. Becataten turned to her as she was rolling the scroll to seal it.

Pygmy Lady leaned into Becataten ear and whispered, "Do you think we can kill him, or at least keep him very ill for a long time?"

Overhearing the loud whisper, the Viceroy's jaw dropped. Maja's eyes grew as large as turtle eggs.

Pygmy Lady glared at them both. "She huddled with Becataten. "There are no kitchen attendants that are pygmies in Pharaoh's kitchen, and I cannot find an ally there, "but it is my guess that your father may know of someone who can help, she snickered."

The two women sat to conspire until Ra's rays left Egypt when attendants came to light the floor candles, and table lamps that burned a refined oil. A light dinner arrived from Pharaoh's kitchen that the Viceroy had ordered. Becataten ignored the food but drank fig wine while Pygmy Lady picked at a few grapes. The Viceroy ate roasted quail and baby eels, ending with a pitcher of dry red wine, Maja finished the flatbread and chickpeas.

After Becataten's long discussion with Pygmy Lady, Becataten found herself exhausted and ready for sleep. Stumbling toward the bedchamber, she reached out for the Viceroy as she reeled from too much fig wine. She stared at the lavish and colorful wall scenes depicting Pharaoh, his symbols, and the verdant Nile. How this all used to impress me.

She swayed as she lifted her wig off her head and handed it to the Viceroy. He helped her out of her shift and appeared aroused by the small tattoos on her thighs of the images of God Bes. Becataten also had an artist apply them for the god's help in birthing. Whispering, he mouthed a quick prayer to God Bes to aid his wife in her birthing. Becataten reached with pleasure for the bed of soft down and fine linens.

Bending down to kiss her, the scent of Pharaoh's strong musk filled the Viceroy's nostrils. It was unmistakably the Living God's essence of Morenga oil.

He stood, hiding his expression of anger. He walked into the receiving chamber, and with authority called, "Pygmy Lady, I wish to speak to you."

Pygmy Lady's face held an expression of indifference when she collapsed onto a pile of nearby floor pillows, but her tone was low and hateful as she whispered, "Princess Becataten is angry, and cannot give her baby to your depraved Pharaoh."

Standing over her the Viceroy snarled, "Of course, I understand that, but you are just inflaming the situation with your lethal solutions. I want these discussions to stop! Don't you think I am angry too when I smell his perfume all over my wife!" He slammed his fist on the table. "I do not know details, nor do I want to, but the plotting I have overheard from you and the Princess sounds like something that could easily get us all killed, or worse, left tortured in a state like Abu, only to suffer with wounds stemming from words of insolence and insurgence! My wife is about to have our child. Please stop entertaining these vile plans and get her back to the relaxed princess she needs to be to keep our child safe!"

Isis and Maja huddled in their respective cubicles, not wanting to know in any detail what was going on.

As Becataten drifted off to sleep, the last images she saw were the wall paintings in her bedchamber of Pharaoh sailing the verdant Mother Nile on his fishing barge. Just before dozing off, she reached for her belly and groaned as her unborn churned. Turning on to her side, the movement stopped, and she fell into troubled slumber.

A vivid dream found her running down the side of the Nile trying to catch Pharaoh's royal boat that was fleeing with her child. She called to him, but he responded by asking the rowers for more speed. His barge sailed faster than she could run. Her baby cried for her. As she ran closer to the river, it became difficult to move through the dense papyrus stocks. Her feet were hard to lift from the deepening mud until she was slowed to a stop. She screamed in panic for her baby, but try as she may, no sounds came from her voice. Then out of the mire appeared the Heka snakes, and the words. *Becataten, you have the power of alchemy, use it, and remember that dwarves and small people will always help you with their mystical gifts.*

Ra's rays were high in the sky when a strong knock sounded on Abu's door. Kombo held his nearly amputated arm with his good arm as he advanced to the entrance. Usually Ahmose tended the door, but he and Ne Ne were out gathering fruit with the baboon, Huni.

A manly looking dwarf, with a large torso and short legs, had to peer high to reach Kombo's gaze. "I have a message from Princess Becataten for Master Abu. I believe he lives here?" said Dwarf Heby.

Abu sat up and cocked his head toward the voice of the dwarf. "Grant him entrance, Kombo," called Abu from his sitting chamber.

With grace, Kombo swept his good arm toward Abu's loud voice. Heby's stride faltered when viewing his past master. The dwarf and others knew of Abu for his supreme power and authority. To see him wearing a linen cloth low around his head that masked his notorious injury drew shock from Heby causing him to weaken at his knees.

Abu boomed, "I remember well your voice, Dwarf. It has been some time since you served me in my Palace apartment. What have you brought me?" Nothing in Abu's strong voice revealed defeat.

"A... a scroll," said Dwarf Heby, who struggled being before Abu now, close enough to notice his scarred arms. A silence ensued, but impatiently Abu tapped his staff on the stone floor. "You say you have brought me a scroll. Did the Princess speak to you about its content?" Abu asked.

The dwarf's short arm thrust the scroll forward then back to his side. "Yes, ah, she told me some of what it said."

"Why did she choose you to deliver her scroll?" Abu asked.

Standing erect, still with an expression of disbelief, Heby's feet shuffled and his eyes averted to avoid Abu's mutilations. "Ah ah... Dwarf Beset and I were good friends, and the Princess sought me out to be her messenger. Pharaoh has a new group of men, called inquisitors who..."

"Yes, I have heard about them," said Abu. "And why were *you* able to elude them?"

"My Lord, a dwarf is rarely distrusted."

Abu nodded. "Read me the scroll."

"You wish *me* to read Princess Becataten's scroll?"

"Most of you dwarfs read, don't you?"

"Yes, My Lord."

The scroll that Dwarf Heby read explained that Pharaoh wanted Abu's grandson for his own and that Pharaoh appeared no longer a strong but a hedonist obsessed with his burial temple and that Becataten was sure he planned to sequester her permanently at his Palace.

Abu stood, held his staff high, and plowed through his sitting chamber striking at anything in his path.

Dwarf Heby and Kombo took to corners in the chamber.

Ahmose, Ne Ne, and Huni returned from gathering fruit after Abu's rage. The site of the house set Ne Ne into tears, and she ran to an exhausted Abu who was sitting in silence, beathing heavily and sweating. Ahmose struggled with Huni, who was pulling hard on his tether to reach Dwarf Heby.

"You can let him go," Dwarf Heby said. "Huni and I are old friends." When the baboon was freed and reached Heby, his slaps and wallops of affection knocked Dwarf Heby to the floor, until Heby stood back up stiffly and allowed the baboon to hug him.

Chapter 15

♊

When warm rays penetrated the high clerestory windows to awaken Becataten, she was reminded that this was the day of Dwarf Beset's funerary ceremony. Her mouth was dry, and her head ached. She lay staring at ankhs painted on the ceiling that echoed the key of life, reminding her that she must protect the child within her. She was pleased her birthing had not yet begun; as it would obstruct a plan she was implementing on this day; a plan that must work. Carefully she rolled over on her large down bed then with some effort sat, waiting a moment before standing. She reached for a bedpost, feeling the effects of too much wine drinking the night before. She was quick to use the chamber pot. With a shaking hand, she grasped a clay beaker of well water and drank it to its finish. Nude, she waddled to the upright, copper mirror and stood before it. Rubbing the small of her back, then the front of her belly she said, "By the God's, I'm the size of the hippopotamus, God Taweret."

Awake before most of the household in her Palace apartment, she quickly dressed in a comfortable shift then entered her sitting chamber. With wavering steps, she moved to a lounge plopped onto it and adjusted the zebra hide pillows for comfort. Looking stern, and with purpose, she called to an attendant who was removing chamber pots. "Send me a sentry, now." The young eunuch did as he was told, but backed away from her in awe, never having taken a direct order from a princess. Next, Becataten clapped her hands that brought a slave girl running from her sleeping cubicle. "Bring me peppermint tea, lotus bread and a boiled goose egg," she said.

A tall Nubian sentry arrived in a leopard skin kilt asking Becataten for his assignment. Still adjusting her pillows, she took a deep breath and looked up. "Go now to Queen Tiye's apartment and return with her son. She knows of my request for him to accompany me today to Dwarf Beset's funerary ritual."

Nanny Maja entered the chamber, not fully awake. "Taten, are you well? Can I get you something?"

"Yes Maja, go quickly to Pharaoh's kitchen with two attendants and have Chef Bakenamen fill several baskets with the foods Beset favored."

"But, I am not sure how to..."

"Maja, I have no time to quibble."

Maja did as she was told, without the time to groom her rumbled wig or change to a shift without wrinkles.

The Viceroy had been out early arranging the procession from the embalming house to Dwarf Beset's tomb. Beset's mummified body would be transported across the river where Pharaoh deemed she would be entombed. The location was within the confines of his eighty-acre, mortuary temple-complex that was under frenetic construction.

"Where is my makeup artist, I want her now!" called Becataten.

"Should I come to you, Princess Becataten? I was waiting for you in your bed chamber." Carefully called the artist, Isis.

"Come to me here, to my lounge. I just got settled. I don't want to get up again."

"Yes, My Lady." The artist shuffled the large chest of makeup to her mistress.

"Paint my face as beautiful as you have ever done, but do not dare to paint my face as heavy as the women of the court paint theirs. Do you understand?" The artist nodded as she proceeded with care to create her masterpiece for the important day.

Becataten watched the makeup artist scrutinize her work, then reach in the chest for a small ball of linen that held gold dust. After lightly touching Becataten's round checks, she said, "Finished."

With her back to the entry doors, Becataten held a polished silver mirror to her face and examined the makeup artist's work. She was admiring the perfectly painted kohl lines around her eyes and the malachite paint on her eyelids, when she saw the cedar doors open. Flanked by two sentries, entered the odd-looking son of Pharaoh and Queen Tiye. Not quite a man, Young Horus was difficult to look at, in body and face. Tall for his age, his long oval head and thick lips gave him a ghostly appearance. He showed discomfort to be out of his realm where his nose was always buried in sacred scrolls, and where religious scholars surrounded him.

Setting the mirror aside, Becataten turned toward the pubescent boy. Holding on to the edge of the lounge, she rose then bowed deeply before Pharaoh's homely son, the boy who had always been disregarded as a student of religious doctrine, and nothing more.

Becataten gushed, "Young Horus, my sweet future Amenhotep IV, how beautiful you look. How happy I am to have you join me for the funerary rituals and burial of Dwarf Beset."

The boy made a small bow to Becataten, continuing to look uneasy.

Pygmy Lady entered the sitting chamber with an expression of revulsion at this ugly court-child that Becataten fawned over. She looked him up and down taking in his sagging belly and drooping pectoral mussels, an image resembling the image of a eunuch.

Becataten noticed the expression on Pygmy Lady's face as she assessed Horus. His physique coupled with his lack of interests in any sport caused Pharaoh to pay little attention to this second son. Becataten knew she must change that. *May all the gods in Egypt help me to make Pharaoh welcome this remaining son as his heir apparent.*

"You are dressed perfectly for Beset's funeral, Young Horus," Becataten said. The boy stood still in slumped discomfort. Becataten continued with her compliments. "But I know you understand funerary costume, ritual and dogma better than most people at court. That is something you must be very proud of."

With hesitant authority, he straightened his posture some. "Have you all the proper texts and have the priests been assembled for the ceremony, Princess Becataten?" asked the Young Horus in a voice of an adolescent that was breaking.

"I believe so, but of course I have invited *you* to oversee the religious practices so they will be properly executed," she said.

Horus' frame puffed briefly while he took in her silhouette. "You won't be wearing that shift, will you, Princess?" he lamented.

"How observant of you, Sweet Horus, I was just about to change into proper dress. Will you excuse me?"

He nodded, and Becataten rushed to her chamber with Pygmy Lady right behind her.

Hands on hips, feet planted apart, Pygmy Lady said quietly, as her long breasts stopped swaying. "Just when I think I have seen the worst of you Egyptians, a little snake like this turns up."

Becataten didn't want to hear negative things about this goat-faced boy. He was obviously strange to look at. What she wanted was his recognition by the court. "Be thankful for him, Pygmy Lady. He is the one we are going to bring to the attention of Pharaoh, to divert him from taking *my* boy child." *This is the way I will use my Heka,* Becataten thought.

Becataten watched Pygmy Lady parade around the room, ruminating, slapping her big feet on the stone floor and rubbing her chin like a man clad in her usual leather shift. "I don't like him. My people say anyone borne as ugly as he is born cunning, too. Where did you find him?"

"No more bad talk about Young Horus. He is Queen Tiye's only son. You know how important she is to Pharaoh. We must shower him with words to make him feel important."

"I knew you would one day prove to be your father's daughter." Pygmy Lady said with a shrewd smile that gave a rare glimpse of her filled teeth.

Becataten's attendant adjusted the straps of her shift over her growing breasts. "Where do you think I got the idea?" Becataten said.

As Pygmy Lady continued her stride around the chamber, she said, "So this is the little fanatic you told

132

me about that we are to charm. Leave him to me. I can charm a hyena."

Becataten stilled her turquoise and lapis lazuli earrings, looking into the distance. "Do not look upon this child as a hyena or a monster, Pygmy Lady. He is a highly intelligent student of religion. However, he isn't much more, we will still pay tribute to that talent and get Pharaoh to do the same. Pray for this!"

Pygmy Lady's face showed no expression while Becataten dressed. But before they left, a rare grin crossed her face again revealing her teeth, sharpened to points.

With the help of her attendant, Becataten settled a long cape around her shoulders that was woven from spun gold. With reserve, she walked to the Young Horus. She took his hand, squeezed it, and produced a maternal smile. He looked pained by the attention.

"Remember, *you* are the expert today, and I want you to see that all the rituals are perfectly executed." said Becataten. He seemed at home with this statement. "You are my hope to conduct a truly proper funerary ceremony for my beloved Dwarf Beset, who was my second mother."

Pygmy Lady rolled her eyes and shook her head as she followed the two out of the chamber.

Eight bearers arrived to carry Becataten and the Young Horus on a large comfortable litter to the entrance of the burial tomb. The grand litter, fixed with chairs and a canopy for shade was fringed with red and blue tassels. Maja and Pygmy Lady sat behind them, holding bowls of Beset's favorite foods.

They stopped at the opening of the long tunnel that descended into Beset's burial chamber. Here she would enter paradise. The Viceroy was awaiting them. His bow was deep to the future Pharaoh. When he rose, he said, "The procession has reached the chamber and includes dignitaries, Priests, friends and mourners." He added, "You, Young Horus, and Princess Becataten are the last to arrive and shall be carried down in chairs. The assent runs deep into Pharaoh's earth."

Becataten was pleased Mosie had arranged that she and Young Horus didn't have to be a part of the funerary procession. She never liked the professional mourners, women dressed in pale blue, wailing, and beating their breasts during the long walk.

Stepping off their litter, they moved to sit in carrying chairs that held plenty of pillows. These were low boxes with long seats so the occupant could stretch out their legs. They were fitted with long poles, one on each side, trimmed with finials. Four bearers at each conveyance carefully moved the two long chairs down the tunnel. As they descended the passageway to Beset's tomb, the aroma of incense and purification oils reached them. "What are these large copper mirrors we are encountering on our way down the passage, Sweet Horus?" Becataten asked.

Young Horus was in the first chair and called back to her. "When a tunnel is dug, light is needed, so Ra's light is captured at the opening on the first mirror and moved to the second and so on. Then in the deepest diggings, there is always light," Answered the boy, as if she was rather ignorant not to know this.

"I have always been interested in architecture and all sorts of building, but I didn't know that," Becataten said.

Young Horus's nod was professorial.

Becataten turned to look at Pygmy Lady who was walking behind her chair down the long decline. Her smug expression remained while she reached for the roughly hewn walls to steady her path. Maja looked frightened because of the steepness of the passage. Only because it was Dwarf Beset's funeral did she attend. She stayed behind Pygmy Lady, reeling with fright all the way down.

The future Amenhotep IV, Horus, arrived first in the burial chamber. Becataten observed the Priests appearing astonished by his presence. They mumbled amidst one another, then quickly offered Pharaoh's only son obeyance. Comments of surprise were also heard among the mourners who recognized him. She watched as the boy began to place the Priests in different order around the coffin and pass on to them many instructions. She saw that he was absorbed and intent at making the spiritual dogma at this funeral perfect. She watched as he inspected Beset's wrappings, her canopic jars and the adze that was forged from meteoric iron. It would be used to perform the opening of the mouth ceremony allowing Beset to eat and drink in the afterlife. Becataten was thrilled to see people she had not expected. Mosie was a great planner and had arranged this well. She had not anticipated the arrival of Lady Nagara and Architect Suti, or her old friend the Heka Priest, his white spikey hair shimmering in the mirror-light like Ra himself in the darkness. This was to be a glorious Ra, and the best way to say goodbye to her beloved dwarf. She caught a glimpse of Maja, wearing a girlish grin, and that meant Sennejem must be near.

Chapter 16

♊

When Becataten returned from Dwarf Beset's funerary ceremony. . . she was exhausted. She thought of the ceremony and how in the dim light her beloved Dwarf Beset's carefully wrapped body was placed in her final resting place. Now it seemed so real, and Becataten sighed over the loss of her sweet friend who had raised her like the kindest mother would. Holding back tears, she was glad once her litter was parked in front of her apartment, her Nubian bearer and the Viceroy had to help her up and out of her litter. In her bedchamber, she threw off her golden cape, handed her wig to her attendant and wiggled out of her shift until it was on the floor. An attendant tried to help her remove her jewelry, but she shook her head and dropped to her bed where she lay writhing about while holding her belly. During these last days of her pregnancy, her unborn was very active.

The Viceroy came in to check on Becataten. He saw her condition, and with alarm the Viceroy called, "Come Pygmy Lady, come quick! I think the Princess is..."

Followed by Maja, Pygmy Lady rushed to the bedchamber and with the eye of a hawk examined Becataten's shifting belly. "No, she is not in her thrusts yet," Pygmy Lady reported. "This kicking is the baby trying to get into the right position," Pygmy Lady added.

"But she is in such discomfort, look at her." said the Viceroy.

"She will be in more than discomfort when the baby comes, leave her now to rest."

Resigned, the Viceroy turned and left.

As Pygmy Lady pulled a nearby stool to Becataten's bedside, she asked, "Tell me what you feel." Maja was standing attentive at the foot of Becataten's bed.

"I feel the head of the child revolving, down here like a melon," Becataten said, frowning and pointing to the lowest part of her belly.

"That is the girl's head churning. She is trying to move to the correct position for birthing."

Becataten wailed, "What is the *right* position, Pygmy Lady?"

"Don't these healers tell you anything in Egypt? I bet Maja knows."

Becataten looked at Maja for the answer. Maja put her head down and her arms in a dive position.

"Like diving into a pond?" Becataten asked, confused. "The baby is turning so the head will come out first?"

Pygmy Lady nodded.

"How do you know it is a girl?" Becataten asked.

"The same way I knew that the Viceroy would marry a princess, I just know."

Becataten looked into Pygmy Lady's small face, where she saw obstinacy mixed with confidence. "You do have the Heka, Pygmy Lady, and Dwarf Beset knew it. I am pleased that Beset choose you to be in my life. I feel confident knowing that you will be with me when I have my baby," said Becataten.

With a raised head Pygmy Lady adjusted her bench. "What you call Heka, I call magic, and there was a man at the dwarf's funerary ceremony that has it too," said Pygmy Lady.

"You must mean the Heka Priest with the spikey white hair?" Becataten guessed.

Pygmy Lady nodded.

Becataten handed her earrings to her attendant and allowed her to remove her golden carnelian and turquoise collar. Eager to indulge Pygmy Lady in a real conversation, she said, "My father must have the Heka too."

Becataten watched Pygmy Lady shake her head with a set jaw.

Taken aback, Becataten sat up. "But my father must have the Heka because I do. Beset told me so."

"Your father is very shrewd, and cunning, but that is different."

Becataten asserted herself with a questioning air. "But he understands much about people. He gave me the idea to groom Young Horus and bring him to Pharaoh's attention when I sent him a scroll telling him Our Living God wanted my child."

"Listen to what I have to say, then I am through talking. Your father can understand many difficult things, and faster than most people, but he does not have what you call the Heka. Your father has guile, and he is the perfect man to outwit someone with the same trait. You must learn in your lifetime that you have this wily trait too. Never use it, Princess Becataten, unless it is against someone evil. If you do, you will find yourself with a fate like your father's."

Disturbed by her words, Becataten watched Pygmy Lady stand and leave the room.

When Becataten woke the next morning, she rushed to her chamber pot then went straight back to her bed, sat on it, and clapped her hands. To the arriving attendant she said, "Bring me a cup of boiled fenugreek with milk and honey, a goose egg, some bread and barley beer, and dates too. Hurry, I'm hungry! And replace the cotton next to the chamber pot, there is little left."

Pharaoh's outdoor kitchen was close to the royal apartment that had been arranged for her stay, and she took full advantage ordering what she liked and getting it delivered quickly by runners. As she was eating her morning breakfast, the Viceroy came to stand at the end of her bed. "You are enjoying your food more than I have ever seen you do so, My Princess."

"Are you saying I am fat?"

"I am not," defended the Viceroy.

"But you watch me eat, and I know you think I am fat." Becataten said, as she struggled peeling her goose egg. Frustrated she threw it to her attendant, who quickly shelled it and handed it back.

"I just came to say you have a visitor, My Princess," said the Viceroy. "A husband knows when he will lose a conversation to his wife, for there is no winning it!" he said under his breath.

"By the Gods, I don't want to see anyone, the way I look!" She ate the goose egg too fast and hiccups followed. Reaching for her barley beer, she took it and gulped it quickly.

"The guest is the Royal Gardener Sennejem, Becataten. He didn't get a chance to speak to you at Dwarf Beset's funerary ceremony and came to pay his respects."

"And I suppose he didn't want to see Maja, just me." Becataten said with irritation.

"Of course he wants to see Maja. You and I both know they have a long-standing relationship. You are very testy this morning, My Princess."

Becataten sat with a mouth full of bread hiccupping. Her eyes welled with tears. "I want to have this birthing over with. I am fat, unhappy, and hot." She motioned for the attendant to take her tray away. She took hold of her linen covering and pumped it up and down for some cool air.

The Viceroy clapped his hands and a eunuch appeared. "Bring a fan bearer to the Princess, immediately," he said.

Becataten took a deep breath, spread her legs apart and pulled her bedding up over her belly and breasts. "You may send Sennejem in after my makeup artist has attended me."

While Maja and Sennejem sat in the sitting chamber, a tall Nubian sentry announced Dwarf Heby. With a frown at his brow, the Viceroy said, "Do we know you, Dwarf?"

"Sennejem stood. "Viceroy, you'll forgive me, I asked Dwarf Heby here to deliver a scroll for me to Becataten's father. I apologize. I thought you knew Dwarf Heby. He was a close friend of Dwarf Beset and worked in the household of the Royal Astrologer, I mean, Princess Becataten's father."

The dwarf and Viceroy made formal introductions to one another, Heby offering a flourishing bow, to which the Viceroy returned a nod. After Sennejem passed his scroll to Dwarf Heby, a concerned Merymose followed the dwarf to the door. "You will deliver your missive directly to Abu?" asked Merymose.

Heby peered up at the Viceroy, nodding slowly.

"Good, may you journey safely, and please express to Becataten's father that he is soon to be a grandparent."

Looking relieved, Dwarf Heby left to return to the Suti Estate, by boat, where he would deliver his scroll to Abu.

The Viceroy went to Becataten where the fan bearer pumped a pole of ostrich feathers over her bed while Isis finished painting her face. Becataten snatched the brush from the makeup artist and threw it across the room. "I hurt, and I don't care how I look. I don't want to be pregnant anymore!"

The Viceroy spoke in soft low tones. "You look lovely my Princess. Is there anything I can get you before you receive the royal gardener?"

She shook her head. "I know I am as irritable as a wet hawk, Mosie, but I so want this child to be born. I'm finding it hard to breathe."

Becataten waved the artist away and Merymose moved to her side. As he elevated her pillows, he said, "Perhaps talking to Sennejem will make you feel better. You haven't seen many visitors of late."

A eunuch passed them with a basket of cotton and an armful of lotus lilies as he headed toward her chamber-pot cubicle.

"Stop, eunuch," said the Viceroy. He reached for a lotus out of the bouquet and handed it to Becataten. "This may help you breathe, my love."

Becataten sniffed the lily. "Who was the other voice I heard when you were speaking with Sennejem?" asked Becataten, her voice calmer now.

"It was an old friend of Besets. Dwarf Heby, I believe is his name."

"Why was he here?" Becataten asked.

"It seems Sennejem had a scroll for him to deliver to your father," The Viceroy said quietly.

"Really, and why would my father want such an envoy?" She shook her head. "Don't answer that, I know why, it's because messengers are being intercepted by our new mistrusting Pharaoh, and dwarves are trustworthy."

The Viceroy nodded.

"So, the dwarf is my father's errand boy, and Sennejem is his informant within the Palace."

The Viceroy nodded. "I believe you have that right, Princess."

"Help me up, Mosie, I want to meet with Sennejem in the sitting chamber." She stood with the Viceroy's assistance, and a rush of water spilled from her body to puddle at her feet.

The Viceroy looked horrified, as Becataten screamed for Maja. Isis left hurriedly to find healers. Pygmy Lady came running from her cubicle to aid Becataten back to her cot in a sitting position, stuffing pillows under her legs.

"Becataten looked at Pygmy Lady and said, "I am afraid! Has it really begun at last?"

"It really has, your baby is coming soon. I want you to take some deep breaths to prepare yourself for the thrusts that will come soon," said Pygmy Lady.

Standing at the end of the bed, the Viceroy asked, "Can, can I do anything Pygmy Lady?"

"Yes. Leave," Pigmy-Lady said, pushing her hand at him.

The Viceroy did as he was told, and on his way out the door collided with three healers. They demanded a table for their wares of ointments, statues of the male

God Bes, incense and copper knives moving about the apartment with an almighty air.

Becataten continued to breathe deeply as she watched a healer paint her belly with an orange-colored liquid. "This is beer mixed with saffron, Princess, and will help with your pain," he said.

Pygmy Lady looked at Maja, shaking her head in disbelief. Meanwhile, two of the three healers stepped aside and began to deliver chants for a safe birth. With the same expression of skepticism, Pygmy Lady watched the healers and checked on Becataten's condition from a distance.

Becataten's belly was now a vivid carrot-color when the Healer said, "You will be happy to know that Pharaoh asked to be notified as soon as you went into your thrusts, and it has been done."

Becataten was taken aback that Pharaoh already knew of her birthing. At the same time Becataten heard Pharaoh was informed, she saw her belly jolt like a lurching chariot. She stared at Pygmy Lady and whimpered, "Scrolls don't tell of this kind of birthing, I need to write a scroll about this experience..." she was interrupted by another spasm.

"You are to be lucky in birthing, Princess, your thrusts are strong and come fast. I think before Ra leaves Egypt, you will have your baby," Pygmy Lady said, as he pushed aside the healer.

Becataten moaned. "But Ra has just arrived, will it take that long?"

"If you are lucky," explained Pygmy Lady. "Now, more deep breathing in between these jolts, and later I will ask you to push. Maja, bring cool water!"

The senior healer grew indignant. "I have been summoned to Princess Becataten's bedside by our Pharaoh. Do not intervene in my work."

"And I have been summoned by Dwarf Beset, from the afterlife. Move aside."

It pleased Becataten to hear Beset's name. It truly made her feel she was with her.

"Humph," said the Healer, staying in his place, but looking uneasy.

Becataten looked up at the offended Healer. "Please allow my Pygmy Lady to attend me," she said. Reluctantly, he stepped aside to give Pygmy Lady room to tend the princess.

Becataten forgot to breathe before the next thrust and the pain she endured shocked her and was excruciating. "Now you will breathe, won't you, Princess?" asked Pygmy Lady.

Becataten nodded vigorously, her face grimaced with pain.

With cool well water, Maja wiped away Becataten's eye kohl and facial ochre, then she helped her sip a cup of pomegranate juice. Becataten took Maja's hand and said in a dry voice, "You were at my mother's birth when Jobu and I were born, weren't you?"

Maja nodded with tearing eyes. "Yes, Taten, I was there." Together they sat holding hands.

Finally, Ra settled into the western sky allowing for the dark time. Becataten was still breathing deeply between her thrusts to manage her pain. But her energy was leaving. She looked like a spent hound after a long hunt.

Ra was sinking fast when Pygmy Lady said, "Push now—and push hard." Becataten had pushed each time she was told, and exhaustion was overtaking her. "This time harder," insisted Pygmy Lady.

Becataten gathered up fistfuls of her bed linens, sat up and with a hoarse grunt, pushed out her baby girl. Pygmy Lady reached for a copper knife and twine to cut the cord, then neatly tied it. "Well, the healers had *something* I could use," she said.

Maja quickly swaddled the wailing infant in soft linen.

"Is the child well?" Becataten asked as she reached out.

"Well? Listen to her howl," said Pygmy Lady as she placed the girl child in Becataten's arms. Becataten looked at her perfect daughter and felt a special connection with her babe instantly. She gazed at her with adoring eyes, admiring her tiny delicate lips and bright eyes.

Suddenly the sitting chamber was abuzz with the sounds of footsteps. The hallway was full of activity as the Living God neared, trailed by Young Horus. Then his voice was heard above the commotion, "I demand to see the newborn!" Everyone grew still in the bedchamber as a healer and the Viceroy entered... The Viceroy walked over and touched Becataten lightly on her arm, as Becataten's eyes filled with tears, her large belly still heaving as she clutched her daughter.

"Don't let him, Mosie, don't let him take my baby. No!" screamed Becataten as she held her baby close. "You cannot take my baby!"

But there was nothing the Viceroy could do. One healer held Becataten by both arms, while another removed the howling infant to be presented to Pharaoh.

Pharaoh received the child into his arms, and with anticipation, carefully unwrapped the linen swaddling to examine the newborn. His face became stern upon what he saw, and he handed the baby girl back to the healer then moved out of the living chamber into the hall. Young Horus walked with his father to a waiting litter, while turning to the healer who was holding Becataten's girl child, and said, "Tell the Princess, what comes after the birthing, I will see delivered to the Mother Nile with the proper ceremony."

In the bedchamber, and with authority, Pygmy Lady motioned Maja for help, pointing to Becataten's birth canal. She gestured to Becataten for quiet, as her thrusts resumed.

Chapter 17

♊

Pharaoh and his entourage soon left the apartment after learning Becataten's baby was a girl. Pygmy Lady rushed back out to the sitting chamber where the healers had been clamoring around The Living God. "Out, out! We need to clean up after the birthing. This is women's work!" Pygmy Lady, called, waving her hands to herd the healers toward the door.

"But we want our implements and..."

Pygmy Lady interrupted them. "They will all be delivered to you before Ra returns, now we must be alone with the mother and care for her and what comes next. Remember, Young Horus said he wished to properly return the birthing sack to the Nile, now go, go, we must prepare for his request.

A distasteful look crossed the face of one healer, another grumbled loudly, and the third exited with arrogance.

Pygmy Lady rushed back to the bedchamber to Becataten and Maja's side. Becataten reclined across the birthing bed, moaning, her eyes closed as she seemed to concentrate. Maja pressed wet linens to her forehead as Pygmy Lady entered, assessing the princess.

"This next birth will need our special help. If the healers were here, they would cut her, but we will reach inside her and bring the boy out. With those useless men gone, nobody will know she has had a boy." Pygmy Lady did a little dance.

Maja eyes bulged. "You know there is a twin still inside Taten... and that it's a boy?" Maja exclaimed, covering her mouth with her hands in disbelief.

As Pygmy Lady and Maja huddled around Becataten in the bedchamber, a bustle of activity ensued in the neighboring room. As the healers reluctantly left after being tossed out by Pygmy Lady, an envoy arrived to summon the Viceroy to Pharaoh's quarters as the healers were exiting the apartment. Told to report to Pharaoh's audience chamber, the worried Merymose didn't want to speculate why he was needed. Pharaoh's demeanor, in voice and stature was different than he had seen in the past. Merymose had served Pharaoh his entire life, in campaigns against the Nubians, and more important oversaw the Living God's gold mines of Kush. The Viceroy's title was second highest in the land, the 'King's Son.' Yet was the Viceroy about to serve the same Pharaoh with the camaraderie he and his King once shared?

Nubian sentries outfitted in leopard skin kilts and gold jewelry announced Viceroy Merymose into Pharaoh's apartment. Pharaoh sat in a large golden chair with Young Horus next to him, his young corpulent body filling a smaller seat. "Enter, my son Merymose, I am pleased to see you. You too are now a father like your King. How does it feel?

Merymose didn't like being called "my son" by Pharaoh, though it was the official way of addressing him. In the past Pharaoh never used that title and had only been applied to scrolls and ceremonies. But Pharaoh had set the tone for he and the Viceroy by meeting in his apartment audience hall where Pharaoh sat on a higher throne, a place where his bureaucrats met for brief meetings. No decor, a stone floored room with whitewashed walls and a few carpets from the eastern colonial holdings but little else. So Merymose responded in kind. "It makes me feel proud, Pharaoh, to bring a child into your royal realm."

Young Horus sat up, his belly wobbling as he spoke. "I hope the Princess is doing well. Please send her my regards and tell her I will pray to Aten and Dwarf Beset for her."

"Thank you, Young Horus. That is most kind. I will relay your words."

The boy nodded, adjusting his heavy golden collar over his chubby pectorals.

Pharaoh raised his hand. "You are to be dispatched to Kush directly, Viceroy. With the recent rebellion behind us, your governance is needed there. I want you to leave immediately, and I want the output from my mines to double. Use whatever methods you must. I require much more gold for the completion of my mortuary temple. Images of me that flank the entrance will be sixty feet tall, and require additional imported stone, more workers and more gold to finance this work."

Pharaoh rose, moving to a table to review elaborate plans for his mortuary temple, a sign that Merymose was now dismissed.

The Viceroy stood straight as a column as he rose from the humble bench he had been offered. "As you wish, My Lord, will there be anything else?"

"No, and congratulations on the birth of your... your daughter. There will undoubtedly be more children, and as I recall you have a son by an Egyptian mother, do you not?"

Merymose nodded "I do, My Lord. As you may know he is one of your governors, born of a noble woman who left us for Osiris in her birthing."

"Oh," said Pharaoh, distracted again by his mortuary temple renderings.

"Will that be all, My Lord?" asked Merymose.

"Yes," Pharaoh said as he waived off the Viceroy.

On his walk back to the apartment, depression filled Merymose. He'd have to tell his beautiful young wife, who had just delivered their first child, that he must leave immediately. He tried to lessen his gloom with the fact that the birth of a girl-child was the best outcome. And the other good consequence was certainly how clever Becataten had been in bringing the strange Young Horus into Pharaoh's recognition. The young boy's presence next to Pharaoh, as odd an image as he was, made it clear he was now the new heir apparent. He set aside Pharaoh's new behavior and tried not to worry now that no grave consequences would affect his wife as she did not give birth to a son.

When the Viceroy returned to the Palace apartment, he sensed eeriness within. Even the slaves were silent, quietly going about moving soiled linens and refreshing chamber pots, but in hushed tones. Merymose rushed to the bedchamber. Opening the door, he stared at Becataten lying still on the bed as a sense of shock rose over him. Her eyes were closed, and her face bore an expression of serenity. There was a mass of bloody linens piled on the floor. Nanny Maja and the makeup artist, Isis, knelt at Becataten's bedside, weeping.

Grasping a bed post, in a choked voice the Viceroy asked, "What has happened here?"

One baby began to cry, initiating the other, and then he recognized Becataten was cradling an infant in each arm. He took a step back, wrestling with the thought of being father to not one, but two babies. *How could this have happened?* he wondered. Confusion engulfed him.

After mustering some control, he went to Becataten's bedside as Maja calmed the babies and knelt. "But the healer brought out just one baby," he said to an unresponsive Becataten.

Pygmy Lady was busy housing the afterlife of the twins in a pot and ordering a eunuch to deliver it to Young Horus's household. She seemed irritated by his question and while wiping her hands on a piece of linen, turned to him. "Two babies are not born together, Viceroy. First one, then the other."

Grasping what had happened, he shook his head, and affectionately stroked Becataten's brow. "Of course, of course, it must have been a terrible ordeal to have given birth to two babies instead of one." He kissed Becataten's brow, feeling proud of her. "How is she? I mean, the babies are crying and she sleeps. It is sleep, isn't it?" he asked, with sudden alarm.

"Yes, she sleeps with the poppy, one of Egypt's potions of value," said Pygmy Lady, who was beginning to show the strains of being the midwife.

The Viceroy smiled. "So, she lives!" His relief was deep. "And we have twins, like she and her brother..." his voice trailed off in remembrance.

Maja's head rose. Her voice strong. "Yes, Taten did not die like her mother, Princess Attah. And do you know that the second twin is a boy!"

Maja's slim dark arms settled on the babies, who seemed to enjoy her touch.

"A boy..." pondered the Viceroy. "I hadn't thought to ask... and of course Pharaoh doesn't know. We must get the child, I mean the twins, and the Princess, to the Suti Estate as soon as possible."

At the Viceroy's words, Pygmy Lady seemed to set aside her weariness and launched into action. She began throwing clothing items and linens into a chest. She muttered. "And I would guess that Pharaoh has probably directed you back to Kush."

Surprised at her knowledge, the Viceroy stared at her. "Yes, he has. How did you know that?"

"I just know," said Pygmy Lady in a mysterious way. "When do you leave?"

"I am to sail immediately," the Viceroy said, looking over to his sleeping wife and children.

"Good! We will all go with you," said Pygmy Lady, as she began giving directives to attendants.

The Viceroy straightened his posture. "You cannot come with me. That is not possible. I will be going with soldiers and taking much equipment. We will be traveling fast and on a military barge."

Pygmy Lady's nod was firm. "Then that will be our deception. You will hide us within the equipment you carry."

He stood staring at her, looking bewildered.

"Start thinking like a father, Viceroy, and get your barge ready for us. Go now, or we will be ready before you are." When Pygmy Lady turned to Isis, she was scowling. "You, makeup-woman, pack up Becataten's things immediately."

The woman had been taking orders all day from Pygmy Lady, and her patient nature was waning. "I have a name, you don't have to call me makeup-woman."

"And what is that name?"

"Isis," she spoke loudly and clearly.

"Isn't Isis supposed to mean beautiful?" Pygmy Lady asked, looking the woman up and down.

With tightened lips, Isis turned to her packing detail.

The Viceroy walked toward the apartment door to leave, then returned as if to protest, but decided to exit, not wanting to get involved in a lengthy discussion with Pygmy Lady, who seemed to be in charge. He looked wistfully over to his new twin children before he left.

Adjacent to the bedchamber, two young slaves cradled and comforted the hungry newborns then handed them off to wetnurses that were called when the healers left. One by one they nursed each baby until both were fast asleep.

After the Viceroy left, Pygmy Lady continued to order the household staff about like a general, when her momentum came to a halt, and a quizzical expression crossed her face. "Maja, can you get Sennejem here quickly?"

Maja nodded, "He lives close."

"Then go. Bring him here now!"

Maja rushed off, confused, but not daring to question Pygmy Lady.

With the help of two eunuchs, the packing was nearly complete when the Royal Gardener Sennejem was announced at the apartment. Maja was trying to explain what events had taken place, and thank him for coming, when Pygmy Lady hailed him toward her.

"Can you get a scroll to Abu, quick and secret?" Pygmy Lady asked.

With some difficulty, Sennejem was trying to deal with her bluntness. "Yes, I believe I can. Maja has explained the situation. Though this sounds serious, trying to get a boy-child away from Pharaoh's grasp," Sennejem added in a whisper, wearing a doubtful and concerned expression on his face.

Pygmy Lady knew little of the Royal Gardener and distrusted royalty in general. Her hawk-like eyes bore into Sennejem's Ka. After her scrutiny, he sighed quietly when he seemed to pass her test.

"I can make our escape," said Pygmy Lady in a low voice. "I want a scroll to go to Abu, and also, alert Lady Nagara. This must be done now! We must *not* reach the Estate before the message arrives. Can you do this?"

The two exchanged intense stares, after which Sennejem said, "Yes. I have a swift chariot driver, and will deliver the message myself, and there will be no need for a scroll, which could become intercepted."

"Good! Tell Abu we shall arrive in the dark time on Viceroy's military barge. Tell him about the twins. Tell him Becataten is very weak, has lost much blood, but will live. Lady Nagara must also be told, and told to quickly find two wet nurses."

Pygmy Lady stopped a moment, her dark eyes staring into Sennejem's eyes. "Also... ask Lady Nagara to have a big litter waiting at the dock. The Viceroy cannot anchor. Your Pharaoh has sent him to Kush. And you know about your demented King who wanted Becataten's boy-child, and more gold from Kush, yes?"

Sennejem nodded, taking in all the pygmy's words with a somber face. "I will explain it all," he agreed. Pygmy Lady offered a firm nod, and Sennejem exited the apartment into the long hallway, his keen mind full of information and chores he must hastily achieve if this plan to save the princess's twin boy from the clutches of Pharaoh would work.

Chapter 18

When Pygmy Lady heard the knock at their apartment door, she was there before the sentries could answer. A crew member stood tall, several men behind him, with a large litter waiting. "On orders of the Viceroy, prepare to leave at once!"

The apartment was in shambles. Chests were open, their contents spilling onto the floor in disarray.

"At once!" He repeated, looking around at the mess. "You cannot take everything. The content of these trunks is not important, for they will be used but to conceal the family of the Viceroy."

Pygmy Lady nodded. "Don't explain that to me!" She said.

She summoned Isis and Maja. "Pack few items separately and close the chests, now! The guards will use the chests to hide the Princess, only. Be quick!"

Moving swiftly, she ordered the Nubians to lift Becataten and place her in a large wicker hamper lined with a pile of linens and animal hides to ease the journey. Then they placed the hamper in the middle of the litter that would transport them to the royal dock. Packing chests were placed around her. Becataten didn't stir, so potent was her poppy-induced sleep. Her hamper lid was carefully propped open a bit with a piece of thick rope squeezed between the frame and lid so she could still breathe

Maja started to ask a question. "How..."

"Not now," Pygmy Lady snapped. Maja fell into silence, a worried and curious look still on her face.

All who were traveling to the Suti Estate were ushered into the massive litter. Maja was settled between two chest and handed the babies to hold, as they were calmest with her and still asleep after being nursed to their full. After walling everybody into the large litter, the Nubians covered the top with a heavy linen tarp and secured it with ropes. The air was stuffy and the litter roof cut most of the light. Pygmy Lady declined going under the tarp and said she would jog alongside the litter as they headed for the docks.

"It's so dark in here, "Isis said, "I'm afraid. Please let me out!" She began to claw around to find an exit.

Pygmy Lady heard her and hissed, "Quiet." "If anyone makes a noise, it will the last sound you make!"

Isis quieted, sitting down holding her head on her knees and rocking herself.

The head Nubian crew member gave the order to lift and the tall muscular men hoisted the poles of the litter onto their strong shoulders. Groans from the men were followed by smiles of relief as they managed the weighty load.

Pygmy Lady followed on foot.

The Viceroy was not on board when they arrived. With caution, the bearers lowered their stacked load next to the walking plank of the military barge as a grey dawn yielded to Ra's bright morning sky.

A man wearing a crisply pleated kilt with a medallion that marked him Dock Master, stepped briskly toward them as Pygmy Lady hid behind the conveyance. "What is this large litter doing here, and where is the Captain to receive these goods?"

"The Captain and Viceroy Merymose are due back directly, Dock Master," called a voice from the barge.

"Hump, the Viceroy?" The Dock Master swiped at imaginary flies with his zebra tail swatter, then stomped around the conveyance. "There are no military goods here. This is a military loading dock. Leave this area immediately," he demanded.

The litter bearers stood silent. With narrowed eyes the Dock Master walked to the head Nubian and thrashed him across the face with his switch. The man flinched but stood firm. A watchdog, sleeping on the barge, awoke and began barking.

Within the litter, Maja held the babies tight, trembling from the commotion, and muttered prayers to all the Egyptian Gods to keep the twins silent. Isis whimpered.

When the Dock Master's order was not acted upon, he stood with a red face, slapping his switch across his palm. Breathing heavily, he walked to another Nubian and struck him across the face. With stealth, Pygmy Lady maneuvered away from the tyrant's view.

The stuttered cry of a newborn broke the air.

Spittle erupted with the Dock Master's words, "What is that noise? A baby! I want this litter stripped now!" He motioned for dock guards. Their sandals slapped the stone as they came running. The second twin started to cry and awakened a bewildered Becataten in her dark hamper.

"Where are we?" She asked in a thin voice, utterly confused and afraid as she tried to fathom her whereabouts. Her mind felt heavy as it had when she had been once been poisoned in her past.

As the dock master began climbing to the top of the stacked goods. The guard dog followed him. "Do I hear more than one baby, here?" He bellowed.

Oh no, they have come for my babies," Becataten thought as she reached for her infants. But they were not there beside her. Carefully Becataten reached up, feeling herself to be inside a chest! She opened the propped lid and found the litter dark also due to the tarp covering. Maja saw the princess trying to emerge and nodded to Isis. She whispered, "Move to her, put your hand inside the crate, pat her. Isis collected herself, reached inside and covered Becataten's mouth with her hand then made a gesture in the dim light showing her to remain silent.

As the dock guards carelessly began to untie the tarp, the cries of the infants grew louder, though Maja tried her best to silence them.

At the far end of the dock sped an undersized chariot down the long, stone causeway. With a fringed canopy dancing in the wind, the vehicle raced past Pygmy Lady. Considering the driver's small stature, he was managing his spirited stallion well. With a corpulent juvenile body and long head, he looked like a composite of two beings.

Pygmy Lady climbed to the top of the dock embankment, shaded her eyes for a view, then jumped from the wall and returned to the trouble at the litter. The Dock Master had climbed to the top of the large litter, poking at the interior with his crop, as Maja ducked her head to cover the babies she had quieted, each sucking on one of her fingers.

"What is going on here?" asked Young Horus as he drew his chariot to a halt. The provoked Dock Master shook his zebra tail at the young man who had halted his chariot at the dock's edge.

"Leave us young man, this is dock business, and you are meddling."

Pygmy Lady ran to arrive next to the chariot of Young Horus.

"You work in the household of the Princess, do you not?" asked Young Horus, looking down at her.

She stood for a moment breathing hard, hands on hips. "Yes!" she said. "And this descendant of a wild ass is trying to stop the Princess and her goods from boarding," she said, pointing at the Dock Master, and hoping she had an ally in the young king.

Young Horus concealed a grin and said, "Did you hear that, Dock Master? I order you *off* that litter," his chubby arms holding hard his dancing horse.

The Dock Master quickly climbed down from the litter, sizing up this meddler and pygmy.

"You will see who is master here, pygmy," he snarled, raising his zebra tail to strike her. Pygmy Lady grabbed his switch in midair and yanked him to the ground. The dog bounded forward to join the scuffle.

"You have been downed by a pygmy, half your size, Dock Master." Young Horus' laughed as his soft belly wobbled.

With a bleeding nose, the official staggered to his feet shouting at Young Horus. "*You*, whoever you are, will be escorted home to your parents, and your chariot impounded for interfering with dock business," he snapped," squinting through his eyes now running with kohl.

"*Who*, Dock Master, do you think my parents are?"

The official glared at the young prince and inspected him more closely. When his eyes rested on his royal ring, he dropped to the ground to prostrate himself.

"My Lord, I had no idea..."

Horus ordered a dock guard forward, "Strike this man twice in the face then take him to the local magistrate for further punishment. He is not fit to be master of the royal docks. Now where would Princess Becataten be with her new girl-child? I must see her. I can hear the child crying now, though it sounds far away."

As the Nubians untied and removed the large tarp, the large litter items came into view, and the young prince trotted his chariot around the conveyance. Once the linen tarp was unleashed, Becataten lifted the hamper lid and rose to steady herself. Isis helped to cover her with a cloak. Becataten offered a weak smile and wave.

"There you are Princess Becataten. Let us get you onboard. You look unwell." Young Horus motioned for more help with the onloading to the barge to make a path for her. Before anyone noticed, Pygmy Lady had scaled the chests like a monkey and was helping a shaky Becataten off the conveyance.

Speeding down the stone-lined quay, the Viceroy arrived, jumped from his chariot before it came to a stop, tossing the reins to his captain.

"Greetings, Young Horus, I see you are assisting my family," he said warily, believing the boy twin had been found and in peril of being returned to the Palace.

"Yes, Viceroy, when I went to your apartment, I tracked you here, and my advice to you would be to sail as soon as possible. The Princess looks most unwell."

Feeling greatly relieved, Merymose formally thanked Young Horus for his intervention, and asked if he could return a favor.

Merymose watched the prince pucker his heavy lips in an effeminate way. "Yes, you may. I'd like a word with the pygmy," he said.

The Viceroy snapped his fingers, a guard showed, and Pygmy Lady was requested.

Pygmy Lady arrived to stand next to Young Horus' chariot, invoking amusement mixed with exhaustion.

"I would ask you to take a ride in my chariot." Young Horus said.

Looking up at him, she said, "Too little time. We must go. It is my regret," said Pygmy Lady. "You have a fine chariot and strong steed."

"Then we will talk but briefly. Walk with me away from the ears of those who would wish to hear us," the young boy said as he stepped off his chariot. When they moved up the quay, Young Horus said, "I wanted to thank you for the delivery of the afterlife, Pygmy Lady. Please inform the Princess that I will perform the ceremony, and I understand that she is not well enough to attend."

Pygmy Lady nodded.

"I admire the Princess Becataten because I believe she places the same amount of importance as I do on religious ceremonies."

Pygmy Lady nodded.

"Also, I ask that God Aten be included in the child's name. When I am Pharaoh, I will request the God Aten will be attached to all my children's titles."

Pygmy Lady began to take seriously this odd young man. "And you, Young Horus, will father five daughters and one son."

"Young Horus's laugh sounded like a cackle. "So you see the future? For such insights, I ordinarily pay gold. Instead, I will offer advice that is far more valuable. When you wish to conceal the birth of twins, do not send a pot with two after-sacks."

Without another word and not looking back, Young Horus strode to his chariot and sped away.

Pygmy Lady stared after him a moment before she mounted the barge.

"It is time," she barked. "It is time to leave, now!"

Chapter 19

♊

By the time goods were transferred to the military vessel and Becataten heard the orders to sail, she was more alert and looked around her space. On board, the Viceroy had his crew create an enclosure of thick linen the size of a small room for her and their new family. She closed her eyes and felt the gentle ripples of the Mother Nile slap against the large vessel resting on her ample bed of pillows and hides as the barge began its voyage. He had the Golden Falcon trail the military craft to the Suti Estate. Originally, he hoped the Princess could be settled onboard his vessel, but she was so ensconced on the barge, he couldn't think of moving her, and knew Pygmy Lady's plans had succeeded.

The Viceroy parted the curtain. "She looks so tired and small," he whispered at Maja, who sat at Becataten's side with a twin in each arm. The babies were sucking well water from tiny pouches and looked to be sleeping at the same time. The grin on Maja's face was broad when she looked up. "Master Viceroy, Taten will be well and strong soon, and you can thank Pygmy Lady for everything," she said, with tears of joy trailing her worn cheeks.

Isis sat on the other side of Becataten, and said, "Maja, I can hold one of the babies," reaching for one.

"No." Maja said, turning away from her. "I have them in hand."

When they were under way, Merymose called to Pygmy Lady. I want to talk..." he began.

"No talking, not now," she said in a loud authoritative voice raising a palm. "Bring me a piece of wrapping linen and a big basket," she barked at a Nubian.

Surprised, the Viceroy shrugged and went to order the barge further away from court.

The Nubian brought Pygmy Lady a large basket and a roll of linen. Once the basket was lined with the linen, it became Pygmy Lady's bed, where she coiled herself inside like a snake. No one had seen her sleep this way other than in the bush. She was soon snoring like a rhinoceros.

The Viceroy had surprised his crew by helping to cast off. When the large barge slid from the docks and the smell of cool morning air rose from the river, it lent an air of calm and relief.

Becataten could feel they were under way and drew her drape open to see a screeching hawk flying overhead with a catch in his talons. It was a good omen, as if Young Horus was offering his final farewell. Her thoughts were confused about the events that revolved around their departure, but she knew the Young Prince had helped her, and she wondered if she would ever see him again,

Their sail south was against the flow of the Mother Nile, so they encountered some pitch, but safely reached the Suti Estate late into the dark time. Becataten slept on and off in between looking down at Maja firmly seated beneath her while holding the twins tight. Becataten became fully awake when they drew near the landing at the Suti Estate. She could hear a commotion of people and felt deeply relieved at the unmistakable aroma of freshly baked bread.

"Maja, tell me what you see outside?" Becataten asked.

"The land is lit by torches. It looks as if Lady Nagara has all her household people doing things for your arrival! There are trays of food and drink, extra litters and people with flowers!" Maja exclaimed.

"Open the curtain wide, Maja," Becataten said, raising herself up on her elbows. Near their mooring she could see Lady Nagara, seated on her palanquin, calling commands.

From the shore, Lady Nagara looked like she was running a huge theatrical event from her conveyance. "Move that litter with Becataten's two wet nurses closer to the dock and ready the chair for the Princess. Move it closer to the boarding plank. Where is Butler?" The Butler stood next to her and bowed. "Ah, there you are. What have we for refreshments?"

"I have baskets filled with warm bread, fruits, cheeses and beer, My Lady," he said.

Becataten smiled. How good to hear Lady Negara's strong voice, and how safe it felt to be back at the Estate. She could never feel Pharaoh's Palace was home again. Not after experiencing that Pharaoh wanted to take her boy child. *How was the boy-twin kept from him,* she wondered? She shivered at the thought of what could have been.

Lady Nagara had the bearers move her palanquin about as she continued to direct orders. "Have the light bearers ignite their extra poles, now! I want it as bright as Ra when the Princess and the babies come off the ship." She said, pulling her shawl around her.

When the Viceroy stepped off the barge, he went directly to Lady Nagara, and produced a respectful bow. Now, the entire area was brightly lit and welcoming.

"My Lady, you have offered us a grand welcome. Princess Becataten and I thank you."

"Of course, I offer you a celebrated welcome. It is not every Ra that my charge, or rather my near daughter, arrives with twins. And thank the Gods she lives. Now, how *is* the Princess?"

"She is still wrought as you can imagine and leaving the docks, she had to endure a stressful incident. I will just add that we are to be most grateful to Young Horus for his intervention."

"Let us speak about that later," said Lady Nagara, with curiosity. "I do hope Becataten is well."

The Viceroy nodded. "Here she comes now. See for yourself."

Becataten was transferred to her pillow strewn chair by a large Nubian. Maja wrapped her with a shawl then settled at her feet. The Viceroy held her hand. "It was but two Ra's ago when you were delivering twins, my love. How do you feel now after your sleep, and our sail?"

Becataten squeezed his hand. "My babies are safe, you are with me, and I am happy." She raised her head to watch the chairs that carried wet nurses with her babies in their arms as they were gently moved toward the Estate house. She smiled. "Did Lady Nagara arrange all of this?"

Lady Nagara's palanquin moved in close. "No more talking, my dear, though I am so glad to see you! You are to rest here at the Estate, eat well and be properly cared for. I will oversee the care of the twins. Now take her to her suite." she said, motioning the litter carriers away.

There were whispers and bows of reverence from the crowd at the sight of the Princess and her babes as her litter was carried down the flower-strewn path toward the Estate. It was no secret that the blessing of twins meant prosperity and good fortune for all who resided at the Estate.

It was almost a race to see which conveyance arrived at the bottom of the Estate steps first, Becataten's litter or Lady Nagara's palanquin. The household staff and many field workers ran with the bearers along the way. Once upstairs with the babies, Lady Nagara became another person, someone Becataten had never seen before.

"Wet nurses! Place one twin here in this cradle and the other one here. Careful, do not wake them. They need their rest. I have read birthing is a terrible ordeal for an infant. Oh, let me look at them. Which one is the boy, and which one is the girl? I think I can see a difference in them. Yes, I can."

Becataten and Maja smiled at one another as they watched Lady Nagara chatter on about the twins.

Then Lady Nagara grew silent, and touched each infant with a tender pat. She stood over them and softly announced, "I am your Grandmama, Mut. You shall live here all your lives, if it pleases your parents, and you shall have all the offerings the Estate and the Gods can bestow upon you."

Becataten whispered to Maja. "The Goddess Mut is the one we see in the form of the mother vulture."

Maja nodded. "Like Lady Nagara."

"I think she likes feeling needed, Maja," Becataten whispered, as they watched Lady Nagara fuss over the twins with a smile on her face.

Chapter 20

♊

When Merymose saw Becataten's litter heading safely toward the big house, he turned to Abu, standing humbly in the background with Kombo at his side. Shyness kept the Viceroy's Nubian son, Ahmose, waiting in the shadows. Ne Ne stood next to Abu holding his hand.

"Hello, my friend," said the Viceroy as he rested his hand on Abu's shoulders. "You have been a grandparent for two Ras, and of twins! Becataten wants you to cast their birth charts and create their names."

Abu stood proud, and with a heaving chest said, "I already have."

"How did you manage that?" asked the Viceroy.

"I'll explain. Come, you and Ahmose dine with me."

The men walked in silence toward Abu's house in the date grove. Kombo guided Abu with his good arm. It was clear Abu had a caregiver for life in the Viceroy's friend, Kombo, and a pupil in Ahmose.

After Kombo led the Viceroy and Abu into the house and when they were seated, he set tables before the three men with large cups of freshly brewed and filtered beer. The men discussed Pharaoh's recent overindulgences, and how it would affect the Kings rule. Amose's face was full with pleasure at being included in the dinner and discussion. The Viceroy's nose soon led him to say, "Is that Suti beef I smell Kombo cooking outside?"

"It is. We fathers' deserve a celebration for our small participation in the birthing of children," Abu said. "And a first son needs to be included, as he will one day father a child," added Abu as he acknowledged Ahmose, whose face flushed.

Kombo soon returned from the outside fire brazier with three juicy steaks, each as big as a man's hand. The men ate in solitude together with only sounds of pleasure as they enjoyed the famous Suti beef.

"I had planned to push off after I saw Becataten safe, but I think I'll remain until Ra returns to light my way. Pharaoh's edicts don't seem as imminent here as they did from the Palace. And, I will return in a half moon to see the Princess."

"Good plan," said Abu.

"How is my daughter, Merymose?" Abu asked.

"Weak, and in need of rest, but she lives after bringing forth twins, thanks to Osiris and all the Gods. I am also told Pygmy Lady was of great help."

Abu nodded. "Yes, Becataten's mother was not so fortunate," he said in a whisper.

"That too was true of the mother of Amos, who left us in childbirth," acknowledged the Viceroy.

Even with covered eye sockets, Abu's expression of sentiment for the woman he had truly loved showed; the woman Pharaoh had denied him marriage, the diminutive green eyed, Princess Attah of Mitanni.

"You know leaving Kombo and Ahmose with me has proved fortuitous," said Abu. "Ahmose has gained the position of Estate Manager, and I have found Kombo to be an able reader of the night sky."

"Ahmose, is that true?"

Ahmose was sitting quietly and listening then nodded, shyly.

Abu continued, happy to talk to a peer. "I keep a large board and place pebbles on it of varying size to represent the stars. Kombo sets the stones according to the heaven's placements, and last night, together we were able to produce the children's birth stories. With relief, I can say that there is not the intrigue that existed in Becataten and Jobutaten's charts. There is much travel beyond Egypt for the boy-twin and for the girl, a strong sense of the Heka. There is a continuing theme, however, that reveals an ongoing connection to royalty which can only mean Pharaoh."

The Viceroy looked assured. "Ah yes and that theme, as you call it, already exists. It is with the Young Horus," said the Viceroy.

Abu appeared deep in thought, planning or just thinking, the Viceroy couldn't quite say.

"Tell me about that, Viceroy?"

The Viceroy motioned to a slave for fresh beverage. New cups were filled with *sma*, the dark time demanded more tallow for lamps, and conversation continued long before sleep was taken.

Becataten awoke rested but in discomfort. Her linens were wet with her mother's milk, and she felt like her breasts were made of rocks. When she stood, her breasts were so heavy, she elevated them, one in each hand. She looked to Maja who was seated on the floor, a twin in each arm. Isis no longer asked Maja if she could hold a twin. The wet nurses were in the back of the chamber eating bread, skewered beef and drinking plenty of beer. Maja looked like she was never going to let the babies go. Becataten stroked them softly as they slept. "When do the wet nurses feed them, Maja?"

"Only when they cry, and I hold them after they take their milk."

"But, Maja, when do you sleep?"

"Do not worry about me. Taten, you have so much milk spilling from your breasts, why don't you nurse them some of the time. You are miserable, I can tell."

"Lady Nagara says I am not to nurse them," Becataten said, her expression sad.

Maja shook her head in disagreement but said nothing.

"Did I dream that we had trouble on the dock?" Becataten asked Maja, as she sat down on her bed.

Maja shook her head.

"And I thought I saw Young Horus, or was that a dream too?"

"You saw Young Horus, and we had big trouble." Maja said.

"Tell me what happened." Becataten asked.

"I do not understand it all, Taten. You must ask Pygmy Lady."

"And when will I see the Viceroy?"

Lady Nagara entered Becataten's suite in a flourish, with several attendants trailing her. "My dear, you look so much better!" she said to Becataten. "Maja, what are you doing holding those babies when they have perfectly good cradles. Put them in there at once."

Becataten frowned, and Lady Nagara added. "That is, if it is acceptable to the Princess."

Becataten stood, holding on to her bed frame, as attendants stripped her bed linens for fresh ones. "Lady Nagara, why don't you hold one of the twins for a while so they can get used to you?"

"Me, why I don't hold babies, I mean I never have..."
Lady Nagara glanced at the infants in Maja's arms.

Maja stood and offered her one of the twins.
Curiously, Lady Nagara removed her wig and handed it
to an attendant. With trepidation, she took the infant
in her arms but stood motionless.

"You can walk with the baby, Lady Nagara,"
Becataten said.

"Walk, I don't walk with babies, I mean..."

"Just try, Lady Nagara," encouraged Becataten.

With a sober face, Lady Nagara took one step then
another, until she was walking around the chamber,
her head held high, exuding confidence as she carried
the girl twin around the room.

Soon after Becataten was cleaned up and refreshed,
a messenger announced the Viceroy into the nursery.
He walked in and saw the beautiful princess dressed
comfortably in a clean loose tunic, looking a bit weak
but mostly recovered, and his twins wrapped in fresh
linens, each sleeping in a crib as Maja sat beside them
ready to reach for them should they awaken. Fresh
flowers gave the room a fragrant scent that pleased
him. He felt as if he could leave his wife and return to
his duties, now that he knew she would be so well
cared for.

"My love," he said, walking to her. They retreated to
a quiet corner of an adjacent sitting room, shooing
away awaiting staff so they could talk privately. Ra's
early rays shone through the high windows above as he
held Becataten's hands.

Becataten said, "I am sure you have been informed
about what occurred at Pharaoh's palace, and how we
fled in secret to keep our boy twin a secret from the
court! Some do know of our precious boy, so our best

hope is that the information never reaches Pharaoh's ears. I have it on good authority that it is being presented as a rumor," she added, to not concern her husband too much. "Let us hope that it remains just a wild story and not something anyone would want to check for themselves!"

"Yes," agreed Merymose. He looked into Becataten's eyes and stroked her face. "If you were not so well cared for here, surrounded by your most beloved and trustworthy family and staff, I would be concerned leaving you. But I go on Pharaoh's mission with little concern for you and the wellbeing of our twins."

Becataten was caught off guard but she controlled the small sob that threatened to rise up. "Oh, Mosie! No! I so want you to stay here with us, with your new baby children!" She held his hands to her lips. "But I understand your duty prevails. If you must go, you must. We will anxiously await your return."

"Thank you, my princess. I promise to return at my earliest opportunity. I am sure these lovely babies will be running about the house soon enough, and I won't want to miss too much of these sweet early days!" He kissed each one of Becataten's hands and rose to visit the babes before he left on his journey for Pharaoh.

The Viceroy returned from Kush well after Becataten's customary fourteen days of confinement. Pygmy Lady had accompanied him to Kush and returned to reside in Abu's ample quarters. Her presence annoyed Abu in the beginning, but delighted Huni. Lady Nagara knew that the Viceroy stayed with Abu from time to time but didn't acknowledge Abu resided in the Estate manager's house, nor that Pygmy

Lady lived there. These were people outside her social realm, as it would always be.

With Ra's early rays, the Viceroy leaped the stairs to Becataten's suite.

"There you are my love," called out Merymose. "You must be feeling well. Lady Nagara sent butler with the message of a feast that she is planning in your honor. I am happy to say that I can remain for an additional moon at the Estate and look forward to the celebration." He swept onto the chaise next to Becataten, who was sitting before Isis, having her face painted for the day. "My overseers in Kush are managing the gold mines with obedient workers who no longer have a taste for rebellion," Merymose continued. "Lady Nagara also said that Suti will be here and maybe even his twin, Hor, for the celebration!"

Isis was finishing Becataten's face painting with a light dusting of honey colored ocher when she turned to him with her striking smile. "Hello, Mosie, I am so happy to see you!" She stood and hugged him, breathing in the scent of the desert that lingered on his clothes.

He smiled at her and looked her up and down. "You are a beautiful mother, even more so than before you gave birth to the twins, I do believe."

"Oh, I feel so much better Mosie, and I am so happy you are able to stay longer."

He took a moment to gaze upon her reprised beauty. "I am happy too, Princess. How are the twins?"

"Come and see for yourself." Becataten said. They went into the nursery and stood doting over their new family lying in cradles carved in the shape of miniature swans. Maja sat on the floor between them as always.

Becataten took the Viceroy's hand and squeezed it. "Lady Nagara demanded her master carpenter finish these beds before the twins reached three moons."

The Viceroy smiled, shaking his head as they returned to the sitting area where Isis waited for her. "She really has become Grandmama Mut, hasn't she?"

Becataten turned to Isis. "You may leave us now,"

"Would you like me to take your wig, Princess?" Isis asked.

"Yes, but put it on the stand for now." Becataten said.

She and the Viceroy talked a bit more and returned to the nursery, where they reached for one another and stayed in an embrace until one baby cried, causing the other to do the same. This promptly brought two wet nurses to accommodate the infant's demands. The women gathered them up to settled behind a partition so the twins could suckle to their fill.

"Do you feel well enough to go for a drive in one of Senzar's chariots?" The Viceroy asked.

"I do! And let's go now before Lady Nagara scolds me for doing so," Becataten said as she placed her wig on her head, evaluate her image in a standing copper mirror, then headed toward the Viceroy with her beaded plaits softly jingling, knowing her twins were in good hands if she left for a bit of fresh air.

As Becataten stepped onto the chariot it rocked some, making her feel a little unsteady, realizing how pampered she had grown. "It is *very* bright outside, or is it that I have been caged in my suite so long that I have forgotten the strength of Ra's rays?"

The Viceroy took her hand. "This canopy should help, stand close to me and you will remain in the shade." Viceroy took the reins and moved the horse into an easy pace.

It was a pleasant ride as the soft sound of the chariot wheels sped them down an earthen path along the Mother Nile. She gazed over the network of canals that held the rich black water that fed Egypt's crops. The flowers, vegetables and fruit bearing trees gave the air a fresh fragrance. Only the soft, distant cattle cries broke the silence while a mild breeze embraced their faces.

"You wanted to talk to me alone, didn't you Mosie?"

"How did you know that?"

"I just did." Becataten said.

"Yes," he said standing firm in the chariot. "I have developed a friendship with your father, and we concur on a few facts that I want to go over with you."

Becataten leaned into him. "Tell me what worries you, Mosie."

He put one arm around her and slowed their ride as the stallion bobbed his head at being reined in. "Pharaoh may still want our boy-child, My Princess, and for that reason I would like you to communicate with Young Hours to keep your friendship with him alive. It is always good to have a friend at court. And I want you to use your father's Dwarf Heby to deliver correspondence with Young Horus. Horus will become king one day, though I fear a strange and unpredictable one, but not one who covets our son."

"I understand, Mosie. Pygmy Lady has advised me about this too."

"Yes, she is always abreast of matters, sometimes well ahead of the rest of us."

"What else, Mosie?" Becataten said as she looked up at him.

"Your father has learned that Queen Tiye has become ambitious and aspires to be her son's regent when he does become King," the Viceroy said as he brought the horse down to a pleasant trot. "Nobody is sure yet," he continued, "but given Pharaoh's new erratic behavior, your father and I believe her taking over the throne even while Pharaoh lives is a possibility." In a rare shady oasis, Merymose reined the horse over to rest and to take shelter from Ra's strong rays. The horse stood in place stamping his hooves some before settling down and staying still. "Meanwhile, Pharaoh's activities have narrowed to feasting and the entertainment of young women. These indulgences are eclipsed only by his desire to build the world's largest mortuary temple. This project has become his obsession, and on more than one occasion, I know he has summoned you to see the work due to your great interest in the building arts. It is believed that the queen handles many court matters and invitations, and apparently the invitations to you have gone by the wayside. This is a concern we need to address." A breeze picked up and Merymose got his horse to start walking alongside the Nile again. He said to Becataten, "As you know, Pharaoh always gave Queen Tiye great latitudes of wealth and privilege. Your father and I believe she is beginning to execute those powers to take the throne from Pharaoh."

"Really!" Becataten was surprised to hear it. "Well I haven't heard that yet," she said. "But I would *love* to see the sight of his mortuary temple!"

"Of course, you would, my princess." He said with a concerned frown. "Hang on!"

The Viceroy cracked his whip, Becataten jerked backward, and they were off for a fast ride.

Chapter 21

Ⅱ

Lady Nagara had Butler summon Merymose to her sitting chamber after his time with Becataten and the twins. This room was her private sanctuary where few people were invited.

The Viceroy entered the comfortable room where jars, filled with large blossoms of lotus stood, imparting their heady fragrance. The walls were brightly painted depicting the Goddess Hathor, an artfully defined face with the ears of a cow. Her image embodied love, fertility, sex, music, and dance.

They sat opposite one another, she next to her new statue of the Goddess Mut. Their chairs were of carved mahogany with deep seats and high arm rests. A large hammered bronze tray separated Lady Nagara and the Viceroy that rested on an ebony stand.

"How is Becataten this Ra, Viceroy?" Lady Nagara asked.

"She becomes stronger every day, and is in a sound sleep at the moment," the Viceroy responded.

"Does she want for anything, Viceroy?" Lady Nagara asked.

"I don't believe so," he said, as he raised his eyes to view the ceiling studded with hieroglyphs of golden ankhs. "Although she does wish to visit with her father to hear the twins' birth stories, and learn the names he has chosen," Merymose said.

Lady Nagara looked indifferent. "Yes, well I suppose he must name them, as well as cast their stories, given his history."

"I see you collect cobalt blue perfume bottles from the Palace glassworks, Lady Nagara," Merymose said, endeavoring to talk about something else, knowing how she disdained Abu. "I was recently in the marketplace and bought a turquoise colored piece for Becataten. That is her favorite."

"Yes, Suti often adds to my collection, but let's not talk of trinkets. Can we discuss the episode regarding Young Horus?"

Butler arrived with a large copper tray holding calcite cups of cool tamarind juice for her, and refined, filtered beer for the Viceroy. The Viceroy explained Pharaoh's covetous desire for Becataten's boy-child, and about Young Horus saving them from a catastrophe at the docks when leaving Thebes, as he savored his beverage.

Lady Nagara sipped her tamarind juice. "We must thank the Gods for Young Horus's help, and that *is* troubling news about Pharaoh latest behavior. When Suti arrives, we will learn if the Palace is gossiping about this incident," she said.

"I think you will find that Pharaoh is a different king than you and I remember, Lady Nagara," said the Viceroy, then downed the last of his beer.

She clapped her hand for Butler to bring more beer, then sat with her hands in her lap, nodding. "You know we were most fortunate to have had a well-timed visit before your arrival from the Royal Gardner Sennejem," she said, changing subjects. "I must say I like that man."

"You liked him?" said the Viceroy with a smile.

"Yes, he informed us that Princess Becataten had brought forth twins, estimated your docking time, and explained what your needs were upon arrival.".

"It was Pygmy Lady who arranged that," said the Viceroy. With gravity, he added, "I have come to learn that she has been the main force in bringing our twins here safely."

With a distasteful look that matched the expression of the vulture Goddess Mut, Lady Nagara said, "Nevertheless, Sennejem was most responsible in delivering that news." With more distaste she added. "Is it true that Sennejem and Abu are friends?"

"I believe Abu was responsible for recommending Sennejem to be the Royal Gardener because of his knowledge of many languages. The laborers that garden for Pharaoh come from many vassal states."

"Let us move on and speak of Ahmose, your son. I have made him my Estate Manager of the growing yards, as you must know by now. He is a diligent worker, and shows promise leading my field staff."

"Ahmose mentioned this to me, and is full with pride about your appointing..."

Becataten's frenzied screaming drew the Viceroy to his feet. Lady Nagara clutched her chest, looking alarmed. The Viceroy quickly excused himself and raced the stairs to her bedside and took her hand. "What is it, my love?"

"My babies, where are they?"

"Maja, bring the babies to the Princess, now!" called the Viceroy.

"They are being nursed behind the curtain, Lord Viceroy," Maja said.

Merymose snapped his fingers and glared.

In quick-step two wet nurses arrived, each holding and nursing a twin.

"Here they are, my love."

Becataten was heaving great sighs and trying to speak. "I, I want to touch them," she said reaching for their swaddled forms. "Are they well, nurses?"

Wide eyed, the two wet nurses, nodded.

"Mosie, I want my father."

Lady Nagara rushed in. "My dear what is it?"

Becataten reached for her. "It was a nightmare, Lady Nagara, as vivid as the one I had when I first came to the Estate."

Lady Nagara looked horrified. The last time Becataten had a dream of terror it foretold of Pharaoh's first-born son's death.

Abu was swiftly summoned to the big house. He and Lady Nagara, not so comfortably, sat on each side of Becataten' bed, ready to hear her dream of terror. Lady Nagara had not seen the scarf Abu wore on his head that was drawn down around his eyes. It disturbed her and brought to mind the hideous torture she saw him endure in Pharaoh's hall not that long past.

The Viceroy had never been privy to his wife's dreams, or her Heka. He sat in a chair at the end of Becataten's bed. Outside Becataten's door stood Pygmy Lady and Butler, out of view. Isis helped Becataten sit up in bed with additional pillows while Maja patted away perspiration on her face with a damp cloth. Once again, a standing brazier wafted fumes of smoldering frankincense from the bark of the sacred tree. Lady Nagara had quickly ordered that the resin burn to ward off evil. A fan bearer pumped his plume above

Becataten's head, and someone handed her a lotus for its soothing and loving fragrance.

"We are ready when you are, Princess," said Abu.

With a glassy stare, Becataten began her tale of her dream. "I was in my chariot and headed for the Mother Nile. In the last light of Ra, I galloped my chariot along the banks. Then I saw the *Ka-em-Maat* in the water. I could see that it had just left the Estate dock. I whipped my horse to gain on the royal barge. I could see Pharaoh was onboard. His guests and I waved at one another.

"But then, I heard babies crying. Estate workers were running toward me to tell me my twins had been stolen. I whipped my horse again to catch up to the vessel because I knew those aboard *Ka-em-Maat* had my babies. But it was impossible for my chariot to keep up with the Royal Barge. The mud grew thicker and thicker, and the chariot wheels wouldn't turn. I fell hopelessly back. Ra was gone, and there was no moon. All was dark. The torches on the barge became small. I called for them to come back, but all I could hear was Pharaoh and his guests laughing at me as the barge disappeared..." Becataten faltered and sobbed.

Abu squeezed her hand, "I will cast this dream like a chart and be able to tell you more, my daughter. Now try and rest."

Lady Nagara patted Becataten's shoulder, "I have invited the Heka Priest for our dinner and he too will interpret your dream for you, my dear."

Pygmy Lady stepped from the hall into the chamber, walked to Becataten and stood with her feet planted widely apart. "That was the dream of a new mother, afraid her babies are going to be harmed, and that is all."

Pygmy Lady had a way of delivering final statements. Everybody looked at one another with no urge to contradict her.

The Viceroy turned to her. "Now that we are all here, tell us what happened at the Palace when Pharaoh arrived asking to hold the first baby," asked the Viceroy as Lady Nagara and Maja comforted Becataten.

Pygmy Lady pushed her hand toward him. "Nothing to tell, Pharaoh took away the swaddling to find a girl-child. He didn't know of the coming boy-child, so he left." Pygmy Lady looked at the women sitting on the bed, lowered her head and in a quieter voice said, "But when Pharaoh learns Becataten has had twins, he will come, and he will try and take them both."

Chapter 22

Becataten called for a chair to have the bearers run her to her father's residence in the palm grove. A runner had been sent ahead of her conveyance to Abu's house announcing her arrival. She knew the cool and generously sized dwelling was perfect for her father, especially as he grew older. It made her happy to know the comfort it afforded him.

The short ride in the fresh air made Becataten feel alive again. How good to be outside, away from servants, and even the twins. To see the pomegranate trees in bloom, the pond full of lotus lilies and jumping fish, the soft sounds, and familiar smells of cattle in the distance. She and Merymose must soon choose a place of their own, but it would be hard to duplicate the comforts of the Estate. She knew she no longer wanted to live within the confines of the Palace, but rather a day's ride or sail away, like here at the Estate.

Becataten had been quite pensive lately about having two babies and decided against more children. She was happy to be shrinking back to her original body. Now that she had a boy and a girl in one birth, that seemed enough to her. Besides, she didn't want to go through that staggering task again. She heard about teas made from herbs that stopped a woman from having babies. She decided she would learn of them and implement them into her routine.

As she stepped off the litter, Kombo stood at the door to greet her, and no longer with a sling on his injured arm, he managed a deep bow of respect when he saw Becataten. "Welcome, Princess! Your father expects you."

"Father, it has been too long," Becataten said, as she rushed toward his chair, reaching out to embrace him. When he touched her shoulders and ran his fingers over her face, it pained her once again to know he was forever blind. He had shed even more weight than she remembered. His voice was not quite as strong as it once was, and her thoughts were carried back many inundations when Pharaoh had stripped him of his title of Royal Astrologer and ordered him brutally tortured. Although not spoken of, it was suspected he had been castrated then. But after a discussion with the healers about this question, they said it made little difference when castration took place after years of manhood.

"My daughter, you have come," he said, as his frame softened into hers. In silence they held one another.

Becataten kissed his forward then looked about the comfortably sized chamber that contained his large sitting chair, some benches, a few tables for candles and food trays, plus a lounge where she chose to sit. She remembered that there were several sleeping alcoves of varying sizes that allowed for servants and guests. She got a glimpse of her father's small workroom crowded with scrolls, and thought she heard someone inside. She wondered who was reading to him, writing scrolls for him, and how had he acquired a library.

Huni distracted her when he placed himself at her side, resting his hand on hers. He whimpered, waiting for her attention. She stroked his head, and his eyes closed. "Huni is still your loyal friend, isn't he father?" she asked, feeling fondness for the primate.

"Yes, he and I have lived through much together, as you well know."

"Where is the Viceroy today, Father?"

"He's testing some repairs and improvements on his vessel for his return to Kush."

"And Ahmose, how does he like being the Estate Field Manager?"

"He has taken well to the position. At Ra's first light, he is out the door and returns only when Ra leaves us. And you remember Ne Ne? She trails after him daily. Since the pups were killed by those Nubian rebels, she has yearned for animals so young Ahmose takes her with him to visit the animal pens. He tells me she is interested in milking goats and thinks she will be a cheese maker one day."

Becataten smiled broadly. "That sounds like a very good trade for her." Becataten paused a moment then asked, "Pygmy Lady stays her too, doesn't she, Father?"

"Occasionally," he replied soberly.

"And you, Father, are you happy here?"

"I am, and happy to be near you, Becataten." He said, wiping his nose with a cloth that Kombo handed him. Then he clapped his hands for refreshments.

The food tray arrived as a helper of Kombo's carried it in, heaped with grapes, pomegranates, figs, melons, date cakes, bread, and goat cheese. Becataten watched as Kombo quickly explained what food and drink was served.

"And Princess Becataten, you please try the goat cheese. Ahmose tells us it is the best on the Estate. It comes from the goat herder that Ne Ne asks again and again questions about cheese making," Kombo added.

"Thank you, Kombo," Becataten said, as he presented her with a filled copper plate of food. "Mmm, this is good cheese, father." She couldn't help but notice Huni's watchful eyes as the baboon observed her eat. "Huni, you would like something to eat too, wouldn't you?" He sat erect and put his hand on her lap as his rear end wiggled. She hadn't remembered him being so well trained. "My, someone has taught you manners, Huni," she said, placing a fig in his palm.

Kombo smiled. "Pygmy Lady has taught him not to beg or steal food."

Abu loudly cleared his throat. "Enough about the baboon! I would like to speak about the twins now."

"Yes, father, I am ready," said Becataten, as she set aside her plate.

Abu put his hand out for a board that Kombo handed him, and Becataten recognized it as a depiction of the heavens. It had been carefully laid out on a grid with varying sizes of pebbles to replicate the sky on the day of the twin's birth. She remembered how the Viceroy had told her of the collaboration between her father and Kombo to work this out. What a wonderful partnership they had arranged; an illiterate but savvy Nubian combined with a brilliant mind who although blind could interpret the heavens using this plan.

Abu adjusted himself in his chair, took a deep breath and began. Holding the side of the board, he fingered it as he spoke. "Your boy twin is going to leave Egypt at a young age to travel the world. He will be intensely curious about all things foreign. He will resemble his grand-mama, Princess Attah, and may have her green eyes." Abu's voice softened as he spoke Attah's name.

"And he will carry the blood of her people of Mitanni more than that of an Egyptian. His appearance will aid him in mingling with people outside Egypt. He will gain and lose fortunes in his lifetime, and have many wives from foreign lands, but ultimately return to settle in Egypt where his wives will bear many children. The Viceroy and he will argue about his way of life, but through it, learn respect and love for one another. I see this boy actively corresponding with someone throughout his travels, and that may be me."

"Father! That is a fascinating birth reading. Did you say wives?" Becataten asked, reeling at the thought.

Abu nodded as he adjusted the tied scarf around his head that concealed his vacant eye sockets. He took a drink of beer and wiped his mouth, then returned his hands to the board.

"Now, your girl twin, she is more complex. This is a woman who will carry much Heka. She will have to learn that this is a force that can be used for good or bad. That will be a difficult lesson for her. But once she learns this, her life will open to many interesting paths. People in high places will pay handsomely for her second sight, and she will be greatly revered in Egypt. Her Heka will also prompt her to travel, but not as extensively as her twin brother. She will bear one child, but not partner with anyone. Her reputation and station in life will become almost sacred. And she will live to be a very old woman."

"Oh, father, it sounds as though I have given birth to two very special lives."

"You have, my dear."

"Do you have names chosen for the twins yet, Father?"

I wanted to consult you about that, Princess. Do you wish to incorporate the Aten into their names, or perhaps another God?" Abu asked.

Becataten thought a moment. "I think ending the twin's names with our God Aten, like Jobu and me, is appropriate."

Abu nodded. "You are probably right about that because Young Horus will become Pharaoh in our lifetimes and covets God Aten above all others. And that reminds me, Becataten, Young Horus *will* play a favorable role in your family's life, one of great friendship. I took the time to do a brief birth chart for him. He will have an almost obsessive favoritism toward women, unlike any Pharaoh that has gone before. He will allow them many privileges and regard them with the same stature as men. He may change the location of the capitol, too."

"Father, you see *so* much," Becataten whispered in awe, feeling gratitude for her father's gifts.

"You will too, my dear, you just won't use the heavens to do so. It is the Heka that provides you with intuition. And I did look into your nightmare. It appears to be a common dream, typically experienced by a new mother."

"Father, what about Pharaoh making one last attempt to take my twins, as Pygmy Lady predicted?" Becataten quietly asked, letting him know she had overheard their conversation.

"I am unable to see that problem using the heavens, but for your sake I will speak with Pygmy Lady about this."

Kombo's jaw dropped and his eyes bulged, never having heard Abu pay respect before to Pygmy Lady.

A few Ras after Becataten visited with her father, a delivery of two miniature scrolls arrived at the Estate. She was thrilled to see the small rolls of papyrus and knew they contained the heavenly stories of her twins, as her father had told them to her. Now the family would have a written record and their birth names. Carefully, she unrolled them and again wondered who was doing scroll work for her father. She had once availed her father with a scribe, but she learned he wandered off. Evidently her father had replaced him.

"Maja, Maja! Come and listen to the birth names my father has chosen for the children!" Becataten called excitedly. Maja paddled in to Becataten's chamber from her alcove where she was resting, her posture more stooped now, her left eye more drooped. Becataten required almost no tasks of Maja any longer, and had to limit her time with the twins, because she exhausted herself caring for them.

Becataten proudly held up each scroll and read Maja the names. "Our boy is to be named Mishai-aten, which means he will be a world traveler and worship God Aten. Our girl will be called, Djezerit-aten, a holy woman who will also worship God Aten," announced Becataten.

Long ago, Maja, who had little ability to pronounce most Egyptian names, had shortened Becataten to Taten and Jobutaten to Jobu. These diminutive adaptations were used to refer to the twins even by Dwarf Beset when she was alive. Maja was quick to do that again having heard Becataten pronounce names that were incomprehensible to her. She would take

Mishai-aten and alter it to Mishi. She would reduce Jezerit-aten to Jezer and forever refer to them that way.

Becataten could hardly wait to share the scrolls that evening with the dinner guests at the party that Lady Nagara had planned in her honor. She was surprised at Lady Nagar's elaborate preparation and how happy it all seemed to make her. The dinner was to be held on the roof, as that was Becataten's favorite place at the Estate.

"Becataten, Becataten, dinner is soon. Be ready!" she heard Lady Nagara call rushing past her open door.

"I am nearly dressed, and waiting for the Viceroy," replied Becataten.

Chapter 23

♊

The Viceroy entered Becataten's suite unnoticed, quietly gazing upon her as he leaned against the doorway. Isis used a paste made from the power of malachite to set off Becataten's green eyes. She was finishing the painting of Becataten's face by patting her cheeks with a small ball of linen that contained gold dust. "Please, do that lightly," Becataten said, "You know how Lady Nagara thinks it is vulgar to use too much gold." Isis pursed her lips, nodded then placed Becataten's new wig on her head.

"This is such a beautiful wig, Princess," said Isis.

"Yes it is, and made of that fine hair from across the Great Sea, not the coarse type from Anatolia. It shines so and see how finely the plaits are woven."

Isis nodded.

"This is a lavish gift from Lady Nagara. I know she ordered it from the royal wigmaker at the Palace. I love the turquoise and gold beads that are woven into the small plates," Becataten said, inspecting herself in a hand-held, polished silver disk when she caught a glimpse of Merymose behind her. "Mosie, how long have you been standing there?"

"Long enough to admire your beauty," he said.

She turned to him. "You look quite handsome too, in your new, long kilt with that woven gold braid at your waist. And I don't think I have seen that gold collar before."

"Yes, well we *are* the guests of honor tonight, aren't we?"

Mischievously she said, "I believe *I* am the guest of honor. After all, all you did was couple with me. I am the one who delivered the cubs."

He grinned back at her and extended his hand. "I cannot deny that Princess. Now before your head outgrows that wig, shall we join your guests?"

"I am so excited to read the birth stories at dinner," she said, as she picked up the scrolls on their way out. "Do you know who Lady Nagara has invited, Mosie?" Becataten asked as they climbed the winding stairs to the roof.

"We shall soon find out, Becataten."

"Do you think this celebration has gotten back to the Palace that Pharaoh may know we have twins, Mosie?"

Before he could answer, they were at the top of the stairs joining the party. Seated on cushions at a low table, the guests looked up when Becataten and the Viceroy entered the room and applauded them. Architect Suti and Hor were there, and next to Suti sat his old friend the Heka Priest. Lady Nagara had invited Sennejem. *The Viceroy was right about Lady Nagara liking the Royal Gardener,* thought Becataten.

Becataten's favorite guest was the priest, with his spikey hair and round belly. He was such a comfort to her after Jobu's death and supported her when she wasn't getting along with Lady Nagara. He was there to talk to when she had no one else, but most important, he had cast true charts for herself and Jobu that told them they were twins who indeed arrived with fortitude.

At the head of the table, Becataten noted a papyrus roll of excellent quality, and she was quite sure it had been secured with a royal seal. *What did that mean?*

"Thank you all for honoring me and the Viceroy, it makes this the happiest day of my life," she said as she reached for Merymose's hand.

"Becataten keeps reminding me that all I did was the coupling," said the Viceroy, smiling at Becataten with a smirk.

Becataten smiled back, and then read the birth stories that her father had produced, and when she was finished she added, "Father says that he marked the birth scrolls with stamps made from clay, but he will replace them with gold seals."

She sat down amid a buzz of conversation on floor pillows to sit at the low table. As Becataten broke off a bit of conical shaped bread to dip in a yogurt sauce, she looked at the Heka Priest and his gaze gripped her. She knew that they must speak after the dinner. The Viceroy reached for a goose leg and a plate of beans. Hor was the picky eater of the group, he always asked for a duck egg, no matter what else was on the table. Lady Nagara was served mint leaves, thinly sliced cucumbers, chopped greens and slivered leeks topped with goat cheese. "Sennejem," she said, who she had placed next to her, "Do try our Suti beef. All the men love it and we are famous for it."

Becataten leaned into the Viceroy and said, "We have been blessed haven't we, Mosie?"

"We have indeed," he said, as he drew her toward him in a tight embrace.

After the savory parts of the meal ended, sliced watermelon, plump figs, fresh and dried dates, grapes, and almonds were served. Gifts for the twins followed.

"Oh, Viceroy, have you ever seen anything so fanciful?" Becataten said, as she opened the first gift. "Heka Priest, where did you have this made? It is charming!" Becataten held up a wooden toy with a bright red platform attached to a row of carved miniature dwarfs that danced when one pulled a string.

The Viceroy shook his head in wonderment. "I never had anything like that when I was a child!" he exclaimed.

The priest smiled. "I was walking through the craftsman village and saw a woodcarver who was making it for the child of a nobleman. I persuaded him that I must have it, and after I bestowed him with several blessings, he relented."

Without a word, Hor handed Becataten two small pouches made from the softest of animal hide. Each contained perfectly fashioned, miniature ankhs of gold. Becataten carefully opened the soft pouches and squealed with delight. "The children can treasure these ankhs and wear them for their entire lifetime. They will come to know life, death, and rebirth through them. Hor, you have such an exquisite eye for lovely things."

Hor's taste in beautiful things was well known. His face reddened with the compliment as Becataten reached for the scroll at the end of the table. "I believe this is to be read aloud," she said hesitantly. Followed by a sigh, she began:

Young Bull Horus extends greetings to the household of Architect Suti and Lady Nagara.

My duties as heir apparent preclude me from attending your dinner.

It was kind of you, Lady Nagara, to offer me an invitation to your Estate to celebrate the birth of Viceroy Merymose and Princess Becataten's girl-child.

Becataten emitted a small sound of alarm as she read girl-child. It was written with red ink, as all-important words were in a script, but the emphasis of a singular birth rocked her emotionally. She covered her mouth and turned to the Viceroy.

Merymose reached for the papyrus to finish the reading beginning where Becataten had left off:

Pharaoh was the first to hold the girl-child and bestow his best wishes. I take this time to extend my congratulations. If the child possesses the fine qualities of her mother, she will indeed grow to be a woman who respects all of Egypt's Gods, traditions, and wisdoms.

I offer but one suggestion, and that is to include the Aten in the child's name. As you know that is the preferred God of our dynasty.

My mother, Queen Tiye, also extends her congratulation to the Princess and Viceroy for a long life of the girl-child.

Your Future King,
Young Bull Horus

In the guest's astonished silence, the only sound was that of the Viceroy rolling the scroll tightly closed.

Chapter 24

♊

After dinner, Becataten stood and said, "I need to walk, I've eaten too much food. Would you join me, Heka Priest?"

"That sounds like a fine idea, Princess."

As they wound down the narrow steps from the roof to the second level of the Estate and then to the bottom of the stairs, Becataten clapped her hands which brought an attendant to her side. She requested a torchbearer for their walk.

Becataten took the priest's arm as they strolled alongside the lotus pond in front of the house. "You have been away too long, Priest."

"Yes, I suppose that is true. I seem to show up when there is some difficulty, don't I?" The priest said as he rubbed his head.

Becataten sighed. "And there is some difficulty now, isn't there?" she said drawing him close.

Before he could answer her, a distressed Maja came running with Becataten's wrap, whispered into her ear then pointed to four sleepy-eyed bearers ready to transport them back to Abu's house.

Becataten pulled the priest toward the litter. "Come, Maja says it is urgent, we must go to my father's house, Priest." As they sped away by litter, Becataten called back, "Maja, tell the Viceroy where we have gone!"

Pygmy Lady was pacing outside Abu's door when they arrived. Becataten and the Heka Priest rushed into the house. "Hello, Father, what is it?" Becataten said, as she went to his side to hug him.

"Greetings, my daughter." Reaching to touch her, Abu said, "Sit."

The priest placed a hand on Abu's shoulder. "Greetings, old man, it is me, the Heka Priest, who has come with your daughter."

"Good, good, have a seat, it has been some time since we have talked," said Abu. "Now, I believe I will let Pygmy Lady speak first."

Becataten noticed that Pygmy Lady had, for the first time, been given status in her father's house. She lived here, as did Ahmose and Kombo, but Becataten hadn't thought her father ever accepted the pygmy. Maybe he had learned that she saved the twins from Pharaoh, or that many inundations ago she had predicted the Viceroy would marry a royal princess. Whatever it was, something had changed his perception.

The Viceroy burst into Abu's house. "What is it Becataten?" he said as he reached for her. "Maja said you were urgently called here." The Viceroy turned to Abu, "What has happened?"

Pacing while she spoke, Pygmy Lady began. "Today, I returned from the barge of Young Horus. He was sailing the Nile trying out his new toy, his boat. When he realized he was near the Estate, he had his crew moor here briefly, then summoned me for a talk."

Becataten was amazed Young Horus remembered Pygmy Lady, and further surprised that he had invited her on board his royal barge. But she remembered the Viceroy mentioned a friendly conversation between

Young Horus and Pygmy Lady had taken place before their problematic sail from Thebes.

Becataten looked at Pygmy Lady. "I have just come from a dinner where we read a scroll from Young Horus," Becataten said.

"Forget that scroll," blurted Pygmy Lady. "Those are old words."

Becataten went silent. She had learned to accept the coarse and abrupt manner that came with this diminutive pygmy, who could quickly take on the role of a tyrant.

Pygmy Lady stood with her hands on her hips and stared at the Viceroy. "Horus told me that Pharaoh knows about the twins, he will take a river cruise to this Estate in five Ras and wants to see them. We are back to the old story, Viceroy. Your gold-hungry king is hungry for your twins." Then she plopped down on some floor pillows beneath her, as if the very words took much out of her.

Abu cleared his throat and in his old strong voice, spoke. "Viceroy, I believe you should take Becataten and the twins on a trip. Hide yourself for a time, but it must appear as though you are taking your family on, let us say, a recuperative vacation."

Becataten was unable to speak and trembled as the Viceroy placed his arm around her to hold her close.

"Pygmy Lady did Young Horus say anything else?" asked the Viceroy.

"No, but his mother did."

"His Mother, you mean the Queen... Queen Tiye?" Viceroy asked.

"Yes, I forecasted her son's future, and told her how she would stand behind him when he became the young king. What do you Egyptians call that?"

"Regent," said the Viceroy, still surprised that Pygmy Lady had spoken to the queen herself. "Is that everything you talked about?"

Pygmy Lady adjusted her hide shift. "Before I left, his mother whispered in my ear to ask me if her son would always have the body of both a man and a woman. I said he would."

Abu interjected. "The queen always liked seers and forecasters. Queen Tiye often had me produce personal charts for people that interested her when I was Royal Astrologer. I am pleased that you have the queen mother and her son as friends, Becataten. If you recall, I predicted this association in the heavenly charts of the twins."

Pygmy Lady spoke up with her loud voice. "Don't be so sure of the Queen as a friend. She is one who can change, and fast as the strike of an asp."

Shaking his head, the Viceroy looked at Becataten, "Yes, it is Young Horus that is our friend. Now, this suggestion of your father for us to be away when Pharaoh arrives, I favor. But where shall we go is the question?"

Becataten was trying to get control of her fear when she heard someone else speak.

Kombo, sitting in the recesses of the room, stood. "Viceroy, remember the small house we built for you that is this side of Fort Buhen? The one we made to conceal from your men so you could be alone when you were... when you were working."

A knowing look crossed the Viceroy's face. It had been where he had spent time, several inundations ago, with the Nubian woman who bore his son, Ahmose.

Becataten caught the Viceroy's look of unease and soon understood that it had been a lover's hideaway. Becataten sat up straight. "Viceroy, I don't care what you did there or who you were with. It is the survival of our twins we are talking about. If we must go there, so be it." Looking toward Abu, she asked, "Oh Father, what do you say, I am so frightened for my twins."

"My daughter, I believe you must go to this place that Kombo describes. We are dealing with a Pharaoh, who is no longer rational. He has become interested in pleasure alone, as proof, just look at the grandeur of his mortuary temple. It covers more space than the Palace grounds."

Becataten went to her father and held his hands and wept. Then, drying her tears, she looked at the Heka Priest. "Priest what do you say?"

"I too say be gone when Pharaoh arrives. He will accept your absence as fate, as he has not announced his arrival. It is Young Horus, alone, who knows he is coming." The Priest rubbed his head in his usual way and added, "However, before you leave, send me back to the Palace with a scroll that heralds the birth of the twins, and a request for an audience to present the children at court in the near future. I must add, Princess, that I foresee Pharaoh claiming the children, but not in a sinister way, and I don't believe for too long a time. He will simply want to own them for a while—like pets—and lavish many goods and gifts upon them. You, Princess, are a fond memory for him, and I believe he has always wished that you had born him royal children, even been his queen."

The Viceroy's face hardened. Trying to show composure, Becataten turned to Pygmy Lady and asked, "What do you say?"

Pygmy Lady lay on the pillows with her hands behind her head. "I say it was a bad day when your father failed to take the crown and kill your Pharaoh."

Chapter 25

♊

A strong hot day illuminated the Mother Nile when Becataten waived off the Heka Priest. He was sailing north to the Palace with the scroll she had written to Pharaoh explaining that she had delivered twins, the family was on a recuperative cruise, and she hoped he would find time to grant them an audience in the future.

Once the Heka Priest arrived at the Palace, he was quick to offer Pharaoh's vizier Becataten's missive, and showed surprise when he had been granted an audience, as well. As he entered Pharaoh's chamber, he began an elaborate greeting and obeisance, when Pharaoh said, "Greetings Heka Priest, my vizier has just read me the scroll from Becataten. Stand, there is no need for such formalities."

The priest stood in silence taking in the heavy scent of morenga oil, Pharaoh's favorite anointment. "When did Becataten and Merymose leave on their cruise, Priest?" Pharaoh abruptly began, followed by much querying about the health of the boy twin and if the babies were on the cruise, or left behind with Lady Nagara.

Pharaoh's anger was evident when he learned late of Becataten's second birth, and that it was a boy. He did however seem genuinely interested in her health, especially after the priest made the most of Becataten's difficult delivery, and how rare it was to aid in the birthing of living twins as well as see that the mother lives.

After establishing that Becataten's residence was at the Suti Estate, Pharaoh summoned his vizier and ordered elaborate gifts be sent there for the twins. He drank fully from his wine-filled goblet and added that a large plot of land be secured for the building of an ample house for the Princess, near his Palace.

Finally, Pharaoh wanted to know if heavenly charts had been cast and names had been given the children. The priest purposefully misstated that he had produced their charts to avoid the mention of Abu. It still was unclear if Pharaoh knew that Abu was alive or dead, begging in the streets of Thebes, or with his daughter, Becataten.

"Did you know that Princess Becataten is very knowledgeable about architecture, Priest?" Pharaoh said.

"Ah, yes, I believe I have heard her speak fondly of the building arts, My Lord."

The resident cat Lady Mui jumped upon Pharaoh's lap and he stroked her soft fur, a cunning gaze in his eyes. "I am going to hold you responsible for returning Becataten to me. I must show her the work I have accomplished on my mortuary temple, and I want these twins with me, soon!"

A far more-portly Pharaoh than from the past stood from his oversized chair. When his golden sandals met the floor, he waved the priest off. Bowing, the Heka Priest left, feeling grateful his own life was intact after seeing how deranged the Pharaoh had become.

Becataten was glad they were underway, and the turmoil left behind. "Mosie, I have thought about it and decided I don't want to go to that place that Kombo described."

Maja and Isis were in the back of the barge when they heard Becataten's words. Their faces showed surprise.

Sitting at Becataten's side, the Viceroy turned to her with wonder. "What do you mean, Becataten? Getting away is about hiding the twins from Pharaoh," the Viceroy said.

Becataten gazed ahead. "I just don't want to be there," she answered.

"Is it because I spent time there with the Nubian woman?" Asked the Viceroy.

"Not really, I'm just tired of moving about. I like staying at the Estate or the Palace. Other places are of little interest to me."

Falling back into his chair he expelled a deep breath. "Well, I wish you would have told me that before we made plans to head south. What do you have in mind now?"

Becataten reached for his hand. "Can we just sleep under the stars for a few nights and stop along the way; maybe have picnics on shore from time to time. This is a very large and comfortable boat, Mosie."

"Yes, we could, but that kind of living could only last a few Ras. You forget about all of the wildlife along the Mother Nile," he said.

As the twins suckled in the arms of their wet nurses, they carried frowns on their brows as though they too had overheard Becataten's words. Seated nearby, Maja whispered to Isis, "I wish Pygmy Lady was here, she would tell Becataten to go to the place we planned."

Becataten spoke in a soft voice. "After a few Ras of cruising, I think we should take your apartment at the Palace. You have told me that it is large and comfortable, and it would be awhile before Pharaoh knew we were there. He's supposed to be cruising and won't be there for a time. Besides, traveling south against the current of the Nile isn't pleasant."

"Listen to what you are saying, Becataten. What you suggest would mean that Pharaoh would soon have the twins in his hands."

Becataten grew resistant, "But remember what the Heka priest said. Pharaoh wanted them in his company, like pets. Yes, he would spoil them, yet they would hardly know the difference at their age," she added.

The Viceroy shook his head. "Only a Ra ago you were in a state of fear over this whole matter, and now listen to you," he said.

The Captain of the barge shouted, "A float of sobeks ahead, Viceroy!"

The Viceroy stood tall and covered his brow straining to look for the crocodiles. When he saw that they were headed into them, he turned to his captain. "Turn this ship about," he called.

Becataten held her breath as she stood, then winced when she saw the swelling white water that defined the movement of crocodiles. She could see their protruding eyes coming into view. Their silence and gaining speed horrified her. She stood and held onto the back of her chair to steady herself while the vessel began the reversing direction. Holding her head high she could see more crocodiles on land up ahead joining the float. Becataten looked behind her at the wet nurses holding their wards tight, fright filling their eyes. *Oh, please God Sobek, spare my babies! Take me if you must, but not them!* She had read accounts of past Pharaohs losing their life to sobeks. She wanted to yell orders at someone but knew she had to leave this matter to the Viceroy.

The giants gained on the ship as rowers worked their oars intensely to turn the craft abouts so they might gain advantage by sailing north with the river. Maja and Isis held one another, both staring at the suckling twins.

Angry and cursing, the Viceroy stood next to his captain. "Get this barge headed north. I want faster drumbeats. Throw all the food aboard at them. If the beasts get any closer, assign two bowmen to fire on them."

Frenzied attendants threw all the foodstuffs they could find at the giant sobeks. The crew reached for their bows and quivers. Cages were opened of live ducks and geese. Feathers flew as the birds were hurled at the gaining beasts, some twice the length of a man. A crewman who was grilling fish for the men cast his food overboard, the women attendants flung all the melons and vegetables, even small heads of garlic and tiger nuts were tossed.

The rowers slowly picked up speed as the giant lizards paused to devour and fight over the cast-off food. The rowers gained significant momentum now moving north with the currents of the Nile. Slow but steady, a distance between the barge and the float of crocodiles grew wider until they were out of danger.

It was silent on board for some time while everyone seemed to be taking stock of the horrible fate they had just escaped when the Viceroy turned to Becataten.

"Where would you like to go now, perhaps the pyramids?"

Chapter 26

♊

The new Dock Master stood looking out across the Nile, slapping at flies with his zebra tail. "That's handy," said the assistant.

"Yes," said the Dock Master, "The rich leave many things behind on the boats we arrange for them." He squinted at a long craft approaching the dock. "And speaking of the rich, is that not Viceroy Merymose's vessel sailing into port?"

His assistant's eyes bulged. "That's a big one, isn't it, Master?"

"Yes, it is called *The Golden Falcon,* and we had better make ready for his disembarking."

"How long is *The Golden Falcon,* Dock Master?"

The master in charge of Palace docks cocked his head. "I'd say she is as long as a row of six standing chariots. Now go and tell the men who are throwing dice that I need their backs."

Viceroy Merymose's vessel, with its raised cabin situated at mid deck, presented an imposing sight. Atop the chamber sat Becataten in one of two chairs, where she and the Viceroy had a full view of the shores of the great Mother Nile.

As the Viceroy surveyed where they were, he had a hard look in his eyes. They had outrun the sobeks, but now they were back in harm's way again. This time at the Thebian harbor entrance to Pharaoh's palacial grounds. A different kind of threat awaited them here. Pharaoh would demand their presence, and maybe take their twins.

As they approached the dock, there was a sharp tone in the Viceroy's command. "Captain, we will moor here at my dock. My rowers are spent after their fierce efforts escaping a float of crocodiles, but we will only stay one night. We are in need of supplies only."

Becataten was surprised at how quickly they had come to be at the Palace waterfront. To cruise here from the Suti Estate usually took a full day. Their arrival had taken half that time. The Viceroy's orders to row away from the sobeks happened with great speed. With relief, she sighed and turned to look at her babies. It felt good to be alive.

From her chair, Becataten caught her husband's eye before climbing down the ladder to his side. She put her arms around his middle. "Mosie, I don't want to go to the Palace grounds, I agree that it would be dangerous, and especially to stay in your apartment. Pharaoh would soon learn we were here, and who knows what he would want of us. I am just happy to have lived through this day, and that we are all safe."

With affection, the Viceroy looked into Becataten's face. "The thought of losing you and the twins..." His voice faltered as he held her close.

Becataten sighed as she leaned against his chest. "I know you were mocking me when you asked if I wanted to see the pyramids, but why not? Do you know that I have never seen them, or the sphinx?"

The Viceroy cleared his throat. "No more talk of going to the Palace, Becataten?"

"None," she replied, with allure in her eyes.

He did not answer, but held her for a long while. "We must bring on water and food stores, then we will sail you to the pyramids at Ra's first light, Princess." The viceroy stood at mid-ship, legs apart, as the vessel maneuvered into his long-established docking place.

"Greetings, Viceroy Merymose, to you and your family," said the new and amenable Dock Master, rushing to the quay. "I have slaves waiting to help you disembark, and I took the liberty of ordering several litters for your needs when I saw you heading for your mooring."

"Thank you, Dock Master but we will not need the transports you ordered."

The man bowed, "Would you like me to notify the Vizier so Pharaoh may know you are in Thebes?"

"That will not be necessary either. We are just here to take on fresh water and a few supplies, then perhaps spend the night on board."

The next thing Becataten saw was a closely woven, rich colored carpet rolled out at the bottom of the boarding ladder, not like Egyptians produced. Probably from a vassal state, she thought. Also, slaves had been ordered to hold parasols for disembarking passengers. She had forgotten what eminence the Viceroy carried.

The Viceroy's attendants disembarked with orders to return with supplies for the sail to the pyramids at Giza.

Dusk arrived. The docks were quiet, birds along the Nile were settling into the thick stands of papyrus followed by their nightly chatter. And a man playing the flute brought tranquility to the evening as a soft current lapped at the hull. No crocodiles lurked near large docks where they could be easily taken as trophies.

"Come!" waved the Viceroy to the cook who would prepare food on his brazier on the after deck. Tossing him a large piece of copper debon, he said, "Find us a nice young goat for dinner, we will dine on board." The smiling Nubian caught the generous-sized piece of debon and smiled to reveal a manifold of gleaming teeth at the prospect of eating goat, and not fish, for dinner. He soon jumped from ship to dock and was off to find a herder.

Becataten and the Viceroy had taken to their chairs and were holding hands, watching the night sky begin to sparkle.

Observing the palatial shoreline, Becataten turned to the Viceroy, "That is a huge harbor we passed that Pharaoh built for Queen Tiye."

The Viceroy nodded, "When you are Pharaoh and take a second wife, that is what you do for your first queen, I guess."

Becataten marveled at its size. "That is her private waterway?"

"The Vizier explained to me that it is actually a boating lake, and perhaps intended to be a diversion for the queen while Pharaoh was preoccupied with his second wife. It also serves as irrigation for the queen's farm lands, and it will increase her yield of products and her revenue."

"Pharaoh has made her very rich and powerful," said Becataten.

"Yes, she has been granted unprecedented gifts," said the Viceroy.

"I have read about her vast landholdings and Beset told me that she is the only one to have a private chef, besides Pharaoh. Is it also true that each brick of her apartment is stamped with her personal cartouche?" Becataten asked.

The Viceroy nodded.

"Do you think she would ever use all her gold and power in an adverse way, Mosie?"

"Only time will tell. I would not be surprised if the queen became regent to Young Horus, as Pygmy Lady predicted, if he is young when crowned," said the Viceroy.

"Do you think that may happen soon, Mosie?"

"The Vizier and Chancellor tell me that Pharaoh has become too obsessed with his mortuary temple and is no longer a functioning king. All the gold I have delivered from his mines in Kush is used for its completion. Also, you may not know, but Pharaoh is growing obese," said the Viceroy.

Becataten's eyes grew wide. "No, I did not know that." For a moment she contemplated Pharaoh as corpulent and thought what a waste of a beautiful man. "I believe we pass Pharaoh's mortuary temple tomorrow as we sail for the pyramids, don't we, Mosie?"

The Viceroy nodded.

With great care, two crewmembers helped Maja up the ladder to the chairs where the Viceroy and Becataten sat. She held one twin in each arm. "This is Mishi," she said as she settled the boy in the Viceroy's arms. "He is very stubborn. "This is Jeser, and she is very peaceful," Maja said as she handed Becataten the girl.

The Viceroy smiled warmly. "These are your special names, aren't they Maja?"

With shyness, Maja's head bobbed. "Like I named Taten and Jobu," she said wiping tears away.

Becataten's eyes welled too, knowing that Jobu was in all their thoughts.

The Viceroy looked into the face of his frowning son. "So, your grandfather, who cast your heavenly chart, says you will be a world traveler, Mishi." His voice was softened for the boy, but to Maja he was louder. "Does he always frown like this, Maja?"

Maja nodded.

Becataten cuddled her baby girl. "Maja, does she remind you of me when I was a baby?"

Maja shook her head emphatically. "Too peaceful," she said.

The Viceroy emitted loud laughter, setting the babies crying.

Chapter 27

♊

The next Ra, after taking on stores for their sail, the dock attendants unleashed lines from a stone posts carved with the heads of lions. Merymose was a generous man and had his captain distribute small pieces of silver debon to the dock workers, requesting that they need not discuss the Golden Falcon's brief mooring to take on supplies. With gratitude and deep bows, the Dock Master and his workers bid a farewell to Viceroy Merymose's vessel. A well-rested crew rowed from the port as long beams brightened the deck. They headed north toward Memphis, where the grand pyramids had stood at Giza for fifteen hundred inundations. And the sphinx, even longer.

Once on the river, the Viceroy ordered they raise the linen square sail for a peaceful 250-mile cruise to the delta. He planned to take one or two days, and maybe longer to reach the Giza plain so as not to tax the backs of the oarsmen. A casual sail would give the rowers more rest from their heroic effort that saved them from the sobeks the day before.

As they headed toward Egypt's grandest architectural marvels, the Viceroy enjoyed escorting Becataten to this place he had visited many times. He had come to understand that although Becataten had lived a life of great luxury at the Suti Estate, it was but a short period of her youth. Her growing years were spent in a humble apartment in a remote part of the Palace grounds, and she had experienced no travel then. All her knowledge and love of Egypt she had gained from the royal library.

At midship the Viceroy and Becataten enjoyed a sequestered environ draped off with heavy linen, where the Viceroy and Becataten slept among down filled mattress laden with pillows. They had made love late into the evening the night prior, but not before the Viceroy asked a question of her as they undressed. "Do you want to have more babies, Becataten?"

She shook her head as she removed her gold earrings and cuffs.

His face became less animated as he dropped his kilt to the floor. "In that case we need to make some changes," he said.

"I already have," Becataten answered, as she shed her shift.

They stood disrobed, opposing one another "And what might that be, Princess."

With a mischievous look, she moved toward him. "Let us lie down and I will tell you."

The Viceroy reached for her and after they had settled into a soft down mattress he said, "I'm waiting, Becataten."

"Well, we will just have to abstain from coupling and be satisfied with fondling one another for our intimate pleasures," she said as she reached for his member. Still with a mischievous look she added, "You know that I may die if I have more babies."

The Viceroy expression was mixed with pleasure and disappointment. Becataten began to giggle.

"And what is so funny," he asked.

"Oh, Mosie, your face has such an amusing expression."

"Really," he said.

"Yes, really, but I won't torture you further."

"Your hand on me isn't exactly torture but say what you have to say."

"Well, I had a scroll sent to me from the royal library that described an interesting concoction of acacia oil and ground dates mixed with honey."

With disinterest, Merymose asked, "And why are we discussing that?"

Becataten sat up on her elbow. "I have placed that formula on a piece of seed wool, then into my birth canal, and now, no more babies..."

The Viceroy looked confused, and she knew she had to be more explicit but also not offend his manhood. "It means, my husband, that the concoction frightens your seeds away."

She stroked him and brought him closer to her, showing him that she was, after all, available for more than just fondling.

The Viceroy looked into her face that was glowing with delight as he rose up over her body. "You have a wicked sense of humor, Princess," he said as he brought himself into her arms, grateful to have his wife back after all she had endured.

Their cabin at the upper deck was the size of a small room with chairs secured within. During the day, the linen drape was removed, and the gentle current of the Nile and the sail captured a modest breeze that allowed for a steady ride in this otherwise draped space. Relaxing in their chairs, Becataten was captivated by the Theban architecture.

"It is so exciting to see the temples of Luxor and Karnak from this height, Mosie. These are the greatest structures in the land. I can understand why Pharaoh moved the capitol from Memphis to Thebes."

"You may change your mind about that when we get to the pyramids, Princess. And don't forget Pharaoh moved the capitol manly to escape the Amun clergy. There is still an active capitol in Memphis dominated by the Amun priests who oppose Pharaoh's God Aten worship."

Becataten nodded and turned her head toward the Valley of the Kings. She jumped from her chair, and with childlike enthusiasm drew attention to a temple under construction. "By the Gods, look at that pair of statues that Pharaoh has erected of himself. They flank the causeway to his mortuary temple! Look, Mosie," she said, pointing in the direction of the crews of workers building what looked like a large town. Becataten's excited voice was new to the attendants on deck and drew their attention.

He nodded. "I hear they are higher than the tallest of any columns in Egypt," the Viceroy said, with a measure of surprise at her elated excitement.

Becataten shaded her eyes, and using her rapid speech of the past, she bubbled, "Look at the grounds that Pharaoh's architects have laid out for his mortuary complex. There is a sphinx with Queen Tiye's head, another with the head of a crocodile!" Becataten became the animated child of her past, a time when she crossed the Nile daily to pore over the sites where architects' Suti and Hor worked. "Oh, Mosie, we must stop and walk the complex!" she said. "Please!"

The Viceroy's expression hardened. "We cannot do that, Princess. It is known that Pharaoh spends most

Ras at his temple surveying its construction. It is dangerous just passing his temple now."

"Can't we just sail close by the site to observe, Mosie?

"No! We cannot, Becataten. I'm sorry, but it is for our safety that I must say no."

As animated as Becataten had just been, she grew silent as she watched the shore from afar, trying to take in as much as she could of the construction that was happening. It brought her right back to her days when she was under Suti and Abu's tutelage, when she was younger, and free to examine the buildings that were making Pharaoh's architectural contributions so great. She sighed, feeling defeated, but understanding why they could not stop to see these marvels up close.

Becataten had been quiet for the rest of the sail to the delta. Maja, who came to sit at her feet, did so with caution. "You like all these old stone places we are passing along the Mother Nile, don't you Taten?" Maja asked.

Becataten nodded. "Yes, but we cannot stop," she replied, repeating what the Viceroy had said.

"You sounded like you were a child again after a long day with the architects. When we go on land again, can we have a picnic at the pyramids, Taten?"

Becataten smiled down on her long-time nanny who had come to Egypt from Mitanni as a slave with her mother so long ago. "Of course we can, and it will be more than a picnic, Maja. The Viceroy has arranged for a tent to be set for us, and we will spend maybe a half moon there."

At Giza where the pyramids stood, their breathtaking view loomed into view from the Nile. Becataten appreciated their enormous scale, but it was the sphinx that excited her. Yet at this place she did not have the same enthusiasm she had for Pharaoh's mortuary temple.

As they floated quietly into a Memphis dock, the Viceroy observed the securing of his vessel then called up to Becataten's chair. "Would you like to walk around the pyramids before Ra leaves us? We can litter there and back, and I will show you my favorite building in Egypt."

"I would like that, Mosie, just give me a little time to refresh myself." Becataten said as she soon descended the ladder from the perch above the cabin. She walked to the twins, who always seemed to be nursing. They were both round and fat from the rich diet the wet nurses were fed. Becataten was happy to find them in Maja's lap, cradled by her thin dark arms, already too much an armful. Becataten reached down and cooed to them. "They are beautiful babies, aren't they, Maja?" Maja nodded and beamed as though she was the mother.

Becataten called to Isis, who entered the cabin where Becataten sat for a new face painting. "I won't need such thick kohl lines around my eyes here, Isis. There are fewer flies at the delta with the sea breezes. Paint my eye lines thinner. It will make the Viceroy happy. He says he likes to see my green eyes, not just kohl. And be sure and use that new dye you found for my lips, he likes that too. Where did you find that?"

"It is from the skins of a rare red grape that I pulverize in a mortar and mix with a little almond oil. It is hard to find, Princess," Isis said proudly.

"Many grapes are grown here at the delta. I will send an attendant to find what you need." Becataten said. "Now help me with that new shift, the red silk one the Viceroy favors."

Chapter 28

♊

When a litter arrived to transport Becataten and the Viceroy from the vessel to the pyramids, she thought their holiday shelter looked small in the distance. As she settled herself in her wicker chair waiting for the Viceroy to take his seat, she watched Maja fuss over the twins and wet nurses. They would follow in their own conveyance. Their attendants would walk to the site with ladened donkeys. One animal lugged a cooking brazier, while others hauled furniture items and chests.

As bearers traversed the sands to their location, Becataten and Merymose were followed by local farmers who ran alongside their chairs, curious to see royals from Thebes. Men in loin cloths left their crops. Women in soiled shifts walked away from their cooking fires and naked children abandoned the herding of goats and geese, all to catch a glimpse of a princess and a viceroy. Becataten was reminded of the time she first traveled to the Suti Estate as a young girl where local peoples followed her litter. The same curiosity surrounded her now. She smiled politely at the people who toiled for Egypt.

Soon Becataten was absorbed with the three main pyramids that shared the vast Giza plain. She knew of the Pharaohs who built them. She knew the lion, bearing the head of the Pharaoh Kufu, was older than anyone could calculate.

"Mosie, I have read scrolls about the great sphinx, yet never learned how old it really is, or which Pharaoh created it. Do you have any knowledge about that?"

As they jostled along, the Viceroy cast a long gaze in the direction of the giant beast with the head of a man, avoiding the men continuing to erect their tent he had kept as a surprise. "My forefathers said that in ancient times, the great lion was a natural stone outcropping. And before Egyptians could read or write, built in stone or even had a Pharaoh, they made this their place of worship. Then when Pharaoh Kufu came to be, he had stone carvers make it his because the Gods deemed it so."

Becataten liked that explanation. She watched as the vast structures neared.

Stirred by the pending arrival of such prominent royals to the ancient site, the atmosphere grew jubilant, if not commercial. Local merchants and tradesmen swarmed around their litter like vultures. Men with pairs of wine jars, suspended on wooden yolks across their shoulders stood to entice the viceroy. "Would you like to taste our wines? A merchant said, lowering his yolk.

The Viceroy raised his eyebrows and smiled. "Those sellers will have the sweet vintages you prefer too, Princess, like palm and date."

"What are all those tags hanging from the jars, Mosie?"

With interest, the Viceroy's answer rang with authority. "The best wine in Egypt has been produced here at the delta for fifteen hundred inundations. All jars are tagged with their type of grape, harvest date and the vineyard. The purveyors are giving me their assessment." Breaking from his seriousness, he smiled and added, "Although I will assess the quality for myself."

Becataten smiled back at him. "I'm sure you will." Her attention turned to a fishmonger traveling with a litter that held a tank of seawater filled with rare shellfish. It made her think of Dwarf Beset, who loved eels, and she wondered if they were found in fresh water or the sea. "Turing to the Viceroy she said, "Do you like ells, Mosie?"

"No, they are an acquired taste."

Before she could guess, her nose was drawn to the baking of bread. A child came near their litter with a basket of warm flatbread. Becataten knew it was freshly baked, but where was the oven?

She turned to notice another woman squatted before a large square of small gray pebbles, who smiled when she saw Becataten's interest. With quickness, she patted a round of dough into a circle, threw it on the small hot pebbles, then deftly plucked it off the grey stones, shook it and turned it to finish baking. With a toothless grin, she waved the finished product at Becataten. Becataten gestured the baker to her side and asked to examine the round to find small brown indentions in the flatbread from the hot pebbles.

"How do they do that, Mosie?" she asked.

He explained as bread baking aromas filled the air. "Women arrive here before Ra, they dig a pit and build large fires in the holes. When wood burns down to embers, they cover them with small riverbed stones. When the stones grow hot and grey like the color you see, they have a cooking service. It is the ancient way to bake bread," he explained. "Have one of the cooks buy what you like. I'm going back to the wine merchants to have some wines delivered."

Sellers of dry goods were angling for space to dawn their wares. They held their arms high, draped with fabrics for shawls, tunics and shifts, many fine imports, thought Becataten. One merchant even had small animal pelts like she had seen traders wear in Pharaoh's grand hall, inundations ago. She remembered that the furs were as soft as Lady Mieu's coat.

Due to the profusion of sellers that surrounded then to present their goods, the prefect of the region had to organize a guard force to keep them back. It was a difficult task, because the merchants of Memphis wanted to sell their goods to a man in charge of all the gold mines in Egypt, and his princess.

Becataten's view of the displays of various goods was halted when their transport lowered before a grayish linen structure that no longer looked small as it had in the distance. *Though it is not very impressive from the outside*, she thought.

The Viceroy stepped off the lowered litter to walk Becataten toward the tent entrance.

"Step out of your sandals so you may feel the carpets beneath your feet, Princess." The runner of silky woven threads felt soft and luxurious on her bare feet. Above the long carpet that led to the entrance, a canopy covered the area creating an outdoor gallery, set with comfortable chairs. When two men parted the fabric at the portal entrance, the melody of a harp and the aroma of gardenias graced the air. She turned to deliver her broadest of smiles to her husband.

More silken rugs lay at Becataten's feet and were also hung as partitions to produce rooms for privacy and sleeping. The inside of the tent was painted with scenes of colorful flowers and wild animals. Bowls of exotic fruit decorated tables, along with honey cakes and imported nuts. A lion cub secured to a post with a golden chain, lay sleeping.

"Oh, Mosie, this is magnificent!" Becataten gushed.

The Viceroy pointed up to a blue fabric ceiling, studded with stars. Becataten looked up with childlike wonder, feeling entirely blessed that she was privy to seeing such amazing sights in such a beautiful world.

Chapter 29

♊

Each Ra was a new adventure of exploration on the Giza plain, and the Viceroy was right the Sphinx and the three main pyramids, built in the fourth dynasty, surpassed the grandeur of Pharaoh Amenhotep's mortuary temple that was built in their eighteenth dynasty.

One morning she dragged the Viceroy from his wine merchants, they hired a chariot and slipped away to the Sphinx. When she stepped off the litter, she walked the long path between the statues enormous legs that stretched out to reveal his huge claws. She had to admit the sight sent feelings of awe through her entire body. That led her to send blessings and ask for some in return under the unreadable face of the sphinx. She poked her head into the chapel between his immense legs but was told it was for the Pharaohs only. She looked up at the painted beard and the statue's eyes circled with kohl and felt she could easily fall over.

The Viceroy was soon behind her. "Don't slip away like this, Becataten, although I am important here, we are among strangers.

"Even though his paint is fading, he remains a splendid site, doesn't he Mosie?" Becataten said as she enjoyed the soft breeze off the Delta and leaned into her husband.

"Yes, he does, and did you know many of his blocks have been restored and his face repainted?

"That I did not know."

The Viceroy nodded. "A thousand years after Pharaoh Khafre built his mammoth lion, Thutmose IV ordered an extensive restoration, and that was 500 years ago. Perhaps another Pharaoh in a few hundred years will do it again. It is far too important not to take precious care of. Would you like to travel on to walk or drive around the large pyramid? It is a short ride."

"No, I am overwhelmed by what I have seen today. I want to return to the tent and reflect and drink some of the chilled wines you bought me. I have realized that all the time I spent in the royal library reading about the Sphinx did little to enlighten me as to its true grandeur."

But the next morning Becataten jumped into the chariot next to the Viceroy he arranged so they may visit the pyramids. Driving toward them, Becataten said, "There are so many, Mosie. Which one shall we circle first?"

"The biggest one, Kufu's, of course!"

"Do you think any of the chambers have been robbed by now, Mosie?"

"Probably not, but it is difficult to keep guards stationed around the perimeter. Each side measures nearly 800 feet."

Covering her eyes and looking up as they drove around the pyramid, Becataten said, "I had no idea how the cap gleams so." "What is that metal made of?"

"It's a mixture of gold silver and copper, and that is what grave robbers are after. But as long as these polished cap stones cover the structure, no one can scale to the top to remove it. The cap would be worth a Pharaoh's war chest."

Becataten shook her heard. "There is so much to know about our glorious Egypt."

"Would you like to move on the Saqquara complex and see the step pyramid and my favorite building in all of Egypt.?"

"No, Mosie, I want to recline in our tent and drink cool wine that you bought me, then retire to our bedchamber.

The Viceroy ordered the charioteer to return to their tent with haste.

Reclining in lounges outside their tent and enjoying the breezes off the Mediterranean, the Viceroy turned to Becataten. "More than one moon has passed Becataten, and it is time that we leave this place of love and sublime living. I must return to Kush, or my Nubian workers will forget who Viceroy Merymose is, not to mention Pharaoh's demands on me."

Lazy and enjoying the pleasant breeze off the Great Sea, Becataten reached for her goblet of wine made from a special date palm. She reclined, dressed in a silk translucent shift belted at the waist with a strap of hammered gold. Every morning Isis freshened her makeup when necessary. Together they had found many new cosmetics in the local markets adding to her chest of paints. Her artfully painted lips pouted in the breeze that wafted over them. "Oh, Mosie, I knew this would come to an end, but couldn't you manage the mines through your envoys a little longer?"

"I cannot, Princess," he said with a touch of sternness. "If we are not careful, Pharaoh will seek me out. And as you know his demand for gold grows every Ra to complete his massive mortuary temple. That means I must return to the excavations and see for myself if the mines are still in full production."

Becataten sighed. "Yes, I understand, Mosie. When shall we go? We have accumulated so many goods to take home." She looked inside the now-crowded tent. "And where shall we call home?" A crease crossed Becataten's brow. "I can no longer live at the Suti Estate. That was only appropriate when the babies were a few moons old. You can no longer live like a bachelor in my father's house in the date grove." Her forehead crease turned into a frown. "And we certainly can't take your royal apartment at the Palace."

The Viceroy was in pensive thought when an envoy approached bearing one of many messages he had received since their stay at Giza. Becataten noticed that the papyrus was secured with architect Suti's clay seal, and she sat up from her lounge, curious. Scanning the document, he seemed amused. "The Heka priest must be right about you having second sight, Princess. Suti sends word that... here, you read it."

Becataten read the missive. In red hieroglyphs it announced that construction had begun on a large house at the Suti's Estate; a gift from Pharaoh to Becataten for having delivered royal twins.

Becataten's eyes grew animated, and she squealed. "Oh, how perfect! I will see that the attendants ready our goods for transport immediately! And Mosie, can we not commission another vessel to take all these fine goods we have accumulated?"

"Yes, we will probably have to do that. I will put the captain in charge of that. I will be sailing alone on a swift and small craft to Kush, so you will take the Golden Falcon. You will have most of my crew. Will that suit you, Princess?"

"Yes, of course," she quickly answered, though she would always savor the memories of their lovely time in Memphis. *And I won't tell Mosie that in the second vessel I will send our twins home to the Suti Estate, so they will be out of Pharaoh's grasp, and I would like to be on my own again for a time.* "And Mosie, can you order a chariot, now, for us to travel to the step pyramid so I can see King Djoser's funerary temple up close before we leave?"

The Viceroy showed surprise. "I thought you forgot about that."

"How could I forget to see Imhotep's funerary temple? Did you not say it is your favorite building in all of Egypt?"

"Yes, I did, some time ago," the Viceroy edged into the conversation.

As Maja headed toward Becataten she was halted by her active armload of twins, now six moons in age. They squirmed and fidgeted in her arms. But Maja showed an effort to stand and listen to her mistress. Isis came forth and stood beside Maja after Becataten beckoned her near as well.

"Maja, give the twins to the wet nurses, and come to me," Becataten commanded. When Maja arrived, Becataten continued. "Have someone shake those carpets of their sand, roll them tight, and secure them well. Use the Viceroy's discarded papyrus scrolls to pack glass perfume bottles that I bought in the marketplace. And the jars of wine must be carefully loaded onto the vessel in the lowest compartment. All my new silks and shawls and garments put in one chest. The clothes I arrived with can be folded and bundled. And, Maja, the pearls and earrings the Viceroy bought me, put in my jewel chest and set under my deck chair." Maja nodded as she backed away trying to remember everything to begin the process of packing up, and noting that Becataten had become far more demanding during this stay in Memphis.

Becataten then motioned Maja to come close and whispered to her. "You and the wet nurses will return to the Suti Estate alone. I along with Isis will follow in a few days after visiting Pharaoh's mortuary temple." Maja took a step back, shocked and saddened by the decision the princess had made.

Becataten didn't like Maja's reaction to returning the twins to the Suti Estate and took it out on Isis. Sharply she called. "Isis, be sure all my new paints are in my cosmetic chest, and that beautiful oil of the gardenia, don't forget that." Becataten headed for the tent while removing her gold belt. "Isis, I also need a new gown, quickly!" She said. Maja and Isis exchanged looks of concern at Becataten's harshness. Then Maja turned away to hide her grave concern.

The Viceroy left to speak to his captain about a second vessel for hauling additional goods that Becataten had acquired, as well as a small craft for his sail to Nubia. Then he ordered a chariot for he and Becataten for traveling to his favorite temple built by Architect Imhotep.

Outside the tent, the Viceroy sat quietly waiting for Becataten to join him for their chariot ride to Saqquara where the step pyramid stood, when Maja approached. She looked sad and ill at ease.

"What is it Maja?" asked Merymose.

"Taten will go away when you leave, Viceroy," she said, with her head downcast.

"What do you mean, Maja? Explain yourself?"

"Taten will go to Pharaoh where he builds his big house for his death."

"Why do you believe this, Maja?" The Viceroy asked sitting straight in his chair.

With hesitance, as though she was betraying Becataten, Maja went on. "Taten told your captain to stop at that place. The twins go in second boat with the twins and me."

A quiet anger came over the viceroy. "Are you saying that the Princess ordered a sail to where the two large statues stand at Pharaoh's mortuary temple?"

"Yes, that place," Maja said, nearly inaudibly.

The Viceroy stared out into the vast delta, controlling his rising anger.

"Thank you, Maja. That will be all."

The two-horse chariot sped along the Mother Nile just outside her muddy banks, traveling as fast as the stallions could carry them. Becataten wasn't wearing a wig, and her golden earrings were flying. The wind on her head and face exhilarated her. Her crisply pleated shift of sheer linen clung to her newly shaped body. After the birth of the twins her breasts had swelled, her hips had rounded and she seemed to be formed anew and even more beautiful, like a finely carved statue. She knew she looked her best, and thought it was probably a good idea not to breast feed her twins. *I wouldn't want to look like those wet nurses.*

"There it is Mosie," she called. "Oh, you can see why all the architects that went after Imhotep were given his name. He was the greatest architect ever, wasn't he, Mosie?"

"Maybe even as great as Pharaoh Amenhotep III," the Viceroy answered, with a bite to his words. Making a swift halt before the temple, his strong arms held the reigns of the lathered horses hard. "Do you want to walk the inside of the building? I can pay a caretaker to let us in," he said with indifference.

"No, I know the columned interior well enough from reviewing the plans at the royal library. What I would like is to drive the perimeter of the step pyramid before we leave, though."

"Yes, I forget how your interest in architecture always takes precedence? You must be very anxious to get to the building of our new house, forgive me, *your* house..."

Becataten interrupted. "Don't be silly, of course it's our house, and yes, I am anxious to oversee its construction. After all, I have to get there before Pharaoh spends all the gold in his treasury on his temple. I want something left for our home," she said playfully.

When the Viceroy turned toward her, it was not to inspect her beauty this time. "Count on me to mine the gold. I am sure I can count on you and Pharaoh to spend it on architecture," The Viceroy said through his teeth.

Becataten was taken aback by his words and the anger that suddenly flared in him. She wanted to soften his sour mood, thinking that he must be jealous that Pharaoh had gifted her with a house. She snuggled up to him, squeezing him around his middle. Her perfume of gardenia surrounded him, but not with its usual effect. She looked into his dark eyes. "Actually, I was thinking about the stone Pharaoh is using for his temple. The boats coming from the Aswan quarries pass the Suti Estate. I don't see why we couldn't appropriate a few."

The viceroy's answer was calloused. "You mean steal."

"That's a bit harsh," Becataten said. "I would just like a few pieces of granite for statuary," she pouted. "Wouldn't it be grand to have a carved image of Imhotep at our entrance?"

But Becataten got no response from the Viceroy. *If I encounter Pharaoh at his mortuary site, I will ask him to gift me the stones.* She watched him turn their chariot around, make a fast run around the perimeter of the step pyramid, then drive the horses back to the tent at a fierce pace. Observing him, she thought she saw both sadness and anger consuming him. Why would that be?

Chapter 30

♊

The night before leaving Memphis, the Viceroy could not sleep. His mind worked like a mad monkey as he reviewed the news Maja had brought him earlier. Finally, he rose from their bed to dress in the dark and quiet. He secured an unadorned leather kilt around his waist, adding a wide collar and cuffs of gold. He reached for a pot of kohl and with haste outlined his eyes with the black sun guard. Pausing for a moment to look down at Becataten, he resisted the urge to kiss her goodbye.

Walking quickly to the far corner of the tent, he drew back a hanging carpet that paneled off the nursery. The wet nurses were asleep in a corner of the enclosure. The twins rested peacefully, swaddled in their baskets, with Maja lying between them on the floor. As he leaned down to see his babes, he touched their checks and whispered. "Until we meet again, my girl child, Jeser. May the God Heka protect you with your second sight. And to my boy child, Mishi, may God Horus protect you, my world traveler.

Then with an abrupt turn he left to seek out his captain on board the Golden Flacon. Accustomed to rising before dawn, the captain was waiting on deck drinking a large cup of fenugreek tea, sitting next to his perched parrot that he was feeding sunflower seeds. "My Lord." the captain said, as he stood offering a bow.

The Viceroy cleared his throat. "I understand that the Princess has given you instructions to stop at Pharaoh's funerary temple on the west bank before going on to the Suti Estate," he said, reaching for a crate to sit on.

"Yes, the Princess did so, Viceroy, I was waiting to tell you this before you went on ahead to the mines," the captain said apologetically.

The Viceroy's hand rose, "No need to discuss this. Let her do as she pleases, just stay with her. If she stays in Thebes, you stay in Thebes. I will not return from Kush for some time," The Viceroy said with sorrow in his voice and face. "Eventually I will expect you to join me in Kush, but not until you have delivered the Princess from Thebes to the Suti Estate," the Viceroy said in an even voice, "and it is my belief that that may be some time from now. You have gold, silver, and copper debon for any expenses that you may incur, have you not?" the Viceroy asked.

"I do," answered the captain.

"The second boat carries the twins and Maja and is packed with goods the Princess collected during our stay?"

"Yes, my Lord."

Standing the viceroy added, "Send me a scroll only if something extraordinary happens, otherwise, it is goodbye."

Then, with a deep bow the captain said, "The crew and I will miss you, My Lord."

After stepping off The Golden Falcon, a litter carried the Viceroy to a nearby dock, where he boarded a smaller craft, built for speed. Sitting stone faced in the middle of the vessel, his oarsmen were asked to row with hast for a full day, so as to arrive in Kush before the sun left Egypt.

Becataten woke when the large linen pavilion brightened. "Maja, Ra is here! Where is the Viceroy, and why didn't you wake me? We need to sail to Thebes now!" she called, sounding like a spoiled child.

Maja called back, "The Viceroy said he had to leave early." Then she bent next to Isis, who was on her knees packing a chest and whispered in her ear, "You take the ginger tea to Taten." Maja feared her face would betray her words to the Viceroy.

"He left already? Without saying goodbye to me?" Becataten asked, a pout forming on her lips. Her sad expression caused Maja to look away.

"Maybe it was too hard for him to say goodbye to his beloved Taten," Maja said in a small voice.

"I suppose that is true," Becataten said, as she sat for Isis to ready her for the day. We had the most wonderful time together here in Memphis," then she grew quiet as Isis began gathering her jars of face paint. Maja sighed, grateful for no more words.

Under sail, Becataten called from her chair on The Golden Falcon. "Captain, when shall we be in Thebes at the Palace docks?"

"We are nearly there, Princess."

Craning her neck about, Becataten smiled. "You're right, of course we are, I can see Pharaoh's giant stone effigies coming into view. And look, there is the beautiful *Kha-em-Maat*," Becataten said, covering her brow for a shaded view of the royal barge. "Can we moor there, Captain?" she asked.

"Yes, Princess."

"Good, as we discussed, I want both boats to dock here. Then I want to send the twins and their wet nurses along with Nanny Maja and most of my attendants and goods to move on to the Suti Estate in the second craft."

The Captain bowed. "I will see that the second craft sails with my assistant skipper, and I will stay here with you Princess Becataten," replied the captain, honoring his orders from the Viceroy.

When Maja heard these words, she drew back. Becataten saw her do so.

"Maja, come to me, I wish to talk to you."

Like an anxious child again, Becataten couldn't wait to disembark and see the mortuary temple site of Pharaoh Amenhotep. She convinced herself that sending the twins ahead to the Suti Estate was for their protection against Pharaoh's desire for them. And slipping in a visit to the mortuary temple could do no harm. The Heka in her was speaking against the plans she had put into motion, but she wasn't listening.

A wet nurse reached for the twins so Maja could climb the ladder to Becataten's chair. Maja looked weary. Becataten raised her head empirically. "Maja, I want you to sail with the twins to the Suti Estate in the second boat. I will be along in a few Ras, no longer than a half moon, and..."

Maja spoke slowly, and in a soft voice. "Taten, I mean you no ill, but I fear you have become a mother who no longer cares for her children."

Becataten looked startled, as though someone had doused her face with cold water. Her voice grew shrill. "How dare you accuse me? Of course I care for my twins!"

Standing as straight as she was able, Maja continued, her voice growing bold. "No, my fine lady, you care first about Pharaoh, then what he builds. You have forgotten that the Lord of the Land wants your babies. And you forget what a good man you marry."

Everything on board came to a standstill. Conversations stopped, crewmembers stood silent, all chores ceased.

Becataten's mouth tightened. "You are dismissed."

But Maja moved closer to Becataten, and she placed a hand on Becataten's shoulder and pleaded. "Taten, please not go to Pharaoh, come home with children."

"Don't touch me, Maja, you have overstepped yourself. I will do as I please."

"You have forgotten, Taten, that I was a slave to your mother. On her death bed she begged me to raise you and Jobu as Pharaoh's children, although we knew you were not. I washed your bottom from time you born and watched over you and Jobu like my own." Maja continued.

Becataten stood from her chair, narrowed her eyes, then slapped Maja's face, hard enough to send the old woman to one knee.

Gasps of astonishment rumbled across the deck.

Becataten quickly descended the ladder to her chamber below. "Isis, come dress me in a fine new silk, the gold one I think," she ordered.

Maja had collected herself and was gripping the back of the wicker deck chair in view of the captain. In the cabin below, Becataten's excited voice was instructing Isis to get her clothes and face paint perfect for her visit to the temple, and Pharaoh.

After Maja dried her checks with the hem of her shift, she climbed the ladder and headed toward the foredeck. "Captain, can you make me a favor?" she asked.

Nodding, the captain motioned her to take a seat opposite him on an empty chicken crate. He and his colorful parrot were sharing toasted chickpeas. His outstretched hand offered Maja some. With a weak smile she accepted a few. The jealous parrot squawked.

"Trouble with your mistress, Maja?" asked the captain.

Maja nodded. "Can you get message to Royal Gardener Sennejem?" Maja asked.

"Are you sure you know him? That is a big title for someone like you and me to know, Maja."

Maja nodded, "I know him. Can you get message to him for me?" she asked again.

"That is easy to do, Maja. A messenger can cross the river and be at the Palace grounds before Ra moves behind the Theban hills."

"With a tired smile, Maja thanked the captain. She knew what she must do.

Chapter 31

♊

It was dusk when Sennejem stepped on board The Golden Falcon, asking for Nanny Maya. A surprised captain reached for his wig as he rushed toward the boarding ladder. "Welcome aboard Royal Gardener Sennejem, Maja awaits you," said the captain with a deep bow.

Maja told Sennejem her story of Princess Becataten abandoning the twins and asked him to send a scroll begging Pygmy Lady to come. I no trust scribe how to get message to Suti Estate, you can."

"This all sounds like it has been a terrible burden on you, Maja, and yes, I can send a message for you," Sennejem said. "Do you remember Dwarf Heby?"

Maja nodded.

"He still runs messages for me to Abu. He uses a boat most of the time but a swift charioteer when the message is urgent, and this sounds urgent. I will do as you ask. Does that give you some peace, Maja?"

With her hands to her face, Maja broke down, nodding and sobbing. Sennejem put his big brown hand on her shoulder, offering comfort to his old friend Maja as she cried.

When Becataten stepped off her transport, Ra was leaving Egypt. It had taken her longer than she thought to make herself perfect for her visit. As she passed between the two colossal statues of Pharaoh, she strained for a view of the glorious architecture throughout the grounds of Pharaoh's mortuary temple, but the light was leaving. Now she realized that her beautiful costume and artfully painted face had been a waste of Ra's precious light. There was simply no light left to see the temple structures in all their glory. There were workers and architects moving about, but they were all packing up their materials to leave. A bulky man in a cape was reviewing plans that he held with outstretched arms to accommodate his aging eyes while a torch bearer stood with illumination. A group of eunuchs were ushering beautiful young women who Pharaoh must be traveling with back to a covered litter, Becataten lamented. A portable kitchen was being dismantled and carted away on donkeys. Becataten's attention traveled back to the large man, who she now observed was grossly overweight. And then she recognized him. It was Pharaoh. Her jaw dropped, and at the same time he turned, and recognized her.

When Pharaoh realized he was looking at Becataten, his smile became animated, if not lascivious. Dropping the scroll he was reviewing, his arms stretched out to her. With trepidation Becataten walked toward him. She found herself wrapped in his oppressive embrace like a giant Horus enveloping her; his hands managing to explore her body in the hug. He was poised to plant a salacious kiss upon her, but she thought his girth wouldn't allow his lips to meet hers. Yet his corpulent frame smothered her. With his heavy cape he ensconced her, his mouth devoured her. Becataten wanted to wipe her lips clean, but dared not show her revulsion, so she lowered her head like a schoolgirl. *He used to smell wonderful, now his heavy use of morenga oil smells like animal fat, and his flesh feels soft and steamy,* she thought, feeling a bit ill.

As Pharaoh took a step back from Becataten, it was to see her more clearly. "You are even more beautiful than I remembered, Princess. Some women are like this after childbirth. You are one of those women. I am most pleased to see you, Becataten," his voice was full of lust, his eyes with want. "Tell me where you are staying, and I will send word for you to come to me this evening. And our twins, I want to hear all about them, too."

Becataten managed a smile, and said she was staying on the Viceroy's ship. Pharaoh took his leave, but after a few steps she saw him look back. "The Viceroy is in Kush, is he not?" Pharaoh asked, continuing to exude lechery. Becataten offered a weak nod. *How could Pharaoh have become such a gross and unappealing man in just a few inundations? I wanted a visit and a tour not him to bed me.* As she returned to the ship, her heart sank. She wondered if her plan would work. Having seen the Pharaoh, she now was filled with doubt.

Later that evening the royal missive arrived onboard, beckoning her to the Palace. She remembered the days when excitement took her breath away at the prospect of an audience with Pharaoh. Now it was fear that took her breath away. And worse yet he still believed, or chose to believe, that she and the Viceroy's children were his. Oh, what had she wrought by visiting his mortuary temple? Instead, how she longed to be in the arms of the Viceroy tonight. With that longing, an ominous question posed itself: *Will I ever see Mosie again?* Shaking off her worry, Becataten shook her head to rid herself of the thought and returned to the present. She needed all her will and savvy to get through this evening with the Living God.

As always, Becataten had taken time to dress impeccably, yet on this occasion her feelings were troubled about wearing a beautiful gown and appear alluring. "Isis, bring a sheer, plain white shift. I will add several pieces of jewelry to enhance my look and bring my gold cape too."

Isis looked perplexed as she sought out the ordinary shift among so many striking frocks to choose from. When Isis assisted Becataten, it was a quiet and pensive mistress she dressed. All of the joy and excitement that Becataten exuded earlier was gone. Gone too was her self-assurance.

"Enter Princess Becataten of Thebes," announced a Nubian sentry, clad in a leopard skin kilt pounding the stone floor with his spear of Pharaoh's entry. Becataten stood at the portal to Pharaoh's magnificent apartment and remembered a time when the experience of seeing all this beauty in furniture, wall hangings and art from Egypt's rich vassal states was mesmerizing. She took in a deep breath and walked toward Pharaoh.

A nude harem girl of no more than twelve inundations was sitting on Pharaoh's lap dropping grapes into his mouth. Becataten had to admit she was nearly that age as well when Pharaoh had intimately taken her. A eunuch sat cross-legged at Pharaoh's feet looking dejected as young girls danced to Pharaoh's command. Bells from chains around their bellies and ankles lent a soft jingle. A flute, a gentle drum and lyre played lilting music. Incense wafted from standing braziers at the four corners of the chamber. Food trays of honeyed fruits and cakes were all placed within

Pharaoh's reach, and the Royal Butler kept Pharaoh's wine goblet filled with sma.

How much it took to titillate Pharaoh now. *My audiences with him when he was a younger king, were not like this,* she thought. How could she now offer him more than he already had at his command? There must be something he wanted, or he would not have requested her presence and so quickly. She prayed to all the gods of Egypt that it wasn't her twins alone that he coveted.

"Greetings, My Lord," Becataten said as she approached him. But he was engrossed in the young girl on his lap and did not respond. She saw his butler tap an ear, indicating that Pharaoh's hearing had lessened. She decided to sit in a nearby chair and see how long it would take for Pharaoh to realize that she had arrived. Becataten prayed to the Goddess Hathor, who was associated with drunkenness, and asked her to help the Living God drink himself to sleep.

Becataten watched as Pharaoh fondled the young girl on his lap, his mouth sucking on her breasts that were no larger than small figs. She had to remind herself that in Egypt lovemaking had to be enjoyed by both. If one person said no, lovemaking stopped. Yet she wondered if this child knew such freedom or how or when to use it.

And how would Pharaoh respond if she, Becataten, refused his desires?

Becataten watched Pharaoh continue to imbibe and pleasure himself until it began to look as if her audience may have been forgotten. But then she heard her name mentioned as Pharaoh beckoned his butler. When the butler indicated where she was, Becataten stood and walked to Pharaoh's large chair filled with soft pillows. He pushed the young girl aside and patted a place for her to sit. *Oh how I remember the patting of the chair. The slave trader taught me that. How long ago?* she thought, memories of another time in this very hall flooding back to her.

Becataten sat and decided to talk after Pharaoh told her to speak. She remembered when she had her first audience with Pharaoh, and before arriving she had the slave trader from the Suti Estate explain coupling to her. But she did not wish to remind Pharaoh of coupling with her, so she said simply, "this hall brings back many fond memories."

Pharaoh beamed with the memories himself, and a small part of him from the past came back to the present. He smiled with his eyes that looked warm and friendly for a moment, then he roared, remembering that first meeting.

"You, Becataten, I should have taken as a queen. Do you know why I did not?" he asked.

I had no idea he ever dreamt of me as his queen, Becataten thought. She murmured, "I confess I do not, My Lord."

"It was Queen Tiye who was against it," Pharaoh continued. "When she and I married, I gave her my oath that she could reject any future queens I might choose, and you were one of her rejections. Then you had twins with the Viceroy," he slurred.

A sense of some relief came over her when she heard his admission that the twins were not his. But she returned to the hope that she may outlast him at staying awake. That is until she felt his hands upon her breasts.

"That's right, relax my beauty," he said as he struggled to get closer to her. "Won't you sit on my member as you did so long ago, Becataten, my lost queen?"

By the Gods, he has become senile. I must try and manipulate him.

"No, Pharaoh, I will not, but I will drink another glass of sma to this night and a celebration of our reunion." *He has my shift down around my waist and is making full use of his hands, but his bulk can't draw me nearer. I can see why he wants me on his lap,* she thought.

"Yes," Pharaoh called loudly to his butler, "More sma for my lost queen. Shush," he giggled. "We wouldn't want Queen Tiye to hear that."

"Pharaoh, I think it is time for bed." Becataten said.

"Yes, yes," his expression remained animated. With the aid of two sentries he was laid on his grand bed, then with care his butler stripped him of his clothing and jewelry. "Come to me Becataten, I want you."

Bare breasted, Becataten walked to his bed and stood over him. He stared up at her. "Oh, Princess Becataten, you have come back," he said reaching for her. Then like an obelisk being erected, his member rose. But soon after, it fell like a lotus too long out of water. The next sound was Pharaoh's snoring. The butler's nodded, whispering, "Well done lost Queen."

Relieved, Becataten exhaled a great sigh, pulled her shift up around her shoulders, reached for her wrap, and feeling freedom, strolled toward the entryway. The sentries opened the massive cedar doors that allowed her exit as the butler came up behind her. "You are to be housed in the next apartment over, Princess

Becataten. Pharaoh wishes you to be at his disposal, and to see the twins as soon as possible."

Becataten nodded as she hurried to the neighboring apartment being shown to her, wishing Isis would already be there waiting for her. But alas, she was not, and Becataten was alone. As she stripped herself of her clothing and wig, she wondered how she would break it to Pharaoh that she was in Thebes alone, and that her twins had been sent off with her entourage.

Chapter 32

♊

Pygmy Lady had Dwarf Heby read the scroll that Sennejem composed and had sent. She left immediately upon hearing that Becataten needed her in Thebes. She knew Maja would not have asked Sennejem to summon her if it were not important. For some time, her magic had told her that Becataten and her twins were facing a menace. Pygmy Lady, with little description but much urgency spoke to Abu about his daughter's need. At Abu's specific command, Stable Master Senzar was assigned to drive Pygmy Lady to Thebes.

For additional speed, Senzar rigged a four-horse chariot he had been experimenting with. Not long into their travel, the animals were not running well together. Soon they were stalled, and Pygmy Lady was holding a torch high for Senzar as he changed his chariot back to a two-horse vehicle. Ra had left Egypt and it was not an easy task to make harness alterations in the dark of an Egyptian night. It seemed that the design of a four-horse chariot had been too ambitious for the horses chosen by the Stable Master. It took all the patience Pygmy Lady had not to go into a scathing criticism of this breakdown, but she held her temper. The horses danced, making the changeover difficult. Once the two-horse rig was complete, Pygmy Lady took her stand next to Senzar in the chariot, holding the lighted pole high. Senzar's drive to the docks at Thebes was unmercifully fast. And although the Stable Master had to leave two horses behind, trained as they were, they merely trailed the chariot.

Pygmy Lady stepped off the vehicle spinning, and standing without equilibrium, holding a pole with no flame. "You drove me here fast, Senzar, with your two-horse rig. Go back to the Estate and stay with a two-horse rig," she said. Then she weaved toward the dock like a baboon that had gotten into a jug of beer.

Sensing she was near the Viceroy's vessel, she queried a squatting man whose round eyes showed surprise at the sight of a pygmy. He affirmed that the vessel she was looking for was near, and gladly rowed her across the river to the east bank, showing her much deference along the way. Everyone in Egypt knew pygmies were magical people.

After a short walk, Pygmy Lady gained her stability, spied the Viceroy's vessel, and jumped on board. It was deep into the dark time. The captain's parrot squawked. She hissed back, which quieted the bird. The captain and Pygmy Lady had been loyal to the Viceroy for many inundations. When the captain approached, it was with a torch, he spoke quickly, realizing who it was. "The Princess is with Pharaoh, he summoned her just after Ra left Egypt, Pygmy Lady."

Pygmy Lady nodded as she stood and rubbed her chin, then she called to a Nubian sailor and asked for a large round basket and a piece of linen for her bed. "Nothing to do until Ra comes," she said, coiling herself in her usual habit like a serpent into the round wicker container to sleep during the dark night.

Dawn soon brightened the river and woke Egypt's water birds. It also brought a messenger in a small boat to The Golden Falcon with a request from Becataten. The envoy said the Princess had sent for her cosmetic chest and Isis. Pygmy Lady quickly saw the advantage of accompanying Isis back to Becataten's new palace apartment. When the large coffer containing Becataten's facial paints and her jewelry was placed in the papyrus rowboat, Pygmy Lady settled herself next to Isis.

Having crossed the Mother Nile and transferred to a litter, the two women jostled toward the Palace. "You who carry us to the Palace," Pygmy Lady said to the lead barer, "How can I find you if I want to go back to the boat?" she asked.

"We will leave a small boy outside your chamber door, you can tell him and we will come," the bearer replied.

Pygmy Lady nodded.

As the bearers came near Becataten's door, the lead man raised a hand. "We have to wait here little pygmy, Queen Tiye is passing with her retinue."

Pygmy Lady watched as Queen Tiye's Royal Guard required entrance to Becataten's chamber. Pygmy Lady hid herself in the crowd for a long wait as Pharaoh's first and most powerful queen to exit the apartment. The sight of the queen and her entourage leaving Becataten's assigned royal quarters created an ominous feeling in Pygmy Lady's gut.

Carefully, Pygmy Lady took stock of what she could remember about the queen. Queen Tiye and Amenhotep III had been beautiful young rulers, marrying for love when they were twelve. Now they were three times that age. Together they had two children, both boys, but only one lived, and that was Young Horus, who Princess Becataten had befriended.

Pharaoh shocked Egypt when he chose her for his queen, as she was from a merchant-class family. Her abilities with language and diplomacy were great. He embraced her and her family with titles and additional fortune. He further shocked his people allowing Queen Tiye more privilege, luxury, and freedom in the Royal Court than any woman in the known world.

Pygmy Lady's eyes followed the queen closely. "Her cheek bones are set high on her face, her skin the color of brown bread, and she has the face of one who carries Nubian blood," whispered Pygmy Lady to Isis, who stood beside her.

A Nubian bearer overheard her. "So it is said, little one."

Pygmy Lady did not add that this was a woman full with secreted ambition and would one day stand behind the throne of Young Horus to run Egypt.

Becataten looked up from rubbing her temples when Pygmy Lady entered with Isis and a Nubian courier balancing the coffer on his head using but one hand. Tension filled the room as Isis quickly directed a Nubian to carry the chest of facial paints, jewelry, and perfumes to the bedchamber. Isis followed meekly. Becataten's clothing and other personal belongings were still on the boat.

Becataten's drained face was as worn as her makeup after Queen Tiye's visit. She felt no better when she saw the expression of disgust on Pygmy Lady's face. "You look terrible," Pygmy Lady said.

"You would too, if Pharaoh pursued you like the jackal hunts the rabbit," snapped Becataten.

"I want to hear about your visit to Pharaoh, and tell me about the queen's visit," Pygmy Lady said, standing next to Becataten chair. "Leave nothing out," she demanded.

When Becataten finished telling all, she was weeping.

"Spare me your tears, Princess, you did this to yourself. Now you must outwit a king, and maybe a queen too," she said, then spit on the floor.

Becataten attempted to speak in her defense, but Pygmy Lady's hand went up.

"Don't defend your desire to be with Pharaoh. I think if he were not such a fat man, you would choose him over the Viceroy?"

"Of course, I wouldn't. I miss Mosie with all my heart and I wish he were here," whimpered Becataten. I was forced here, I mean summoned here, and thought if Pharaoh wanted to see the twins I could say that they were suffering an ailment and I returned them to the Suti Estate.

Pygmy Lady's eyes bored into Becataten. "And let me guess, he didn't ask about the twins. What did the queen want?"

Warily, Becataten shook her head. "I was told she had her attendants examined my quarters to see if I had all I needed, but I could tell she had some ulterior motive," Becataten said.

"Amazing, Becataten, you are beginning to listen to your Heka. Where did her attendants poke around?" Pygmy Lady asked.

"Everywhere, I think, but mostly in my bedchamber." Becataten said, trying to remember the movements of the queen's servants. "She said she was leaving me some linens and covered cushions for my bed..."

Becataten followed Pygmy Lady into the chamber and watched her pull apart her bedding, even lifting the goose down mattress off its frame. "What are you doing to my bed?" called Becataten. "It was just freshly made!"

"Quiet!" called Pygmy Lady, ". . . and somebody, get me a spear!"

Becataten, Isis, and several attendants gathered at the entrance to Becataten's bedchamber. With concern, they all stepped aside as two Nubian sentries came running forward with their weapons held high. But instead of handing Pygmy Lady a spear, a guardsman flung his arms out, motioning everyone back. Becataten watched Pygmy Lady bend to scrutinize a red floor pillow, when a guard lifted her by the waist and set her down several feet away. Becataten motioned Isis back as the Nubians circled the red cushion. Stepping forward Pygmy Lady yelled, "Kill the serpent, kill it!" she shouted. The attendants stood perfectly still, then stepped forward with care to see better. Isis began to scream. Becataten put a hand to her mouth, as she saw the Nubians repeatedly stabbed at the crimson colored cushion until a wounded asp slithered out.

The Viceroy's vessel that Becataten had sent to the Suti Estate with the twins and her overabundance of goods docked. It had been a leisurely sail and had taken two days. Many of the field workers came to celebrate their arrival. The disembarking passengers were Maja, the twins, and wet nurses. Attendants followed, helping to carry the magnitude of cargo from Becataten's buying trips.

Lady Nagara sitting on her litter looked worried. She had not heard from Becataten nor did she know of

Pygmy Lady's mission to the Palace. She motioned for Maja. "Where is the Princess, Nanny Maja?"

Not raising her head, Maja remained silent. nervously working her sandals into the sand.

"Answer me Maja. Is something wrong?"

Nodding her head, her eyes downcast, Maja's voice was nearly inaudible.

"Speak louder and tell me at once where Becataten is, Maja," demanded Lady Nagara.

Maja did not raise her head but spoke more clearly. "You must ask Becataten's father, Master Abu," she said, and then Maja spoke no further, but turned away and went back to watching the twins.

Chapter 33

Ⅱ

Kombo offered Abu his good arm and said, "This way, Master, we are following the butler to Lady Nagara's receiving chamber." They crossed the stone floor of the Estate entry where Lady Nagara waited. The two broken men moved about until Abu was seated and placed his walking stick on his lap.

"Do you need further assistance, Master?" Kombo asked.

Abu shook his head. Kombo's bow and exit were followed by an uneasy silence that stilled the air.

Lady Nagara watched Abu finger the fold of the linen cloth that covered his mutilated eye sockets. *How long would it take him to engage in conversation?* She could barely observe him as he adjusted his chair pillows and fiddled with his walking stick, using those mutilated hands. The time returned to her when she had witnessed the execution of Abu's blindness. It made her shudder. She felt relief from her thoughts when she heard his voice.

"It has been good of you and Architect Suti to allow me the house of your previous estate manager," said Abu in his old strong voice.

"Yes, it has. I assume you are comfortable there?" said Lady Nagara.

"I am," replied Abu.

"Well, after all you live in that house with my new Estate manager, Ahmose, do you not?" Lady Nagara asked.

"I do, and of course with Kombo as well. Pygmy Lady comes and goes,"

Lady Nagara sat straight in her chair adjusting her beaded collar, her chin held high, not really wanting all of that information that felt beneath her to even know about. "From my understanding, the Viceroy's son, Ahmose, has proven to be an efficient manager of my crops," Lady Nagara said in a cool voice. "And I presume Kombo is your man servant. But I cannot grasp anyone's affinity for Pygmy Lady."

Not waiting for a reply, she continued, "I must tell you that I have asked you here because Maja says you know the whereabouts of Becataten." She clapped her hands for refreshments. Servants jumped to serve them.

With a downcast head, Abu seemed to be struggling with his response. "Pygmy Lady is with the Princess as we speak,' he said.

"And where, pray to the Gods, is that?" asked Lady Nagara.

"I believe Pharaoh has cloistered Becataten in a royal apartment for his pleasure and requires that the twins come to live there also." Abu said.

"What!" said Lady Nagara, shocked by this news. "And where *is* the Viceroy?"

With apologies, Lady Nagara's Butler entered the room with a missive, explaining its urgency. "My Lady, a scroll from Queen Tiye has arrived. The envoy says the Queen wishes an immediate reply," he said, handing her the papyrus scroll bearing Queen Tiye's seal.

After reading the content, Lady Nagara wilted, "Abu, you best listen to this as well."

Lady Nagara cleared her throat and took a sip of wine to calm herself before reading the scroll aloud:

Dear Lady Nagara,

As you and I have been friends since we were children, I feel obliged to inform you of the status of your ward, Princess Becataten. Currently she resides within the Palace due to the benevolence of Pharaoh. It seems the Viceroy has abandoned her. She is without attendants other than a woman named Isis who is but a face painter, and a strange pygmy who claims to have seen an asp in Becataten's apartment. The Princess also has forsaken her children by sending them away. She appears most unwell, and I find it necessary to return her to your Estate. She will arrive traveling in a modest boat within a moon.

I hope you are able to restrain this woman who obviously needs care and confinement. Know that in her lifetime Princess Becataten of Thebes is unwelcome at the Palace, or on its grounds. Further, the house once proposed by Pharaoh to be erected on the Suti Estate for her is no longer valid. I remind you purely as a friend that you and the Architect Suti were lent the Estate you most profitably operate due to Pharaoh's royal generosity.

I wish a response to this missive.

The First Queen,

Queen Tiye

Lady Nagara dropped the scroll in her lap and expelled a great breath. "Well, how does one respond to those threatening words?"

Abu's posture grew bold. "You respond simply and immediately, Lady Nagara. First, agree with her in every way. Acknowledge Pharaoh's benevolence, the Viceroy's justified leave, and say that Becataten is a negligent mother in need of your care and that you understand she should be returned to the Estate without ceremony," his words were animated as he spoke.

"One can clearly understand why you were Pharaoh's chief advisor for many years, Abu," said Lady Nagara.

"This has nothing to do with Pharaoh, My Lady, this is Queen Tiye speaking. These are her words. Pharaoh often had me soften the Queen's bluntness in the scrolls that I wrote for her. I advise that you write this response quickly before Pharaoh becomes involved, or you will see your ward and my daughter, as well as the twins, sequestered indefinitely at the Palace. And be not deceived, the mention of the asp confirms that a threat was made upon Becataten's life. Pygmy Lady does not lie and knows her snakes."

Lady Nagara placed her hand upon her chest and motioned for a nearby servant to begin fanning her with an ostrich feather as she began getting ready to reply to Queen Tiye's thinly veiled threats.

Chapter 34

♊

Lady Nagara was impressed with Abu's suggested response to Queen Tiye's scroll, so much so that she allowed him her library and household scribe to quickly complete it.

Rolling out a fresh piece of papyrus, the scribe had just gathered his inkpot and stylus when Abu began. Abu's words were quickly dictated to the sitting recorder, who wasn't accustomed to such speed and competency of speech when taking dictation from Lady Nagara.

"The return scroll is ready," said Abu clapping his hands. This brought the sound of slapping sandals across the stone floor of Lady Nagara's library. "Yes, Master, I'm ready," said the envoy.

It was clear that Abu had enjoyed dictating the answer to Queen Tiye's scroll. Lady Nagara watched him relax back in his chair. Having been brutally blinded by his half-brother, Pharaoh, he was damaged in body only. His ability to make quick and sage decisions was still his talent. When he addressed the envoy, his voice was one that compelled people to listen.

"How would you like a swift ride to the Palace in a chariot, messenger?"

With an expanded chest the man said, "I would like that very much, Master."

"Good, we shall see that you return by that means. But first you must carefully listen to what I say."

Lady Nagara's interest piqued at his remark, as she waved to her butler to arrange a chariot to drive the envoy to the Palace.

Abu continued. "When you arrive at the Palace you will deliver this scroll to but one attendant in the household of Queen Tiye. Do you understand?"

"Yes, Master," he replied.

"You will ask at the queen's door for her secretary and place this scroll in his hands only. This man is squat, wears a henna colored wig and is fat. Do you know of him?"

"I do not, but I will find him, Master."

"Yes, you will, because the chariot driver will accompany you to the queen's apartment, and when the scroll is properly delivered, the driver will see that you receive a piece of silver debon the size of your thumb," Abu said.

A vague smile crossed Lady Nagara's lips as she saw Abu enjoy himself. She was relieved that the answer to Queen Tiye's scroll was to be executed with speed and efficiency, not to mention delivered to the right hands. She knew her next task was to find Suti and explain this all to him.

"Abu, what do you think is the safest way to get word to Suti about Queen Tiye's threatening message?"

It didn't take Abu long to answer. "Send no scroll. After this missive is delivered, have the charioteer inquire with the director of public works as to what project Suti and Hor are working on. Instruct the driver to tell Suti to return home at his earliest convenience. Do nothing more."

Becataten called, "Isis, Isis! The door sentry says I am to go to Pharaoh very soon."

"My Lady, you have no change of dress," said Isis.

"Yes, yes I know. Just paint me a face and bring me my finest jewelry pieces as well." Earlier in the day, Becataten had asked for a porter to retrieve clothing from her waiting vessel but there had been no response. This was her second night in her Palace confines, and she had just seen Pharaoh the night prior. She felt unclean and sickened to return to him. Becataten stood after Isis had done her best to paint her face and sponge her body with a small piece of linen. Poised at Pharaoh's apartment, flanked by Nubian sentries, Becataten breathed deeply with false confidence as she waited.

Smoothing out her shift, she stood at the King's door and heard her name. "Princess Becataten of Thebes," called a Nubian of the Royal Guard. The huge chamber had lost all of its enchantment for her, and based on the night before, she could only agonize what was next.

"Becataten," slurred Pharaoh. "Come to me," he motioned. "Come to me!" he said as he pushed away a server with a tray of cooked peacock, decorated with the bird's colorful feathers.

Becataten bowed deeply. "Pharaoh, how nice of you to call for me," she said.

He took her wrist and gently pulled her to his lounge. "Becataten, we did couple last night, did we not? I seem to remember that it was wonderful."

Becataten nodded, thinking that it was best to let his memory be. Her words of last night rescued her from copulating, so tonight she would try the same again. "Pharaoh, how far along is the completion of your mortuary temple?" she asked.

"Ah, you still love architecture like your Pharaoh," he said as he pulled her shift off her shoulders and began fondling her breasts.

The butler offered her pomegranate wine in a gold goblet, which she eagerly reached for. "Are those plans on the table for the temple, Pharaoh?" Becataten said, as she stood and walked to the large papyrus of drawings. Maneuvering the few steps to the table, she shuddered while pulling her shift up around her shoulders. *Please, Goddess Hathor, bring drunkenness to our king as you did last night!"* she whispered.

As Becataten reviewed the architectural plans on the heavy papyrus, she thought she heard something behind her. She turned but no one was there. She took a moment to observe the elaborately painted wall; a painting of Pharaoh fishing and hunting birds on the Mother Nile. It depicted him standing in his boat, and Lady Mui with her dark eyes looking up at the flocks of birds overhead.

Pharaoh rose and staggered to the temple plans, then drew her close to him with a firm arm. "Did you know that I am having Goddess Sekhmet figures carved, one for every Ra of the year?" he asked. His voice was slurred but not as heavily as the night before.

Becataten turned to face him. "My, that will be magnificent to see so many lion-headed Goddesses. Where will you place them Pharaoh?" She pointed to the map drawn that was open on the large table.

Pharaoh called for a chair to sit before the drawings. "You can see it all, can't you my Princess? Not everybody reads plans as clearly as we do," he said,

266

reaching up and caressing her breasts while reviewing the renderings of Goddess Sekhmet. "More drink!" called Pharaoh, "I want my special cup. Becataten, won't you join me?"

Pharaoh was now so interested in his plans that he forgot about fondling her. Becataten nodded, glad for the opportunity to get more drink into him.

"Yes, Pharaoh, thank you," she said, but as the butler went off to prepare Pharaoh's request, she caught the servant's eye and shook her head. She knew he understood that she had no desire to share Pharaoh's special cup that was made from poppy tears.

It wasn't long after their last drinks, Pharaoh was in his bed and relieved Becataten was in hers. Before sleep came to her, she thanked Goddess Hathor once again for avoiding having to bed Pharaoh. Then she thanked God Osiris for the milk that came from the scored seedpod that had put Pharaoh into his slumber.

No summon came from the court for several days, nor did little else. She was at a standstill. Thereafter she and her servants were denied movement outside the apartment, and with no walled garden attached, her quarters became stifling at midday. When she asked Palace attendants for fresh clothing from her boat, they placated her, but no items arrived. A limited amount of daily water was delivered to her, making bathing impossible. Even a request for papyrus and a pot of ink was denied her. They were served but one meal a day from Pharaoh's kitchen. Becataten had little interest in eating, unlike Pygmy Lady and Isis who savored all the food.

Then when her final visit did come, nothing had changed. She looked down at Pharaoh in his bed, and he said, "Becataten, my lost queen. I must have you come up onto me!" he ordered, but he was not awake enough to pursue the thought.

"I fear my life may be in danger," she whispered in his ear. "I hope you remember me saying this and can help me. And Pharaoh you do not want my twins, do you?"

"It is you, you my forgotten queen that I want."

Now it was clear, this man was capable of nothing. Realizing it was the Queen who commanded all, Becataten knew she would not be safe if she continued to see the Pharaoh in his bedchamber. She had to figure a way out of the Palace, for good. And her heka told that her very life depended on it.

After her last visit to Pharaoh, Pygmy Lady sat at her side to ask about every detail of the three evenings. "We are missing something," Pygmy Lady said. "Tell it all to me again." At the second telling Becataten mentioned the sound she had heard behind her while looking at the plans. At this bit of information, Pygmy Lady jumped from her chair and bullied the sentries to let her out.

Returning late that evening, Pygmy Lady looked angry when she stood before Becataten. "I have learned that we are in the hands of your Pharaoh's first and vengeful queen."

"I believe you are right Pygmy Lady, but please explain what you have learned," asked Becataten.

"It is simple! The queen spies upon you and Pharaoh through holes in his chamber walls. She watches you both through the cat's eyes. She did not stop with the asp. She will soon have you dead. We have to get out of here."

In the ensuing days, Pygmy Lady managed to craft her way in and out of the apartment. But it was clear that her powers were limited in this place. One stifling afternoon she approached Becataten. "I have convinced the Nubian sentries to let us out of here in the dark time. They know I can place a curse on them if they do not," she said.

Becataten shook her head, "That is not possible, Pygmy Lady. It is too far to the river and I have no debon to hire a chariot even if we did leave. If I just had some ink and a papyrus, we might be able to get help."

In the corner of the room came whimpering from Isis. "Please, Princess, let us leave. You are out of paints, I can't bathe you and your only shift is so soiled. Please," she whined. "This is not befitting of a royal princess like yourself!"

Becataten shook her head. "We must wait and see what comes next. I am sorry to have put you both into this situation. I know I have acted badly, and I hope you will one day forgive me." The three sat in silence in the apartment that had become more like a prison. Speaking almost to herself, Becataten said, "I came here to convince Pharaoh not to take my twins only to realized he wanted me alone, and his vengeful queen now wants me dead."

For the next few Ras, Pygmy Lady was found pacing the floors of the pent apartment while a whimpering Isis huddled in a far corner. Becataten warded off tears most of the time, but her heart ached due to the damage she had done to the people around her, and she longed for her children and the Viceroy.

A half-moon had passed when Queen Tiye's secretary pushed his way into Becataten's apartment, paying no respect for her rank. An effeminate man, his actions were steeped in pomposity. Becataten thought he looked like a huge pomegranate on sticks as he tottered toward her chair. Like some appointed court ministers, his haughty demeanor was accentuated, his drawled words mimicked court speech. "Greetings Princess Becataten. Queen Tiye sends me to tell you that arrangements have been made for your return to the Suti Estate."

Becataten attempted to cover her soiled shift with her only other article of clothing, her golden cloak.

"Many thanks," she said, trying to maintain some dignity. The secretary's address to her was condescending. "You are to exit the Palace by litter, and then on to the Mother Nile," he said, waddling back and forth before her chair, and switching at imaginary flies with his zebra tail.

Pygmy Lady's eyes narrowed into slits. "You should have a servant dye your fly switch red to match your wig," she said, curling her lips with each word.

"I do not address pygmies," said the secretary, speaking into the air.

Pygmy Lady bore her teeth like a wild animal. "But my guess is that you would copulate with one, if he were young enough."

Becataten intervened, afraid they would never be allowed to leave the Palace if this conversation escalated. "Please, let us not argue, I am interested in your instructions as to how we are to travel to the Suti Estate, Secretary," said Becataten as she forced an angry look at Pygmy Lady.

Pygmy Lady backed down from the fight as Becataten hurriedly used whatever charms she could muster to cover up the argument and get out of Pharaoh's cage.

Chapter 35

♊

Queen Tiye's reach throughout Egypt had grown wide and strong. As her husband's interest in building projects expanded, his involvement in administrative matters lessened, and his use of the poppy grew allowing the queen to expand her authority. She eagerly took on her new power.

The first queen commanded that the captain of the Viceroy's vessel move distant from the Palace docks. Knowing it broke the promise that was made to the Viceroy to wait for Becataten, the captain had no choice but to obey the queen's demand. The captain had the vessel moored down river in wait, should Princess Becataten still need the craft.

Queen Tiye further instructed her secretary to arrange Becataten's journey home be in a small papyrus boat, a common craft that fisherman used for short distances only. Two rowers, and a sail tender manned the meager boat. The three men were illiterate slaves wearing loin clothes and who knew little of sailing. It was a tight fit for six people. Pygmy Lady took a place at the bow, watching the two oarsmen and looking aft. Becataten and Isis sat next to one another in the middle of the tiny craft behind the rowers, facing forward.

This was sure to be a frightening trip and maybe a fatal one, as they knew they could encounter crocodiles along the way, especially when the Nile grew quiet after passing fishing activity alone the shore. Gripping the sides of the reed boat, Becataten now understood the disdain and vengeance that the queen held for her. Pygmy Lady was right. The queen wanted her dead. Heading south against the current, the ripples of the Nile became stronger. The women traded glances, about the dangers ahead.

After sailing a short distance, Becataten watched Pygmy Lady scan the river, then with alarm, sit erect. Becataten noticed her nod to the boat's stern as her eyes swelled. She was signaling toward the boat's wake. Becataten turned to see just the hint of a crocodile's head surfacing. The beast was well behind them but gaining. His tale had begun to sweep the water, propelling him closer. The sockets that held the giant beast's eyes rose above waterline and glistened as they came into view. Isis and the slaves had not yet seen the massive sobek. Becataten began to shake. She held her hands in a knot trying to deal with her fear. Pygmy Lady's face turned into a savage mask as she focused on the sail tender's knife. Becataten watched Pygmy Lady rush to the tender, then as fast as the sand viper takes a rat, grab the blade from the man's waist. Becataten covered her mouth to muffle a scream. Before the man could defend against Pygmy Lady, she had circled his head with her small arm. Her rapid slash across his neck splattered blood across Becataten and Isis. The man's legs danced, his arms flew to his neck then he slumped down like a sack of grain. The shocked rowers sat like stones at Pygmy Lady's speed and skill. They barely moved as she heaved the corpse off the side, nearly toppling the small craft. "You, rowers, pump those oars faster! His body will save us from that killer swimming lizard!" she said, pointing to the river with the bloodied knife. The rowers obeyed her like children. Isis, who was always quick to scream at anything was frightened into silence. The beast charged his new-found prize. With giant jaws, the crocodile gripped then thrashed his trophy about in the bloody water like a happy puppy with a toy. Becataten stared at the horrific event, hardly able to grasp what had just happened. The two remaining slaves rowed with speed upriver. Isis clung to a stunned Becataten while Pygmy Lady gloated over the outcome.

Scanning the waters, Becataten suddenly recognized the claxon sound of the Viceroy's ship; a low and long tone from an animal horn sounding across the river.

"It's about time they found us!" Said Pygmy Lady. "Head this boat toward that horn," she ordered the rowers.

As the rope ladder lowered into the Nile from the Viceroy's boat, it was with a worried look the captain reached to help Becataten climb up.

"Many apologies, Princess Becataten. We saw the sobek take a man... you, you are bloodied. Are you injured?" He pulled the princess aboard and she was offered a linen wrap by a servant. "I waited for you to return, but orders from Queen Tiye sent me away, so I waited in the rough waters of the Mother Nile."

Becataten interrupted him. "I am fine. It was in no way your fault. I am so grateful you found us, and that you waited! We are not yet safe, so let us get quickly to the Suti Estate, Captain," she said, with a drained expression. Suddenly feeling faint, she sat down and was attended to by the crew.

The Viceroy's ship was a refuge she had never really valued until this Ra. She took in the thick papyrus bundles that made up the vessel's framework, lashed together with heavy duty ropes, so unlike the shabby boat she just left. She retreated to her comfortable cabin with a cedar floor caulked with linen and beeswax and felt at home. Its bank of rowers standing by with their oars were reassuring. She had been saved from her erroneous detour and would live to see her children. Only the Viceroy was missing. *Where was he? Have I damaged our relationship that badly? Yes, I may have,* she realized with a sad heart.

Isis and Pygmy Lady trailed Becataten up the woven ladder then scurried for barley beer. While Isis quenched her thirst like a spent donkey, Pygmy Lady made demands. Becataten began to tell their horrific story to the captain, only to be interrupted by Pygmy Lady, after she greedily downed her drink.

"Jugs of water for my body," yelled Pygmy Lady as she stood in a blood-soaked leather kilt. Her command sent several Nubians to her side with splashing pots. When the containers were emptied over her, she called, "More water," showing her teeth with a mock thrust of her knife. Her pluck triggered a roar of laughter, and the towering Nubians showered her again.

Becataten then returned to settle herself on the top of her cabin in her familiar chair, turning to lament the empty seat next to her. She looked down on deck at the jovial sounds and for the first time saw Pygmy Lady laughing, gleefully exposing her filed pointy teeth.

Isis came to Becataten. "There is plenty of water on board. Would you like me to bathe you, Princess?" She said handing her a cool barley beer and a damp linen cloth.

"Yes Isis, but first listen to my words. I must say them. I know you told Pygmy Lady that I was cruel to Maja. I was, and I must apologize to her. And the children, I have neglected them too. I so want to see the twins and make it up to them," she said turning away. "I have behaved so poorly."

Isis nodded and returned to the deck where the liveliness had ended. The Nubians were back at their duties and Pygmy Lady was coiled like a viper, snoring in her linen-lined basket.

Relief and exhaustion came to Becataten as she sat above deck waiting for Isis to bring her bathing supplies. The horrendous events of the day pervaded her thoughts. Her life had not been taken, and for that she thanked all the Gods of Egypt. She envied Pygmy Lady who lived in the moment and not troubled by thoughts of the past. She said a special prayer to God Sobek for saving her. Sitting stiff in her chair, she intermittently wept, and then fell asleep, unbathed, for the duration of the sail home.

Becataten was awakened when they landed at the Suti estate. Stepping onto the docks at the Estate, she saw no one. But how could anyone know she had come when her arrival was unknown. She surveyed the richly planted land with the nearby sounds and smells of animals. A relieved sense of being home combined with a great sadness surged over her at having been such a fool to think she could indulge herself with Pharaoh and gain anything. She must get to the twins, her children that she had paid little attention to for most of their young lives. In shame, she began the long walk to the grand house with Pygmy Lady and Isis.

The three women trod in silence. Isis spoke first. "Do you think your chest of paints with all your beautiful jewelry will be returned to you, Princess Becataten?"

"Never," shot Pygmy Lady.

"I think Pygmy Lady is correct, Isis," said Becataten.

Becataten's face was unpainted, with the exception of heavy smudged kohl lines that circled her eyes. Her tattered cloak partially covered her dirty and bloodied shift. She looked down at her bony wrists, feeling older than she was. When the queen's secretary had seen her off in the small craft, she said that the cosmetics coffer must be examined for items that might belong to the court, and that perhaps it would be sent along at a later date. She was saddened that her lovely inlaid chest that Lady Nagara had gifted her had not arrived with her, but mainly because it contained the beautiful necklaces and earrings that the Viceroy had given her. *Will I lose the jewelry, and him too?* she wondered miserably.

As they walked, Abu's residence came into view first, nestled within the shaded grove. "I will go to Abu's house," said Pygmy Lady. "You, Princess, go on to the big house."

"Maybe I should stop to see my father first," said Becataten.

"No! Go to your children and go apologize to Maja. Isis told me how you hit Maja. Life always makes you pay for hurting someone innocent, so expect to be paid back." Pygmy Lady said, breaking into a run toward her home among the palms.

Becataten was struck with the many foolish things she had done and wondered what her payback would be. Would it involve the Viceroy?

Becataten stopped to take off her silver sandals that hurt her feet and were ill-serving on the long walk. She handed them to Isis. "Come, let us go and see the twins and Maja," she said.

At the mention of Maja and the children, Isis produced the smile of a jackal, "And the Viceroy, Princess! You must have missed him too," she said, then immediately covered her mouth after blurting her words.

Chapter 36

♊

Standing in the doorway at the top of the stairs, Butler pointed into the dusk, holding a small torch above Lady Nagara's head.

"What is it?" she asked, squinting at Ra's last light.

Two figures were headed toward the house. A pair of weary and dirty women came into view. A barking dog trailed them, along with curious attendants and a night guard who approached them with suspicion.

"By the Gods, it's Becataten and Isis," said Lady Nagara, running down the length of the steps, something no one had ever seen her do.

Becataten put up a hand as she saw Lady Nagara approach. "Don't touch us we are filthy!" she said.

"My dear, what has happened, are you unwell?" said Lady Nagara with a horrified look.

"We are well enough! It is so good to see you! We are grateful to be alive! And, we in are much need of baths, as you can surely see, Lady Nagara," Becataten said in a weary voice.

"You certainly are! You need tending to immediately," Lady Nagara said, unable to conceal her aversion to their shabby appearance and foul smell. She snapped her fingers for Isis to run ahead and begin preparations for Becataten's bath.

As Becataten reached the house, she saw that Maja was having difficulty navigating down the long stairway, looking as though she had become crippled.

"Maja, I am pleased to see you. What has happened?" Becataten asked! Alarmed, Becataten stepped toward her. Maja tried to bow but did not speak, and in the limited light Becataten saw that half of her face didn't move. Becataten reached out for her, turning toward Lady Nagara with a questioning look.

Lady Nagara's expression was resigned. "The healer said that her left side has been struck by a spirit. She cannot move as she used to. Speaking is difficult for her also, but Maja says there is no pain."

Becataten looked at Maja's sad face. "My Loving Nanny, I am so sorry for the pain I caused you. I hope you will forgive me."

With a nod, Maja was able to show a partial smile at Becataten's words.

Familiar attendants came forward to welcome Becataten home. The Butler paid her his respects. When she reached the top of the stairs, she saw Suti shuffling toward her. He was not looking like his old robust self and wore a shall around his shoulders.

"Suti, it is good to see you."

"And I am pleased you are home, Princess," he said, accompanied by a man who was helping him walk. "We have learned from Abu that you have had a rough time of it. Your father always seems to know what is going on at the Palace. We must talk soon, Becataten."

"Yes, we can talk after I am properly tended to," Becataten said, watching him hobble to the library with his attendant. The sight of the great man struggling made her heart hurt.

Once on the second floor, Becataten anxiously followed Lady Nagara to the nursery chamber where the twins were sleeping soundly. "Oh, they have outgrown their cradles and are so big. It is hard to believe that they have lived though one inundation. You have taken such fine care of the children, Lady Nagara," Becataten said with a lump in her throat.

"I hired very capable nannies, and they have been a blessing. They spent the day in the fishpond with them, which they adore. Do you know how much work twins require, Becataten?"

Becataten was ashamed to admit that she did not. "I shall never be able to thank you for all your help," was all she could think of to say.

"You may start by immersing yourself in a tub, Becataten. The pair of you smell like wet baboons. Then we will hear about what you have been through. But that need not be tonight. You look as though you need rest."

"Is Suti all right?" asked Becataten.

"Suti is well enough, but a nasty cough has plagued him for some time. He's been home resting for a while," said Lady Nagara

"But is he getting better?"

"A bath, Becataten!" exclaimed Lady Nagara, shooing here away.

With the help of three slaves, Isis had prepared a tub for Becataten that was laced with the oils of peppermint, lemon, and rosemary. This would be a blend to relax her mistress and encourage her to linger in a luxury that she had long gone without. Thick towels from Anatolia were stacked on a nearby bench. Copper tweezers, shaving tools, a stone of pumice, and various picks of ivory were laid out for hair removal, a pedicure, and a manicure. Lotus blossoms filled nearby vases sending a sweet aroma into the bathing chamber. The bathtub of hewn stone filled with fragrant tepid water awaited Becataten along with Isis and attendants.

Becataten rushed into the room, stepped out of her badly soiled shift and into her bathwater. "Isis you may shave my head but never mind tending to my hands or feet, just quickly bathe and oil me. I want to return to the nursery and see if the children are still asleep." Becataten lowered herself into the bub. *I know they won't remember me, but I will stay with them every Ra of their lives and watch over them until they do.*

"But I have to scrub you with natron first," said Isis. "You are so unclean."

"Yes, yes I know, but do hurry."

Isis did as she was asked, leaving behind the untapped glass vials of rose and iris fragrances. An alabaster effigy of a dwarf carrying a pot on his shoulder stood near the tub. "Would you like a little marjoram cream?" Isis asked as she reached into the container with a cosmetic spoon.

"I have no time for unguents Isis, I must go."

Avoiding the help of the attendants, Becataten quickly dried herself with the imported thick towels. She rushed away, slipping into a linen robe when she heard Isis politely call to her. "Princess, may I use your bathwater?" Attendants stood by with siphons to transfer the water to jugs, then transport the bathwater to garden plants.

While fastening her robe with a golden clasp, Becataten turned to see a weary Isis. She took a moment to observe the effort Isis had taken to make her bathing and grooming perfect. "Isis, you may, and you may also use some of the fragrances you so thoughtfully set out for me."

With a homely and grateful grin, Isis smiled broadly.

Becataten stood at the entrance of the bedchamber to find but one lit candle and the twins still asleep. Their beds had been well-draped for the night with sheer linen, a protection against insects that pervaded Egypt. *Thank the Gods the children are out of Pharaoh's grasp.* But had Pharaoh really seen her children as possible royals? Or had he just become acquisitive about everything? Queen Tiye was taking more control of the crown, and Becataten breathed a sigh of relief to know that meant no future interest in Jeser or Mishi. The queen was grooming her son, Young Horus, to be the future king. Suddenly it became very clear why the queen-mother was eliminating Becataten and her twins from court life. Wasn't it odd that she and the queen were destined to be enemies, while Young Horus had become a friend? How would that contrast be played out in her future?

Hearing the sound of soft snoring, she walked closer to the children's cots to find Maja asleep on the floor, positioned between their beds. Dear, sweet Maja had been a devoted slave to her mother, an anchor of love in her own childhood and was trying to be the same for her children. *How could I have been so cruel as to strike this kind old woman?* Becataten shook her head to ward off the pain of the memory.

Chapter 37

♊

Stepping closer, Becataten raised the thin curtain to view the golden body of her son. So, this was the young man her father had said would be the world traveler, Mishaiaten. She found him stocky and a handsome boy, saddened that he would never know Jobu, his uncle. Nor would her blind father ever see a resemblance of himself in his grandchildren. She would ask Maja if she saw any traits from their grandmother, Princess Attah, in the children. Maja was the only person alive who knew what Becataten's mother had looked like. All she knew was that Maja and her mother had traveled by caravan from Babylon to Thebes when they were twelve, and somehow a brief love affair between Abu and Attah had ensued after the princess arrived. It had happened in the temporary Royal Harem, making it a sacrilege. Often, Becataten had been reminded that her eyes were a sparkling green like her mothers.

With care, stepping over Maja, Becataten pulled the linen back from Djeseriaten's cot to see the young girl who would carry all the Heka. What a lean child she was, with skin the color of carnelian, darker than her brother. *I hope she can manage her Heka well. Like a sack of gold, the gift could be of great value but also a heavy burden*, Becataten thought.

Quite tired, but not ready for sleep, Becataten decided to visit with Lady Nagara and Suti in the library. The grandeur of the house sparked nostalgic memories, and once again she felt like the mentored child of so many inundations ago. In her soft linen robe and finely woven leather slippers, Becataten descended the stairs.

Walking down a long hall, she paused at an opening then poked her head into the chamber where household records and correspondence were kept. Lady Nagara and Suti were lounging peacefully sipping pomegranate wine amid all the papyri. "I just came to say thank you for caring for my children. I won't stay long, I *am* exhausted," said Becataten to Lady Nagara and Suti.

"Come and sit. I was hoping you would find a little time for us," said Lady Nagara. "We know you have had a harrowing time and that story can wait until our next Ra. But the children have been a pure joy for us to care for."

Suti set his goblet aside. "We are happy to see you back home, Princess. And it has given us much pleasure overseeing the children's care. Mishi is a bold young boy who already has taken to wondering off, as your father predicted he would," Suti said with pride.

"And Jeser shows much kindness to others. She is a patient child who likes to please people," broke in Lady Nagara as though her appraisal was absolute.

Becataten was amused hearing Lady Nagara and Suti use the diminutive names for the twins that Maja had assigned them. "And you can tell all of that when they are but one inundation old?" said Becataten.

Suti smiled and nodded, like a proud grandpapa.

"Well, I think I am now ready for sleep," said Becataten, covering a yawn. "I have much to tell you about the trip to the delta, the pyramids, my encounter with Pharaoh and so much more, but that will all have to wait." She knew she wouldn't tell all that happened to her with Pharaoh, and she would abridge the telling of the sobek encounters. That could all wait.

"Goodnight my protective mentors," Becataten said as she walked to each one, kissed them on their heads, then left for her bedchamber.

"And where is the Viceroy?" Lady Nagara loudly whispered to Suti.

Picking up a scroll of plans to review, Suti shrugged. "You might ask Abu. There is little that the old astrologer doesn't know."

The following Ra Becataten rose with the sun god and dressed in a blue silk shift, grateful to have a choice of clothing. "Isis, paint me a face that won't scare the children," she said. When Isis was finished Becataten rushed to the nursery. The twins were being fed thick, cultured milk mixed with finely chopped dates. "Hello, nannies, I am Princess Becataten, mother of the twins," Becataten said as she stepped eagerly into the nursery. The two women exchanged surprised glances, then bowed.

"This is Jeser and this is Mishi," Maja said with some difficult maneuvering around the children as she stepped forward. The girl hid behind Maja, but the boy stood firm to assess Becataten. His eyes were as green as her own and much larger. Walking to her with a bland expression, he ran his hand down her long silk shift.

"I am going outside for a walk," Becataten said. "Would you like to come with me?" Shaking his head,

Mishi returned to the nannies, and Jeser tugged at Maja's arm to pull her away from Becataten.

The Butler showed in the doorway. "Princess, you are called to Master Abu's house."

"I will be with you presently, Butler," she said turning to the children. "Could we go outside tomorrow and maybe walk in the mud and pick flowers?" The children looked at one another as Mishi nodded his head affirmatively. Jeser shook her head with a scowl.

As bearers settled Becataten's litter before her father's entry, she could hear arguing within, and even Huni the baboon was shrieking.

"What is it?" asked Becataten as she entered.

Pygmy Lady asserted herself. "Ahmose wants to go with me to Kush and see the Viceroy."

At the sound of the Viceroy's name, Becataten was taken aback. She hadn't heard or spoken of him since he left her, several moons ago. Why was Pygmy Lady going to see the Viceroy?

Ahmose and Kombo were in the room and it appeared that they had all been voicing heated opinions about this.

Hearing Becataten's voice, Abu straighten in his chair. "I am pleased you have come, daughter," he said, reaching for her.

"Why are you going to Kush to see the Viceroy, and what are you all arguing about?" Becataten asked as she went to embrace her father.

A brief silence filled the room until a red-eyed Ahmose spoke up. He appeared to have come from the fields and stood in a dirt-soiled kilt. "A messenger brought news that my father is dying, and I want to go to Kush with Pygmy Lady, but she says it is too dangerous," he blurted.

Becataten turned to Pygmy Lady. "Who says the Viceroy is dying?"

Abu cleared his throat. "My dear, we have had word that your Viceroy suffers the worst of the fevers that comes from the small buzzing fly. The one that injects their victims."

"Where did this information come from?" Becataten asked, alarmed, as she looked around the room.

Kombo struggled to stand straight and answer her question. "A fellow tribesman ran the news here early this Ra," Princess," Kombo said.

Becataten collapsed in a chair of pillows. "Do we know if he can be brought back, or even where the Viceroy's vessel is? After the captain sailed me here from the Palace, I assumed the crew sailed the Golden Falcon to Kush. What craft would we use to search for him?"

Abu's head shook in frustration. "That is part of the problem. The Viceroy's vessel did sail for Kush. That of course would have been the safest and most expedient way to search for and return the Viceroy."

"I am going alone," Pygmy Lady said, standing firm with crossed arms and staring at Ahmose. "And if you try and follow me, you will be eaten by sobeks or killed by a tribesman, who hate half-bloods."

With bulging eyes, Kombo's head bobbed, affirming Pygmy Lady's words.

A knock at the door brought Stable Master Senzar, who quickly bowed to Princess Becataten, as though surprised to see her. He turned to the astrologer. "Master Abu, as you asked, I have inquired and there are no boats or rafts to commandeer at this time. But I have been thinking. I could carry one passenger, and driving my chariot hard, I believe I could find the Viceroy's vessel by surveying the Nile along my way."

Pygmy Lady's body tensed as she turned to Senzar. "I will go but not with that four-horse rig you drove last time."

Ahmose fled the room, slamming the door.

Abu and Pygmy Lady agreed that she would travel the along the edge of the Nile with Senzar to find the viceroy's ship. Becataten watched helplessly as her father and the diminutive black woman sat talking about her trip with the Stable Master. Senzar's words were gentle.

Abu interjected. "I believe Senzar may well catch up with the Viceroy's ship. He is a capable driver. The Viceroy's ship and crew would have to moor at the first cataract for the best possible time to drag the vessel passed the giant falls. After you board the ship, send Senzar home, then you know you must forge the second cataract where Fortress Kor stands. There the captain has to sail the Viceroy's vessel against the tides of inundation now, and that is a slow and dangerous sailing."

Becataten knew the Nile flooded every twelve moons when a giant lake overflowed and spilled its water down the Mother Nile that was well beyond Egypt. This was when the colossal boulders that defined the cataracts were inundated and ships could sail over the 'belly of stones.'

I could go to Mosie and return with him, but is he alive? And could I be away from the children again? Becataten wondered, her eyes filling with tears. Her thoughts were interrupted when she heard Pygmy Lady bark, "We leave when Ra rises, Senzar."

"Becataten stood. "I will accompany you, Pygmy Lady."

"You need to be strong!" Pygmy Lady said, boring her eyes into Becataten. "But I think you will be. And you owe the Viceroy much."

Chapter 38

♊

They left at dawn. Becataten and Pygmy Lady gripped the rails of the oversized chariot as the stable master drove his two spirited stallions toward the shores of Fort Kor. Senzar sped furiously alongside the Nile with all eyes on the river scouting for the Viceroy's vessel. He drove his animals hard as Ra grew stronger and brighter. It took skill to drive around the muddy shoreline that the inundation caused and not become mired in the black mud. Twice, Becataten saw resting floats of crocodiles that Senzar had to avoid. The sight took her back to encounters with the sobeks and caused her to shake with fear at the memory.

Pygmy Lady loaded her bow, and with swagger stood square in the chariot, aiming at the giant crocodiles but not firing. "They can't outrun a chariot," she said with her toothy grin.

In the late Ra the horses were moving at a trot when Senzar spied the Viceroy's vessel. His powerful arms slowed his steeds, and after bringing them to a stop, he reached for an animal horn to hail the craft. The captain responded immediately and had his bank of oarsmen slow the large boat and navigate toward them. As Senzar drove his chariot to the muddy shoreline, some of the crew waded through mire and with ease carried Becataten, Pygmy Lady and their few possessions aboard. Once the women were settled,

Becataten explained their mission to the captain. Stable Master Senzar was waved off, and the vessel continued south, what the Egyptians called upriver, toward Kush.

After two Ra's of pounding through rushing waves, they passed the stronghold Buhen where she and the Viceroy had tried to make their first home. The mounting Mother Nile had covered the first cataract. She knew they were in the 'belly of stones' now. The last time Becataten saw this place it was a raging waterfall. Now, only a handful of rocks showed above the water. With the captain's skill, as well as the brawn of his oarsmen, they maneuvered around the huge stones, when the Viceroy had said they couldn't. The decks were awash with waves until they arrived at the second fort. The captain's skill had guided them through the belly of stones toward shore with ease.

"We are at Fort Kor, Princess Becataten, and where I believe you will find the Viceroy," the captain spoke loudly over the sound of the rushing river.

"Can you be sure, Captain?" Becataten called back. Becataten saw Pygmy Lady throw a look of disgust at her, then jump off the boat. With her bow and loaded quiver slung over her shoulder, a cloth bundle of her meager possessions in her hand, she trudged through the water toward shore. The crew quickly put together a litter for Becataten, loaded her small chest, held her above the water and when they reached shore trotted her overland toward the fort.

To be on land was a relief, even though the heat was oppressive. The movement of the boat had been tumultuous and the chariot ride, jarring. Becataten thanked a Nubian who handed her a piece of bark, showing her its use as a fan. As Pygmy Lady walked alongside the litter she appeared comfortable in this dry and desolate land.

"Inside fortress soon," Pygmy Lady said, walking at a steady pace under Ra's scorching rays. "If the viceroy is still alive, you will see him before light leaves," Pygmy Lady said, moving into a jog, as though always wanting to move quickly toward the problem to solve it.

This fortress was cooler and smaller than Fort Buhen, as Becataten remembered her brief stay there. Probably due to thicker mud brick construction, she thought, always with an eye toward construction. She was greeted by an Egyptian official and designated a chamber with two beds, but obviously not the one the Viceroy occupied. *He must be too ill for me to join him in his quarters,* she guessed. But for the first time, Becataten was hopeful because he was near.

When Pygmy Lady popped in, threw her bundle on a cot, and settled her goods in a corner, she said, "When you go to the Viceroy, do not be surprised what you see."

"He's alive, and you have seen him?" asked Becataten.

Motioning Becataten to follower her, Pygmy Lady headed out the door. "He is alive."

They stepped into a large square room that was ill-lit with smoldering pots of animal fat, making the air dense and unpleasant. A tall Nubian standing behind Mosie's bed pumped a large fan, doing little to improve the air. She was offered a stool to sit at his bedside. With concerned faces, Egyptian and Nubian officials milled about. Becataten slowly grew accustomed to the darkness as she made out a woman who was systematically keeping her Mosie's body damp with applications of wet linen. An acrid smell filled the room.

She wasn't sure if it came from his sweat, or maybe herbs in the moist wraps.

As he lay unconscious, Pygmy Lady came closer with a small torch, giving light to Merymose's gaunt face and emaciated body. Becataten hid a sob as she looked at her beloved husband, who now seemed to be near death. *Is he going to live?* she wondered, feeling doubt that he could, given how wasted away he was. He looked dead already.

A Nubian healer solemnly attested to an Egyptian official how grave the viceroy's condition was. Across from her was his nurse. She was a beautiful woman with luminous black skin. Their eyes met. Becataten noted that her face was filled with pain and concern as she wiped the Viceroy's brow with what Becataten could only describe as love. As the Nubian woman stood to fetch more water and linen, it was clear she was full with child.

For five Ra's Becataten sat at the Viceroy's side across his bed from his devoted attendant. On the sixth Ra, the Viceroy's fever broke. His head turned toward the Nubian woman with a wan smile as she lifted his head and held a cup of water to his lips. "So, you are going to live, you old digger of Pharaoh's gold," Pygmy Lady said with a smile exposing her spiked teeth.

Turning his head toward Pygmy Lady's voice, the Viceroy's face went rigid when he saw Becataten next to her. His tone was hollow. "Why are you here?"

"Because I love you, Mosie," Becataten said, tears welling up at his harsh words.

"It is late for that sentiment," he replied.

"It isn't for me."

The Nubian healer standing at the back of the room came forward to have a brief discussion with Pygmy

Lady, which ended in clearing the room so Merymose could rest.

In three Ra's the viceroy was walking about, using a cane looking like a starved prisoner. Before he was advised to walk about, it was clear that he was planning his exit from Kush. As he began his plans, he refused Becataten's aid in favor of his Nubian woman, surprising his Egyptian staff and even some of his highly stationed natives.

On the fourth Ra, Merymose ordered the captain to ready his vessel. On the fifth, he and his two wives sailed for Thebes.

Becataten found the trip back to Egypt swift, as this time they were traveling with the Mother Nile. The voyage would have been a happy one if the circumstances had been different, but that was not to be on this trip.

Becataten stood looking over the Mother Nile, the breeze cooling her as the boat sailed quickly along. Her heart was heavy as she thought of all the misunderstanding that had brought her to this place. She knew she had to find a way to bring Mosie back to her and the children. He must know that although I went to Pharaoh, he thinks it was just to see his mortuary temple. He doesn't know that I had to go to Pharaoh to dissuade him from taking the twins. No one knows. Not even Maja. In retrospect that was such a foolish decision. Her pain at slapping Maja, at losing her husband, at having everyone think she was selfish when her reasons were anything but that caused her deep pain in her Ka and heart. She had never felt so alone on a boat full of people.

At each attempt to speak to the Viceroy, Becataten was repeatedly rebuffed in favor of his Nubian wife, who showed no hatred to her, and great devotion to the Viceroy. *This is a difficult kindness to receive, and I wonder if I could be as kind if the conditions were reversed,* she thought miserably.

Finally, Becataten found the Viceroy alone. Climbing the ladder above decks, she sat on a stool at his feet. "Mosie, may I please speak to you about our children?"

"You mean the children that you exposed to Pharaoh, who wanted them for his own."

"I did not do that, Mosie."

"What did you do Becataten, just give yourself to Pharaoh?"

"No, I did not do that either. Mosie. Please let me speak."

"We are nearly at the Suti Estate, so speak quickly then. This is where you get off."

Chapter 39

♊

Becataten was unceremoniously helped off the Viceroy's ship with a farewell only from the captain. As she stood at the Suti dock and the ship sailed, she and Merymose stared at one another, until both were out of sight. Her heart ached with a sharp pain as the boat got smaller and smaller. Breaking down, Becataten dropped to her knees and sobbed.

It wasn't until a litter bearer offered her a ride that she returned from her sadness and realized Pygmy Lady had remained on board. Was Pygmy Lady's allegiance with Mosie, and not her? Would Mosie forget her and devote himself to a new life with the Nubian woman who carried his child? *Becataten! Think of your children, not this!* she told herself.

As she stepped off the litter at the stairs of the Estate house, Butler greeted her. From his expression, she immediately knew something was wrong. "What is it, Butler?"

"Greeting, Princess Becataten. I am sorry to say that Master Suti is gravely ill. Lady Nagara is upstairs with him now."

Forgetting her own tiredness and despair, she raced to the second floor. She witnessed something she had never seen before: Lady Nagara was on her knees at Suti's cot. Next to her was Hor, standing over his brother in bent posture. It surprised Becataten that

Maja was nearby too, half of her face looking pained. Becataten walked to Lady Nagara, putting a hand on her shoulder, feeling her quiet sobbing. Reaching for Hor, she looked into his long sorrowful face and squeezed his hand. How sad it was to see a twin grieve for his equal. The loss of Jobu came to her. Becataten wept.

Shuffling to her side, Maja whispered, "Suti has been asking for you, Taten."

Butler brought chairs for the women. "I am glad you are here, Becataten," Lady Nagara said in a voice thick from crying. "Does the Viceroy live?" she asked.

"He does."

Lady Nagara nodded. "Is he with us here?"

"No, he sailed on to Thebes," Becataten said, new pain rising up in her at the words.

Nodding again, Lady Nagara offered nothing more, and the room became uncomfortably still until the healers began their chants.

A Sekhmet statue, the goddess of healing, had been placed at the foot of Suti's cot, and curative incantations could be heard as braziers wafted medicinal scents.

"Do the healers know what Suti suffers from?" asked Becataten.

"Something in his lower stomach is growing, and they are trying to drive it out with spells. At least his pain has been relieved with the poppy potion," Lady Nagara said.

Becataten motioned Maja to her side, noticing for the first time that Ra had left, and the dark time had arrived. "Are the children asleep, Maja?" she whispered.

Maja nodded.

"I want to see them," Becataten said.

The women walked the hall to the nursery. Jeser had climbed into the second cot with Mishi where together they slept soundly, Jeser's arm around her brother. Becataten was transported to their humble apartment growing up with her twin as she looked at her children.

"Just like you used to protect Jobu," Maja mouthed her words with difficulty.

When Ra showed himself again, Becataten quickly dressed and without a painted face went to Suti's chamber. Lady Nagara's bed had been moved into the chamber; she too was without cosmetics and was sitting at Suti's bedside.

"The healers just told me that it has become more difficult to dull his pain with the poppy," Lady Nagara said, her own twisted face in pain. "In past Ras he has asked for you and the Viceroy."

"The Viceroy is with Pharaoh. I will write for him to come," said Becataten somberly.

Lady Nagara nodded.

Becataten went first to the nursery and bent to hug each child. They were surprised to see her but did not thwart her as they had in the past. "I will be back to take you both outside so we can play in the mud," she promised. Their faces showed a guarded interest.

Once in the library, Becataten struggled with how to address a husband who had obviously abandoned her. Then she decided to speak as her heart dictated.

Dearest Mosie,

When I returned to the estate, I found Suti gravely ill. The healers are doing all they can, but his condition is worsening. He has requested to see you. Lady Nagara and others believe that he may be dying. I beg you to come to his bedside if it is at all possible.

There are many misunderstandings left between us. What you are thinking is not the truth of the situation that separated us. I hope that if you come, you will allow me to explain.

Your Loving Wife,
Becataten

Outside the library door where she was finishing up her scroll, she heard her father with Kombo heading for the stairs. "Father!" she called.

"My dear, you have returned!" Abu said, reaching out for Becataten. They hugged. "And how is the Viceroy?'

"He lives and has gone to the Palace, Father, but there is more to it than that. I just wrote a scroll to him and will have Senzar deliver the message by a swift chariot."

She greeted Kombo and the two led her father upstairs to Suti's chamber. "Did Pygmy Lady return with you, Becataten?" her father asked.

Before Becataten could answer, her father's step paused at the sound of a deep masculine voice at the entry. Abu's face lit up with recognition.

"Who is it, Father?" Becataten asked.

"If I am not mistaken, that is General Nesu," Abu said in a booming voice that the general could hear.

"Royal Astrologer! I never expected to encounter you at the Suti Estate!" said the general as he approached, following Abu's voice.

It was clear that there was a longstanding friendliness her father had with this general as they greeted one another, yet she didn't know this man.

What a striking individual he is, Becataten thought. Tall and mahogany-skinned, but from Ra's brightness, not from his ancestry. She stood looking at this man with his eyes as blue as the Great Sea and was relieved when her father interrupted her staring to introduce her.

The general took her hand and held it as he gazed into her eyes like no man had in more moons than she could remember. "I am honored," he said quietly.

And I don't even have face paint on. What was I thinking when I awoke and didn't ask Isis to apply my cosmetics?

"Let us go to Suti," Abu said.

It had been five Ras since she sent the scroll to Mosie. Suti's decline was now steady. He recognized Becataten only briefly when she visited his bedside, and he no longer asked for the Viceroy when they spoke. Time saw no recovery in Suti's condition. Becataten checked in on Suti and Lady Nagara, who remained at his side day and night.

Otherwise Becataten was making friends again with her children. "Isn't it fun to stomp in this mud?" Becataten said as the three of them followed a drainage canal, a water supply for a huge flower crop.

The children wore no clothes, as was the custom in Egypt for young babes. Becataten held up her sheer shift to keep from splattering it with mud. When Mishi saw his sister slapping at the water with a stick, she said, "I want a stick too."

"Maybe you can get a real javelin at Grandpapa's house!" Becataten said.

"Oh, I would like that, MaMa," Mishi said. Becataten was sure she could feel her heart jump when her child called her MaMa for the first time.

The trio finished their journey trudging to grandpapa's house.

Abu called out playfully, "Do I hear my Grandchildren at my door, or is it just rats looking for the grain storage?"

"No, Grandpapa, it's me and Jeser!" Mishi called.

Huni began to jump up and down and call out with screeching sounds for the children. "Kombo, chain Huni! He could hurt the twins without meaning to," Abu called.

They all burst into the house as Kombo secured the baboon. Becataten was immeasurably pleased when Jeser and Mishi ran to her father to hug him. "Can we touch Huni, please, Grandpapa?" asked Jeser.

"Yes, you can, with Kombo close by to see that Huni stays gentle," Abu answered with fondness in his voice.

Huni wiggled and danced in place as the children approached him. Kombo was on guard with the eye of a hawk as Jeser, then Mishi, reached out to pet the baboon.

"Nice Huni, nice Huni," said Jeser, who showed no fear of the animal. After she spoke, to Huni he settled to the floor like a puppy, adoring her with his brown eyes as she ran her small hand down the rough hair of his head.

"Where is Ahmose, Grandpapa, I have come for a javelin!" Mishi called out.

"Did I hear someone ask for a javelin?" called General Nesu, as he walked into the sitting chamber. "I know something about that weapon."

"Becataten, General Nesu is staying with me for a few Ras. He and Suti grew up together, and of course I knew him well before he became a famous general."

Here he comes with those penetrating blue eyes, and once again I am without facial paint, thought Becataten.

"Greetings, Princess, how nice to see a mother who plays in the fields with her children."

"Yes, well that's what we have been doing," she said looking down at her mud splattered legs. Only because she had her children with her, did she not feel like a dirty attendant. "I am afraid I am less than presentable at the moment," Becataten said, her cheeks reddening.

"Nonsense, you appear to be having great fun with your family," the general said with a slight bow.

She could feel his magnetic eyes absorbing her and needed to turn away. "Father, is Ahmose about? Mishi and Jeser want a javelin to play with, and I recall that..."

Jeser found herself more interested in Huni and no longer seemed interested in a mere javelin.

The general interrupted. "Allow me. Young man, let's you and I go outside and make a throwing stick." Mishi followed him like a cub follows his lioness.

"Father, how old is the general?" Becataten asked as they stood outside watching Mishi looking for a sturdy stick.

"Ha, so you see him like most women do," Abu said.

"What do you mean?" Becataten asked.

"Nesu has always had his share of women, and in answer to your question, he is close to my age. I think he and Pharaoh were borne under the same moon."

"I see." Becataten said as she enjoyed the soft breeze that picked up and cooled her.

"I know you won't go flying after the general because of your separation from the Viceroy but be careful of him. He has a reputation with women," Abu said in a quiet voice so the general would not hear.

"Father, of course I won't. I think I am just missing having a man in my life," Becataten replied with a sigh. "I miss Mosie."

"And what of the Viceroy, have you heard anything?"

"No, Father, he did not respond to my scroll, even with Suti on his deathbed," Becataten said in a sad voice. "I fear he has left me forever."

"I'll see what my sources can learn of him."

"Please do, Father, I miss him so..." Becataten wiped a small tear as her son held up a long stick to practice throwing.

Chapter 40

♊

The Viceroy did not respond to Becataten's summons to come to Suti's bedside, but Becataten soon learned that instead he wrote a compassionate scroll to Lady Nagara, which seemed to satisfy her.

Suti's death was one moon after Becataten return from Kush. After his body was transported to the 'House of the Dead,' Lady Nagara walked the halls of the big house in silence, especially at night when she couldn't sleep. Her appetite left her, and she began to lose weight. Her demeanor changed from a self-assured woman to a recluse, communicating only with her butler, and never leaving the Estate.

Becataten visited her in her bedchamber after too many days of this behavior had gone by. "Lady Nagara, we are all concerned about your health. What can I do to help you?"

"Just leave me be, Becataten," Lady Nagara said in a frail voice as she sat on her bed.

"But Lady Nagara, the Estate cannot run without you!" Becataten reminded her.

"Then you run it," Lady Nagara said, taking Becataten by the hand and looking at her with sad eyes. "I have not the heart to do it any longer without my beloved Suti."

"I have no training for this huge task!" Becataten protested.

"Neither did I, Becataten," said Lady Nagara. "Now leave me to grieve." Lady Nagara insisted.

"Lady Nagara, Suti would not like to see you like this. You are the heartbeat of this Estate," Becataten said.

"No, Suti was my heartbeat, and I deeply regret that I never told him so, and now I want to be left alone."

How sad it was to see Lady Nagara suffer so for never embracing Suti as her loving husband. She had been a responsible partner in many ways, but it was true, Becataten had never seen Lady Nagara show Suti much affection, when he obviously adored her. This too made her think of how she put her own plan to try and control the Pharaoh above her love of Mosie and her children and what a fool she had been to let Mosie get away from her without ever explaining herself to him so he would know her heart had always been in the right place.

It wasn't long before Becataten learned from Butler that the managers of the growing fields, the cattle herders, the producers of beer and other products were falling rapidly in their outputs. She went to her father for answers.

Abu listened intently. "What you have told me, Becataten, can be remedied, but it must be done quickly. I had no idea that Lady Nagara had ceased in performing her duties. Together we must put this Estate back in line. Now, I want a meeting with the head managers, I believe there are seven?" said Abu.

"Yes, Father. The herding and dairy overseers are the most in need of direction. The vegetable, flower and date managers await instructions too. And of course, the grain and brewery supervisors are also anxious to be directed. Is Ahmose going to be able to help, Father?"

"No, not as a manager of the entire Estate, but I have in mind to advance his responsibilities substantially. Now, I am going to need the resident scribe that Lady Nagara uses for accounting to come here to live. Can you make those arrangements, my dear?"

"Of course, Father. Will there be anything else?"

"Yes, take control of the operation of the house and expand the authority of Butler to make decisions, just be sure he reports those decisions to you. Find him a young and strong assistant. And find yourself a house scribe for personal correspondence. I can give you my dwarf, Heby, as a help in running the house for a time. And by the way, I believe you have a liaison with Young Horus. He will be king one day soon. By scroll, cultivate that relationship."

"But Father, after the way I was treated at the Palace, it's clear his mother, Queen Tiye, dislikes me very much, Father. She would see me dead!"

"The queen mother dislikes many. We won't worry about that now. Just begin communicating with Young Horus. Perhaps you could begin by writing him about Suti's death and his coming funerary ceremony."

Abu stood and paced his receiving chamber with newfound energy. "This is a job we can share my daughter, and in the end, we will make this Estate more profitable than it has ever been."

Becataten looked at Kombo, who was smiling at her father.

"Stay for the evening meal, my dear, and Kombo, fire up your brazier and have one of the butchers brings us some tender steaks," Abu said rubbing his hands together with an enthusiasm Becataten hadn't seen in her father since his return to the Estate.

"Isis, dress me well, I must look perfect for Suti's funerary services. And paint me a face that is rich with color, like they do in Thebes." Isis did not fail her princess when she chose a tight fitting, low-cut shift woven of silver threads and a wig adorned with beads of gold and turquoise. Becataten's facial touches with the colors of peaches and pomegranates shone with vibrance. Isis also made sure to use finely ground malachite mixed with a little almond oil to rub on Becataten's eye lids. The effect was stunning, as the ground stone matched her green eyes.

"MaMa, MaMa you look beautiful!" she heard the voice of Jeser as both children entered. "Can we come with you?"

"No, my little cubs, not this time, but I will return very soon. I do not like to be away from my beautiful children," she told them. As Isis finished painting Becataten's face, the children leaned into their mother and pleaded for the scents that were being lavished on her. "Isis, give them some drops of the rose oil," she said, remembering it was the Viceroy's favorite with a pang in her heart of missing him.

After receiving Suti's body, the morticians released his mummy in ninety days for the burial ceremony. The burial took place in Thebes on the west bank of the Nile, and although the number of people in attendance was small, the individuals attending were esteemed. Lady Nagara remained a withdrawn and altered woman, most believing it was because she was mourning her husband's death, but she made an appearance for her husband's burial ceremony.

Becataten now saw her as a woman who still couldn't forgive herself for not being a loving wife to Suti. With Lady Nagara's new-found reclusiveness she was of no help for funerary arrangements so Becataten handled everything regarding the planning of Royal Architect Suti's entombment.

Just as Becataten was noting that things were going smoothly and according to schedule, she saw the Viceroy enter the tomb. Her heart skipped a beat. She smiled at him, and she was sure he saw her, but he looked away and found his station as the ceremony began.

Even Young Horus made an appearance to bid farewell to Suti, and although Becataten had little conversation with him. He was cordial and insisted they correspond. Her father had been more correct than she knew. Young Horus had already heard that she was operating the Estate with some success and complimented her. It was particularly gratifying to Becataten that his queen mother Tiye had not poisoned him against her.

Once in the tomb chamber, Becataten settled Lady Nagara into a comfortable chair next to Hor. The priests performed their rituals, offered food for Suti's after-life, and the Book of The Dead was delivered. Then amongst the wafting of incense, the long ceremony ended. Becataten stood to bid farewell to all who had attended. General Nesu passed before her in his full military regalia, with lustrous gold bees awarded for bravery, pinned to his chest.

"Thank you General for attending today, it was kind of you to come."

"May I be of service to you and Lady Nagara during this time, Princess?" he asked, standing attentively.

Becataten looked to the corner of the burial chamber to see the Viceroy watching her and decided to produce a captivating smile for the general. "Yes, if you don't mind waiting until the mourners have left, I could use your assistance."

"I am yours to command, Princess Becataten." The general took up a place behind her standing like a possessive bronze lion.

When the Viceroy passed before her, she looked directly into his eyes with a neutral expression. "It is nice to see you again, Viceroy," she said, noting that he looked thin and still not fully recovered from his illness.

The Viceroy's arrogance toward her had lifted some. "As you are in Thebes, may we speak later in this Ra?" he asked.

But she saw little contrition in him and there was still anger in his eyes. "I do not have much time, but I do have some things to say to you. We must speak now, as General Nesu is arranging our travel back to the Estate."

It was clear the Viceroy didn't expect to be rushed. "Very well," he said, extending his arm to let her leave the area where everyone gathered. They walked a ways toward a sandy hill and stood in the shade behind it.

"You did not answer me when I sent you a scroll," said Becataten, speaking first before she lost her nerve. The Viceroy's expression remained stern. "I have to tell you that while it seemed I was being petulant and impulsive by going to Pharaoh, the real reason is not what you think. My plan was to try and convince him not to take the twins away, and especially not Mishi so we could live in peace when you returned from Kush."

"And did you succeed?" asked Merymose.

"At the last moment, I choose to send the children to the Estate. Then when I met with our Lord, it was not what I expected," replied Becataten. "Pharaoh is addled by the poppy seed and not in his right mind. I only saw him three times, and we did not couple, before Queen Tiye held me prisoner. I am lucky to have escaped with my very life."

Merymose's expression softened just a little. "I did not know that to be the case. You should have sent me a scroll to tell me."

Becataten nodded. "I thought of it, but in the wrong hands, it could have looked like treason on my part. I did not expect to find you with a new wife at the time I was trying to save our family. I would have acted differently if I knew our love was so fragile."

Merymose looked truly regretful but he shrugged. "I cannot go back and change time, my Becataten. I have a new life now. I thought you abandoned our love, and I moved on." He looked up to see some litters leaving the tomb entrance. "If I had known, I would have made other choices. But I did not know."

"Our time in Memphis will always give me joy to think about," Becataten said in a sorrowful voice. Merymose straightened up.

"Yes, I agree. But what is done is done. But we will have to talk more another time. I have some business to attend to before Ra's end."

"Yes, perhaps we can talk more when you find time to visit with Djezeraten and Mishiaten," she said.

"Yes, perhaps," he said as they returned to the group of mourners. He threw a resentful glance at the General Nehu, who appeared stalwart next to the faded Viceroy. For just a moment Becataten, felt sorry for Mosie.

It took many moons, but together Becataten and her father put the Estate into full production and ultimately had the land producing more than it had under Lady Nagara's watchful eye, as her father had promised. Becataten had always enjoyed going into the fields and seeing firsthand what was growing and being harvested. Abu had appointed Ahmose to be her assistant, and the two traveled the various production areas by chariot every seven Ras. Ahmose would step off the conveyance, ask Becataten's questions, and thus gather all the information she needed to compile and later discuss with her father. The two would then make administrative decisions.

One early Ra, Becataten and Ahmose were driven on dry ground passing workers shoring up irrigation basins where tubers were planted. "I want you to remind the workers that we want more basins filled this year, especially for flowers. We were short on deliveries to the Palace of Iris, Chrysanthemums and corn flowers last year, and I have learned that waterlilies are needed to stock all of Pharaoh's fish ponds," Becataten told Ahmose, as he stepped of the chariot.

As warm rays encouraged the lilies to open, fragrances poured into the air, Becataten sighed, "Oh, and smell the mint, it's clear we have reached the herb growers, isn't it?"

Ahmose nodded. "Do you still want more henna planted, Princess? They are grown here with the food and medicinal herbs.?"

"Yes, we must always plant an abundance of Henna bushes, Egypt always has many needs for henna; for dyes and the healers need a supply for curbing fevers."

Ahmose spoke up quietly, "And for mummification, too."

Becataten nodded approvingly. "Very good Ahmose."

A visit to the Estate granaries showed sacks stacked in abundance of emmer wheat and flax ready for transport to the docks. Nearby, the humming sounds of grinding on large flat stones by men, a job too laborious for women. This flour was for the Estate, whereas the grain that went to the Palace was not ground but placed in grainers awaiting shipment to the Palace. The aroma of flat bread for the Estate staff and workers wafted through the air as women patted circles of tough before slapping them onto hot clay. A nearby brewery utilized yeast from the bread dough for beer making.

Becataten and Ahmos stopped for a sample and deemed the beer never better.

Toward the end of the day, Becataten and Ahmose ended their seven-day tour at the cattle platform and counting station. "Did I ever tell you, Ahmose, that I was severely punished by Lady Nagara for coming here as a young girl?" She didn't wait for a response but stood in the chariot recalling in silence the kneeling on small pebbles until her knees blead for coming to this place when she first came to the Estate for mentoring.

The livestock counting included oxen, sheep pigs, goats, and donkeys, all being tallied by a scribe. Dairy production was steady, and where Ahmose proudly told Becataten that Ne Ne had become an able maker of goat cheese. They discussed the rise in production of dates at the end of their tour because her father had sent for a congregate of baboons where he had long ago acquired Huni. The male animals arrived castrated with their eyeteeth removed and were trained to scale palms for dates as well as sort the crops. A handler came with them who lived on the Estate and managed their care. "I'm sure you have heard Huni when his brothers are in the palms and he gets so excited he howls to them. When he causes the ruckus, it makes all who can hear it smile."

Chapter 41

♊

As Becataten readied herself for the day, her children were nearby on the floor. "Who would like to ride with me to grandpapa's house?" Becataten asked her children. The response was squealing and jumping. Becataten was impressed how the children held fast to the rails as she trotted her one-horse chariot to her father's house.

"You little goats didn't arrive by chariot, did you?" asked Abu of the children.

"Yes, we did," answered Mishi, standing tall.

Jezer went straight for Huni, who no longer had to be leashed, especially when she came near him. He was complacent next to her and rolled over on his back like a dog so she would scratch his chest.

"So, you have tamed Huni, and at your young age," a voice said that Becataten knew well.

"Greetings, Pygmy Lady," said Becataten, turning to see her enter the room. "Did you finally decide to leave the Viceroy's side?" Becataten said, her voice sharper than she meant it to be.

"I left his side long ago, Becataten. I have been visiting my own people."

Sounding annoyed, Becataten turned to Pygmy Lady. "Really, you could have sent us word, especially my father."

"I could have, but I didn't."

"And why was that?" asked Becataten.

"Because there was a war, and my village was destroyed. I got out with only one thing."

Jezer, a silent child, took in much of what was going on around her. She walked to Pygmy Lady and took her hand. "What did you get out with?" Jezer asked softly.

"My life, little one."

"That is a good thing, Pygmy Lady," Jezer said, hugging her.

"Yes, that is a good thing, little wise one."

Becataten felt ashamed about being unfeeling to Pygmy Lady. They talked more, and their old comfortable way with one another returned. Becataten invited her to live in the big house with her and Maja and Lady Nagara and the children.

Pygmy Lady declined but said she would visit her in a few Ras.

Pygmy Lady kept her word and leaped the outdoor steps to the house one early morning.

"Hello Butler, still looking down that nose at me?"

"Why, no I don't ..." Butler began, but Pygmy Lady squeezed in through the door underneath him.

"Is Becataten in her chamber?"

"Yes, My Lady, I mean, Pygmy Lady!" Butler looked flummoxed as Pygmy Lady grinned with her sharp teeth at his error.

Pygmy Lady climbed the stairs and walked into Becataten's suite. Jezer came forward and took her hand.

"Greetings, little wise one," Pygmy Lady said, looking down into the child's round black eyes. "How many inundations have you lived through now?"

Jeser held up four fingers.

"You know you have the Heka, don't you?"

Jezer nodded. "MaMa and Maja tell me so," she said.

"I'm here to talk to your mother."

Becataten entered her chamber carrying a basket of kittens. "Children, look what one of the servants brought for you!" Becataten handed the basket to their outstretched arms, their faces aglow with excitement. "Treat them with love and care, children." Turning to Pygmy Lady, she said, "Let's slip away for a walk in the garden.".

The two strolled around the large lotus pond forever stocked with fish. "I want to apologize for being rude to you at my father's house, Pygmy Lady," Becataten said.

Pygmy Lady waved a hand. "I didn't come to talk about that. I came to tell you I had a portent dream that two men want you. And I believe you already know which two."

Becataten nodded, a wistful look in her eyes as she thought of the general and Mosie.

Becataten went silent. Pygmy Lady, in her crude way, always went to the heart of a matter.

"You are now strong and rich and can run this place. Your father helped, yet you have done most of the work. Men like to conquer powerful women. But I do not believe you wish to be conquered."

Becataten nodded. "Pygmy Lady you are right. I do not want to be conquered. In my life, many requirements have been made of me, to be groomed for Pharaoh, to put my father to death, to bear the torture of my father, to accept the Viceroy as my husband, to bear twin children, to make a mistake trying to protect my children and nearly dying because of it and losing my marriage, and now to manage this Estate. None of these did I choose to be my fate." She watched bubbles rise on the pond surface as a group of fish swam below.

Becataten continued. "Today I would like to make my own decisions. When Pharaoh asked me to condemn my father to death, I did what my heart told me. And where would I be now if I had not kept Father alive? Today, my heart tells me to stay put, and to work this land." Becataten expelled a big breath. "But I do want a father for my children."

"Having both a father for your children, *and* your freedom, may not be in your future."

"When they are older, I was thinking I could send them to visit their father," Becataten said. "I feel they must know him and learn to love him. As I learned to love my own father, Abu."

"Then that's what you will do," Pygmy Lady affirmed, with conviction.

Becataten looked over the estate as they continued to walk on. In the distance, she could see the colorful flower fields, and beyond that, the pastures where the cows grazed. She had her own world here, and even though Mosie was not by her side to enjoy it with her, she was content to be here, with the aging Maja, Lady Nagara, her father, and even Kombo and Ahmose, even Ne Ne. This was her home, these were her people, this was her life. She was content. Even without the blue-eyed general or the man she once loved beyond all.

"And life here will be good, won't it Pygmy Lady?" Becataten asked with concern as she admired the work she and her father had done to restore the estate to its original glory.

Pygmy Lady nodded. "And life here will be good, Princess Becataten," Pygmy Lady agreed as they strolled together along a winding path under a grove of date trees.

The End

Glossary

Sma ⚊ blended wine from preferred vintages
Nome ⚊ Provence
Ka ⚊ Spirit or Soul
Debon ⚊ Various-sized pieces of gold, silver, or copper for trading prior to coinage
Kush ⚊ Probably modern-day Sudan (sometimes referred to as Nubia)
Nubian ⚊ A native of Kush
Land of the Bow ⚊ What natives called Kush
Nehesy ⚊ What the Egyptian called the Nubians
The Great Sea ⚊ Mediterranean Sea
Heka ⚊ Magic
'Son of the King' ⚊ Title (only) of Viceroy Merymose, half-brother to Pharaoh.
Isis ⚊ Ubiquitous female name in Egypt
Young Horus ⚊ Born Amenhotep IV, changed his name to Akenaten

*Many half-brothers were born in Pharaoh's Harem from various women; however, it was rare when one of those males rose to become Pharaoh. Usually, Pharaoh had to have a royal mother.

To My Readers: A Request!

Dear Readers,

Thank you for taking the time to read *Harem Twins Book II,* and of course I hope you were able to also read my first book in the series! I am in the midst of writing book three in this series and contemplating a fourth.

As an independent book writer, I depend even more so on you, the reader, and the reviews you that you pass on. Every sentiment shared regarding my novels and comments from you mean more than you know.

To find the series for purchase or to leave a review on Amazon, google Dolores Maria Davis and Harem Twins.

Thank you

DMD

www.ingramcontent.com/pod-product-compliance
Lightning Source LLC
Chambersburg PA
CBHW060519180626
46817CB00002B/417